The Deal

"Take the offer or leave it, Kathleen," he clipped. "I haven't got all night."

"All right," she said with a sigh that made him want to take her into his arms.

"All right," he echoed, and stepped closer.

"All right," she whispered, and moved away as if she had only just now discovered that she'd sold her soul to the devil.

Feeling hurt and unfairly accused, Nathan picked up his coat and began walking doggedly toward the prison matron.

"But this is an even trade," Kathleen assured him as she hurried to keep up. "Please don't think my feelings have changed, Mr. Cypress. I still consider you—"

"An opportunist and a gold digger." Nathan bleakly dared the matron to say a word as they entered the door of the office to finalize Kathleen's release. "Don't worry, my dear. I couldn't possibly forget."

D1213723

Dear Reader:

February has a reputation for being a cold and dreary month, but not at Silhouette Intimate Moments. In fact, so many exciting things are happening this month that it's hard to know where to begin, so I'll start off with *Special Gifts* by Anne Stuart. Anne is no doubt familiar to many of you, but this is the first time she's done a novel for Silhouette Books, and it's a winner. I don't want to tell you too much, because this is definitely a must-read book. I'll say only that if you think you know everything there is to know about love and suspense and how they go together, you're in for a big surprise and a very special treat.

Another name that many of you will recognize is Linda Shaw. In *Case Dismissed* she makes her first appearance in the line in several years. If you've been reading her Silhouette Special Editions, you'll know why we're so glad to welcome her back. This is a book that literally has everything: passion and power struggles, dreams of vengeance and, most of all, characters who will jump off the page and into your heart. Don't miss it!

Award-winning writer Kathleen Creighton treats a serious subject with insight and tenderness in *Love and Other Surprises*, the story of two people who never expected to find love again—much less become parents!—but are more than capable of dealing with such unexpected happiness. Finally, welcome bestseller Naomi Horton to the line. In *Strangers No More* she gives us a whirlwind romance and a momentary marriage between a heroine you'll adore and a hero who is not at all what he seems. Figure this one out, if you can!

No matter what the weather's doing outside, February is hot at Silhouette Intimate Moments!

Leslie J. Wainger
Senior Editor
Silhouette Books

Case
Dismissed

LINDA SHAW

Silhouette Intimate Moments

Published by Silhouette Books New York

America's Publisher of Contemporary Romance

SILHOUETTE BOOKS
300 East 42nd St., New York, N.Y. 10017

ISBN: 0-373-07324-0

First Silhouette Books printing February 1990

Printed in the U.S.A.

LINDA SHAW

the mother of three, lives with her husband in Keene, Texas. A prolific author of both contemporary and historical fiction, when Linda isn't writing romantic novels, she's practicing or teaching the piano, violin or viola.

To Yvonne Miers of AT&T
Thank you

Chapter 1

Sentinel Takes Heat from Sterling Interbank. Stands Behind Reporter—Headline, page one, *Washington Sentinel*, November.

It was Nathan Cypress's habit to perpetuate the rumor that he was a tough son of a bitch. To his way of thinking he had no choice. Self-preservation was not an elective in life.

The myth was that a handsome man had it made. He had the world by the tail, it claimed, and held four aces in his hand.

Wrong. A good-looking man might as well be a convict. He was marked. Like Cain. A good-looking man could never go out for a night on the town with a buddy; what sane man wanted all the women ogling the guy beside him? As for women, all the really nice ones mistrusted a handsome man on principle, secretly believing that he reduced life to the common denominator of a stacked nyphomaniac. Employers were the worst of the lot. They invariably gave the best jobs to plain old Joes, because any boss worth his salt knew that handsome men were nothing more than worthless playboys or cat burglars.

Hellish all around, Nathan thought.

He stood in the door of his outer office, one hundred eighty handsome pounds on a six-foot frame. A thumb was hooked in the slash of a trouser pocket, and with the other hand he spanned a firm, paunchless waist. He brooded behind gold-rimmed, John Lennon glasses that, at thirty-eight, he didn't require but wore anyway. Beneath the mustache, which, unlike the brown curls on his head, was beginning to gray, he hid a mouth that had been described as everything from devilish to divine.

Before him stretched the *Washington Sentinel* newsroom, an acre of desks on bright, sturdy carpet. Usually the room crackled with creativity; today gloom hovered like a toxic cloud. His reporters had one nervous eye on the television sets and one on his reaction as he stood in the doorway.

The host of *Good Morning, Washington* was introducing the owners of Sterling Interbank.

Jack Pardue's opening question to the city was "Is the *Washington Sentinel* really on a glorified witch-hunt, as some people are claiming it is? After this commercial break, we'll find out."

The station paused for the merits of dishwashing liquid, drain cleaner, life insurance and panty liners, during which time Nathan slid his fingers beneath his glasses and wearily pressed his eyelids.

Returning, Jack said to the camera, "Our guests, Gloria and Curtis Sterling, owners of one of Wall Street's most fashionable and prestigious investment firms, have virtually been accused by the *Washington Sentinel* of perpetrating a fraud. How would you retort to that, Gloria?"

"Ah, Nathan Cypress again." Smiling, Gloria lifted her famous, oft-photographed chin. "If you want to learn about Gloria and Curtis Sterling, Jack, why don't you ask the National Symphony Orchestra? Ask the patients of Children's Hospital. Those at the Kennedy Center for the Performing Arts, the Eisenhower Theater.'' Gloria raised diamond-encrusted hands. ''The question is, Jack, would swindlers keep a whole ballet company from sinking into bankruptcy? The evidence speaks for itself. Some of the most famous, respectable people in the nation invest in Sterling. And we, in turn, are dedicated to community involvement. Nathan Cypress wouldn't know a fraud from a fig.''

Every head in the newsroom pivoted toward Nathan. Nathan felt the bones of his grinding jaws reverberate inside his skull.

Jack Pardue was replaying clips from yesterday's news— a shot of federal judge Richard Kelsey, who was an investor with Sterling Interbank. ''Nathan Cypress is insane!'' the jurist stormed. ''In all my years I've never seen such shabby, irresponsible journalism as the *Sentinel*'s. Me guilty of tax evasion? Outrageous!''

''Mr. Cypress is entitled to his views, of course.'' Another clip showed the financial consultants at Munger, Haverson & Jewell. ''But the *Sentinel* has made a radical departure from the ideals it once held when Lee Bradford Case was at the helm. It's unfortunate. The *Sentinel* was a fine newspaper.''

The bottom dropped from Nathan's stomach as he saw Lee's beautiful face in a still shot.

''Lee Bradford Case,'' Jack Pardue was saying, ''heiress to the *Sentinel*, the ex-wife of acclaimed author William Case and mother of four, who married Nathan Cypress shortly before her death eight years ago.''

Nathan's own face followed Lee's upon the screen—a handsome, lifeguardish, hustlerish photograph that Nathan despised. The host explained how Nathan had married Lee and assumed publication of the paper. He saw the rerun of himself saying to the television's minicam, "We stand behind our story."

Yet the headline that flashed on the screen next brought the most pain: Handsome Playboy Gains Position by Marrying Boss.

Nathan wondered if it was insanity to wish that a bolt of lightning would strike TNC News and kill everyone at the studio.

"Of course," Curtis Sterling was adding with his twitching squint, "I'm not going to reveal how we make so much money for our clients. I will say this, Jack, it's going to revolutionize foreign currency trading as we know it."

The phones at the *Sentinel* would never stop ringing now.

Nathan was smoldering when his frail, scholarly District of Columbia editor walked past his office door: Harry Parkinson, having just come from brunch with one of his friends at CBS.

"Are they going to support us, Harry?" Nathan asked, and plowed a hand into his shock of unruly curls.

Harry touched the dark green bow tie that spread its butterfly wings beneath his chin. One could predict the barometer of Washington's moods by the tie Harry wore.

"I doubt it," he said.

Behind Harry, Jerry Franks, the *Sentinel's* metropolitan editor, shuffled scruffily along in his Bass Weegans, nursing coffee in a cracked cup. A veteran of Vietnam, Jerry was a black man with an incredible sense of Washington's ghetto streets and of what would work and what wouldn't. He had been the first to raise the question of Sterling's legitimacy.

"I predict the editorial meeting is going to be a replay of Watergate," he told Nathan as he adjusted a black eye patch—a trophy of Vietnam—and cast his good eye upward. "I hope you like walking on hot coals."

Spinning on his heel, Nathan returned to his office. By the time he reached the inner sanctum, the telephone on his secretary's desk was ringing. Rose Perrin answered and appeared almost immediately in his doorway.

Rose had been the perfect secretary for Lee before he and Lee married, and she'd stayed on after Lee's death eight years ago. A handsome woman whose ivory suits and silk blouses and real pearls spoke of old money, money that meant the luxury of working strictly for the satisfaction, Rose was his girl Friday, his nanny and guardian angel rolled into one. Nothing of a romantic nature had ever passed between them, but the possibility hung there nonetheless.

She put his suit jacket on a hanger and placed it in his closet, then plunked several bottles of vitamins and minerals beside his phone. She filled his coffee maker and plugged it in.

"William Case's attorney is on the line," she announced.

Nathan worked his chin against his cardboard-stiff blue collar. "Is he cursing?"

"Only in a very polite way."

"Didn't waste any time, did he? Spotted the circling vultures immediately."

"Mr. Case is demanding a meeting. What should I tell the lawyer?"

With a sigh, Nathan drew back a cuff to look at the wafer-thin Patek Phillippe gold watch Lee had given him when he had agreed to marry her. "Tell Case I can meet him the end of the week. Then get ahold of Jeff McBain and tell him the *Sentinel*'s going to need some legal help with Case."

He looked up with a wry grimace. "When this is all over and the theoreticians poke through the ruins and ask 'I wonder who dealt the final blow?' tell 'em it was William Almighty Case, will you, Rose? You know, the man hardly comes around his three youngest daughters for five years, and now, at the worst moment of my life, he moves in to finish me off. I think it's been a diabolical plot all along, Rose. What d'you think?''

''I think you should take your vitamins.'' Smiling, she turned to leave, but said as an afterthought, ''I almost forgot. Mr. Abramson at the Department of Corporations said he has the information about Sterling Interbank you wanted. It sounded good.''

''For me or Sterling?''

''You, I think. Abramson is an inveterate rat finder.''

''So is a snake, Rose.''

She laughed. ''Take your vitamins.''

''What did Lee ever see in that bastard she married?'' Nathan grumbled as, in the same motion, he clawed the knot of his tie loose and began rolling up his shirt sleeves. He stepped through the reception area and out the door, where several heads lifted.

It's me, remember? he wanted to shout.

Less than two weeks ago, after Nathan had published Jerry Frank's first piece on Sterling Interbank, the whole newsroom had witnessed William Case sweeping grandly in, sporting a gray fedora, a pink cashmere scarf and a silver-tipped walking cane, with which he stabbed the floor to punctuate his announcement.

He was a world-famous author—*thump*, Case had proclaimed. *He* had as much right to the *Sentinel* as Nathan—*thump*. His attorney was, even as they spoke, drawing up papers to sue Nathan on the grounds that Lee had promised the paper to *him*.

''And *you*, sir—'' he'd brandished his cane like Moses accusing Pharoah ''—you are a charlatan and a rogue and a dastardly villain who took advantage of Lee when she was sick. However you tricked her, you've robbed Lee's daughters of their God-given inheritance. You've mismanaged the paper with this Sterling disgrace—attacking respectable

people like Curtis and Gloria. The Sterlings will bury you, sir, and I'll dance on your grave. I'll be canonized!''
Thump!

Too much was too much. Nathan wanted the thorn of William Case out of his side. Today.

He scanned the room for heads bent over word-processing terminals and located the shaggy one he sought, then yelled, ''Escavito, get in here!''

Chapter 2

Judge Mason Cites Attorney from Public Defender's Office for Contempt—Headline, page nine, *Philadelphia Reporter*, November.

From deep within the folds of her dream, Kathleen Case floated as lightly as thistledown. Her wings of watered silk fluttered gently, carrying her high into the sky, where a breeze captured her in its safe, peaceful flow.

Soft voices echoed through glassy corridors as she drifted, until the wind caught her in its eddy and propelled her earthward. She wafted down, down, down, trailing gossamer and tiffany in her wake. Lightly, on tiptoe, an evanescent ballerina coming to rest in reverence before a judicial bench, she lifted her head and found herself surrounded by faces.

Crowds were waiting with bated breath for some grave pronouncement to be made. Standing, she faced the judge, who leaned over from behind the ponderous oak bench. To

Kathleen's surprise, the face wasn't that of the Honorable Helen Mason at all but her own mother, Lee Bradford Case.

"Guilty." Lee's verdict echoed through space.

An awed hush fell over the courtroom, for even in dreams Lee Bradford Case was accorded the same reverence as Jacqueline Kennedy Onassis or Katharine Meyer Graham.

"Your crime is punishable by death, Miss Case," the majestic tones proclaimed. "You will be hanged. Sentence to be carried out immediately."

Slam went the gavel.

Panic riddled the dream, and Kathleen realized she was wearing only a wisp of panties and her breasts were quivering. Her nails were bitten into the quick.

Mortified more by her telltale nails than her nakedness, she crossed her arms and backed away. Then the thought came that she was only dreaming. Why was she afraid? In dreams, who cared? Things like this happened all the time. No one was going to hang her, and she could explain to the court that she'd actually been protecting the confidentiality of her client when Judge Mason had ruled against her.

"I only wanted to find a place where I belong," she shocked herself by arguing. "I only wanted to be important to someone. I only wanted to be loved. Is that so wrong?"

The courtroom gasped in amazement.

Miraculously she was dressed again. She hastily smoothed the lapels of her suit—the tailored green shantung because it showed off her slim waist and long legs and complemented the rust of her hair so nicely. It also made the hazel of her eyes appear more green than brown and drew attention from her face, which was pleasant enough but not beautiful by anyone's standard. At least she'd worn her hair in a twist today—appropriate for a twenty-eight-year-old lawyer being cited for contempt.

"Out of order," said Lee Case.

"I object, Your Honor," Kathleen retorted lamely.

As a matter of fact, she was quite weary of the dream, Kathleen thought. She would pull very hard and drag herself out of it as she'd done countless times before. *It's a dream, wake up.*

But she didn't awaken. Instead she turned to find the hangman looming over her, his black robes rustling. Upon his head was a dunce-cap hood with slits for eyes, like one of the Ku Klux Klan's, only black. In his hand was the fearful hangman's noose that she'd seen in half the Western movies ever made.

"No," she said, protesting with waves of her hands. "You're not supposed to be here. This is a dream. This isn't real."

Turning, she found the judge no longer her mother but Helen Mason, the very real nemesis who had caused it all.

"This is no dream, Miss Case," Judge Mason angrily declared. "You think you can intimidate this court by becoming a martyr? Do you think that you, a mere public defender's assistant, can intimidate me by going to jail? John Tortorelli is a contract killer for Vincent Carboni, Miss Case. Do you have any idea how long the law has tried to bring down Vincent Carboni? And now you dare tie my hands. I find you not only guilty of contempt, but of obstructing justice, as well. Hang her!"

This time the explosive slam of the gavel made Kathleen know that, waking or dreaming, she was alone with the decision she had made. She had committed the unpardonable sin. She had dared to question authority.

Hard fingers gripped her shoulder, and she heard her own wail keening in her ears. She could not move. The hood was slipped over her head, suffocating her, and then the noose. With great effort she tried to lift her arms, but they were too heavy. Her feet were leaden. The more she struggled against the hood and the noose, the more she suffocated.

"Hey you—lady!"

"No," she begged. "No, no, no—"

"You in there!"

"No!"

With all her strength Kathleen lunged upward, gasping and fighting her way from beneath the pillow that covered her face—a Philadelphia County jail issue with rough, striped ticking, whose pine-disinfectant stench made her gag.

Hurling the pillow at the wall, she whimpered and covered her face with her hands. She was in the cramped cell of women's detention. There was no courtroom, there was no hangman, only the results of her own supercharged idealism.

Limp with exhaustion, she drew herself up to sit. Her fingers shook as she combed them distractedly through her hair and tried, for the hundredth time, to figure out where to go from there.

But she didn't know where to go. At the time—was it only twenty-four hours ago?—she'd had no choice. Her stand had been so right, so simple, so commendable. She'd been a champion valiantly upholding principle, giving her client the best defense possible irrespective of her own personal opinion. She had been brilliant; everyone had said so.

But the system was too gargantuan to notice one hungry assistant district attorney. It sank its teeth into the throats of people like her, burned them out, then moved on in a search of new blood.

"Are you all right in there?" a raspy smoker's voice asked from the next cell.

Trembling, Kathleen waited for her equilibrium to steady. She came to her feet, wiped her face upon her sleeve.

"What time is it?" she asked huskily.

"Six o'clock," the voice said.

"In the morning?"

"In the evening. Jeez, where've you been?"

To hell, Kathleen thought sadly. And she was still there.

Chapter 3

Lee Bradford Case to Wed *Sentinel*'s Managing Editor in Private Ceremony—Headline from *Washington Sentinel* eight years before.

At eight-thirty in the morning, the ring of the telephone on Nathan's desk bore all the promise of an air-raid siren during a blitz.

"Mr. Cypress, this is Gaye Chasteen," a voice said when he lifted the receiver. "The school nurse at Lockesbury."

Nathan leaned forward; his chair shrieked as if it knew what was coming. On his desk were stacks of books and periodicals detailing the intricacies of foreign currency markets and shell banks, Eurodollars, national regulatory agencies, the Bank of England.

"Oh-oh." Without thinking, he scooped up the vitamins Rose had placed on his desk. "Don't tell me."

"Annalee has had a little accident, Mr. Cypress."

"Again?"

"Please don't be alarmed."

After having the sole responsibility for Lee's daughters for five years, Nathan considered himself an expert at not being alarmed. He squinted at the trio of hinged picture frames that resided permanently beside his Outgoing Mail rack.

"Let me have it, Ms. Chasteen," he said with a resigned sigh. "Both barrels."

"Annalee claims she's in no discomfort, but I did want you to know that she's been taken to the Haney Orthopedic Clinic on West Fir. Do you remember the place?"

"Remember? Annalee's injuries have established the man's practice." Nathan rattled the vitamins like dice in his palm. "What did she break this time?"

"Her foot."

"Right or left."

"Right."

"Again?"

"I'm afraid so."

"Have they changed the rules since I was a kid? Is basketball now a contact sport?"

"Dr. Haney's giving her a sound lecture this very moment."

"He has my sympathies."

The nurse made a commiserating sound that Nathan felt he deserved. Hell, what he really deserved was a medal for service beyond the call of duty.

"I'll have someone take her home, Mr. Cypress," Gaye said. "She'll be here for another half hour while the doctor finishes putting on the cast. Will anyone be home when she gets there?"

Frannie, the maid who had been with the house in Georgetown as long as Rose had been with the office, was mother to them all. Nathan didn't tempt fate by considering life without her.

He said, "Tell Annalee I'll meet her at home. It's the quickest way."

"Very good, Mr. Cypress. We're very sorry this happened."

"Don't be. Annalee adores pity."

Gaye Chasteen laughed. "Knowing our girl, by Friday she'll be hobbling around the court on her crutches. You do have crutches, don't you?"

"Does a dog have ... well, whatever?"

"Oh, by the way, I saw you on television. You should have been a movie star, Mr. Cypress."

Not again. Nathan came to his feet. "Thank you."

With the telephone in one hand, he glanced at his wristwatch, then at his office door for Pauly Escavito, who was five minutes late. "I take care of everything, Ms. Chasteen. Thank you again for calling."

Replacing the receiver, Nathan shook his head ruefully at the photograph of Lee's thirteen-year-old. If someone had told him ten years earlier that he would be in this office, juggling power as if it were so many oranges and playing father to three rambunctious girls who had taught him much more about life than he'd ever hoped to teach them, he would have laughed himself silly.

Some office, yes, and one with power; from the day he'd arrived at the Capital as an ambitious young taker, he had schemed and planned and driven himself to achieve power. No more filthy back alleys of Philadelphia. He'd let nothing deter his purpose. With a large, unwieldy bitterness weighing down his shoulders, he'd done a stint in the military as the U.S. was mopping up its mess in Vietnam, he'd put himself through college on the GI bill and for a year he was a rookie police-beat reporter, and found he had a knack for it. So he'd polished his skills as a political reporter and earned his stripes on the coveted bureau of *Newsweek* magazine. After that he'd planted himself in the path of the

Sentinel's owner, Lee Bradford Case, and shrewdly exploited the one asset he had besides ambition: his face.

Ah, Lee. Beautiful, wealthy, pedigreed Lee. Ex-wife of renowned author William Case, mother of four daughters: Kathleen, Victoria, Annalee and Polly. Lee—ten years his senior.

Months after he'd joined the staff of the *Sentinel*, Lee had called him into her office and invited him to dinner.

The invitation hadn't come as a total surprise. In his midtwenties at the time, he'd been studying Lee much as oldtimers used to study the land and speculate where the oil pools lay. First he'd learned her habits and who her friends were. He discovered what kinds of foods she ate and what plays she saw when she went to New York. He memorized her jewelry and made himself an expert of its value. Lee had always made a point of knowing who did what at the *Sentinel*, and when the paper lost an endorsement by a conservative faction of government, he shamelessly seduced the secretary of a subcommittee chairman to get it back.

Lee took the bait. When she called him in, he expected her to announce she was moving him up to managing editor—at the expense of Bud Lumens, naturally, but those were the breaks. The last thing he anticipated was for her to take him not only to dinner but dancing afterward.

Nervous, for he had less than fifty dollars in his pocket, he agreed. It was when she was in his arms and the lights were low and the orchestra was playing Gershwin that she told him she was dying.

"They give me six months, Nathan," she said as calmly as she would type a tag line. "I haven't told anyone, and neither must you."

He was speechless, unable to move. Couples circled them, and the music seemed to blur. Her jewels caught the light of the mirrored ball revolving over their heads. He felt as if he were a rat caught with the cheese in his mouth.

"This is a joke, right?" he said. "You found out that I've been trying to ingratiate myself and you're paying me back."

Her laughter was light and musical and healthy sounding. "I've always known you were trying to ingratiate yourself, Nathan. That's what attracted me to you in the first place."

Chagrin burned fiery paths up the sides of his neck. "You're serious, aren't you? About—"

"Dying? Oh, yes, very serious."

He closed his eyes. "Sweet Christ."

Oh, how smart he'd thought he was, and how Lee had outmaneuvered him at every turn. "I don't know what to say," he said. "I feel like a jerk. Hell, I am a jerk."

"Aren't we all in the end? I want you to marry me Nathan."

When he stepped on her feet, she caught his arm and replaced it about her waist, leaning upon his chest, her cheek on his lapel.

"It isn't at all complicated," she added matter-of-factly. "Don't be so nervous. What I want to do is leave you the paper, and in return you must keep it out of William's hands after I'm gone. The *Sentinel* is all I have left to leave my daughters, Nathan. God knows they've gotten little enough of me. Especially Kathleen."

If he had been ten years older, he would have refused on the spot. But he was young and too smart to be wise.

"You don't look sick," he said. "It's incredible."

"This won't last very long." She reached up and touched his face with something resembling pity. "It won't be easy for you. Oh, you may think you're selfish, but you're a tender man. Believe me, I've thought about how cruel this is, but I need someone. I won't hold you to anything sexual, rest assured of that."

Laughing, she amended, "Not that I haven't considered it. You're a very desirable man, you know." She shook her head. "My only condition is that you remain faithful to me until it's over. For the sake of my daughters and the paper." She pulled a face that only made her more beautiful. "And for my reputation, such as it is."

Nathan couldn't have smiled if his life depended on it.

She continued. "When the end comes I plan to go to a hospital. Please don't imagine some grisly bedside scene, Nathan. It will be very clean, very neat."

"Lee, I don't think—"

"But you must promise me that you'll never tell anyone about this conversation. As far as the rest of the world knows, we've fallen deeply in love and will have a normal marriage in every way. You have to promise me that."

When he finally regained the use of his arms and legs and began to dance, she leaned her head upon his shoulder and pressed her breasts against him in a gentle invitation. So he'd entered into one of the most lucrative business deals of his life. Their marriage was a classic case of convenience, yet to the outside world they were devoted lovers. People understood Lee's marrying a younger man, especially one who was so handsome and so elusive.

But some of Lee's peers were offended. To this day they placed the blame not upon her, but upon him.

When Lee became ill, she didn't go to a hospital. Having come to respect her by then, having grown devoted to her daughters—though he hardly knew Kathleen except for their misunderstanding at the wedding—he had refused to let Lee die with strangers. Nurses came round the clock. He spent every possible minute with her, seeing that she had the best of care and the most humane, dignified ending of life. He comforted the girls as if they were his own. He had, he supposed, grown up. Finally.

When it was over and the hospital bed and accompanying equipment were removed from the room, he'd had the suite cleaned and redone, but exactly as it had been before. A shrine?

No. But a reminder of what he could stoop to, he supposed, given the circumstances. He had closed the door, but something of himself had remained inside—that human ability to risk everything for love, that primitive hunger of the heart. When he picked up his life again, he wished for that hunger back, but it had never returned.

When Pauly Escavito trudged into Nathan's office, he looked like something from the gutter in a Dickens novel. His tie was mangled, his shirt was wilted and his creases seemed to have wandered from the front of his pants to the sides. Not yet out of his twenties, Pauly's talent lay in being the kind of nonthreatening young man whom politicians felt good about taking under their wings, but with his short, stout legs, thick fingers and shaggy head, he remarkably resembled one of George Lucas's unkempt little Ewoks.

Before his furry fist could connect with the door facing, Nathan waved him in. "And close the door," he said.

Pauly stood at attention, then sneezed.

"Bless you." Nathan leaned back to study the reporter, who was also allergic to almost everything, himself included, probably. "And don't tower over me. Have a seat."

When Pauly lowered himself to a leather divan, Nathan fetched a plastic foam cup and poured strong, bitter coffee into it. Pauly squinted from behind his own wire-rimmed glasses. Unlike Nathan, he really needed them; the lenses were thick as Coke bottles.

"You should change to real cups," Pauly solemnly observed, and pushed the glasses higher with his pinky finger. "Plastic foam pollutes the environment."

While Pauly sipped, Nathan opened the blind of a window that looked out on Connecticut Avenue and a gray sky. The drizzle nearly obliterated his view. Out there were things that no longer impressed him: the brooding face of Lincoln, the pristine needle of the Washington Monument, the great white dome of the Capitol, which housed such insatiable ambition.

He was an expert on ambition. "What have you learned about William Case?" he asked.

Pauly ruffled through his tiny black notebook. "I talked to my friend at Harper and Row." He skimmed from notation to notation. "Case is apparently living off royalties he earned on *Shoot the Man in the Moon*. His last four novels haven't even earned back their advance." Looking up, he fished a wadded handkerchief from his pocket. "They rejected his last proposal."

Removing his glasses, Nathan cleaned them with his handkerchief. "Twelve years ago this man and Lee divorced. He took Kathleen and moved to Philadelphia. All these years he hasn't said ten words to me. Why now?"

"He's having a bad time." Pauly blew his nose.

"That's not my fault."

"He's the father of your stepdaughters. He's worried."

Scowling, Nathan replaced his glasses and filled a second cup with coffee. He tore open a packet of artificial sweetener, dumped it in and crimped the packet into a tight paper wad.

"That's a strong word—'stepdaughter,'" he said. "I consider myself more of an older brother."

"A technicality."

With a flick of his thumb, Nathan struck Pauly in the chest with the paper wad and, smirking, sipped his coffee. Victoria was fourteen now, Annalee thirteen and Polly eleven. When he and Lee married, Polly hadn't even started first grade. He had enrolled the child in school himself after Lee died. He hadn't begrudged it. If the truth were known, he'd loved it. But that didn't make him a stepfather.

"We still grew up together, the girls and I," he admitted sourly.

"Which answers your own question."

"No, it doesn't. How can I, in good conscience, wage war with their father?"

Pauly squinted at his hieroglyphics and said without preamble," Kathleen Case is in a Philadelphia jail."

The information hit Nathan in the middle like a fist. Disjointed memories caught him off guard, and coffee went sloshing down his shirt in a scalding brown stain that spread like an epidemic.

"Aggh!"

Rose Perrin was immediately at the door, and Nathan gasped as tears collected in his eyes, "It's all right, Rose."

He slammed the cup to the desk, spilling even more. With a disapproving lift of brows, Rose disappeared, and Pauly gave an appropriate sneeze.

"Kathleen?" Nathan rolled the name on his tongue when he could breathe again. He unbuttoned his shirt and peered sympathetically at the patch of scalded skin. "In jail?"

At Lee and William's divorce Kathleen had been sixteen, but he hadn't known her then. The first time he'd ever seen her was at his wedding. She had been standing on the steps in the sunlight, with the wind catching her silk dress and tucking it sensually between her legs, one hand clapped to the back of her hat to prevent it from sailing away, while the other battled her skirt.

Disturbing memories—those trim ankles and gleaming panty hose and legs that never seemed to stop. He strode irritably to his bathroom and stripped the tie from his neck. Flinging it aside, he removed a fresh shirt from a drawer.

Pauly waited in the doorway.

"When did you find out about Kathleen?" Nathan angled a look Paul's way. "Are you sure about this?"

Offended—Pauly read a dozen morning papers before coming to work each day—the reporter raised his hands in a gesture to stop the doubts. "It was in the Philadelphia papers."

"Bottom line."

"A Philly judge got her on contempt."

"Why?"

Pauly shrugged. "Miss Case refused to divulge—even in chambers, it seems—the source of information the judge deemed vital to the apprehension of a known killer. A man named Tortorelli. John Tortorelli—a hit man from New Orleans. The judge now says Miss Case is lucky she didn't have her disbarred."

"A *woman* judge?" Nathan unzipped his trousers, revealing pale blue Jockey shorts, tucked in his fresh shirt and rezipped. "Who?"

"Mason. Helen Mason."

Pausing in the process of buckling his belt, Nathan tipped back his head and let his laughter rumble. "Well, well, well."

Pauly didn't share the amusement. "Pardon me, sir, do you know Judge Mason?"

"Well enough, Pauly. Well enough." Nathan slipped the leather belt through its clasp and gave it a pat of finality. He motioned Pauly back into his office and commenced mopping up coffee.

"It's not complicated, Pauly. Before Lee died, before people knew she was even sick, Helen Mason caught the political virus and fixed her sights upon a nomination to the House."

Soaked napkins struck the bottom of the wastebasket with an unappetizing splat.

"Lee opposed her on the basis of some states' rights thing. I don't know, it doesn't matter." Nathan tapped his mustache as he recalled. "When Helen didn't realize her dream, there was a certain amount of bad blood between the two women. It went on until the news got out that Lee was dying. Then Helen called and said she wanted to make peace with Lee, and she wanted me as a go-between. I suggested that she go straight to Lee. Helen didn't want to do that. She said if *I* would make things right with Lee *for* her, she would owe me one."

Pauly scribbled in his book and looked over his notes as he fished absently in his pocket for his handkerchief.

Nathan grinned. "Payback time, Pauly."

"How so?" Pauly blew his nose.

"First we get Kathleen in our corner. Second Kathleen talks to Father. Father sees light of day, talks to lawyers. We have one less distraction, bring down Sterling. End of story. Case dismissed." He tapped Pauly's notepad. "This is good stuff, Escavito. You sure you're getting it all?"

"You think that Judge Mason will drop the charges of contempt against your stepdaughter?"

Nathan drew his brows sharply together. "It bugs the hell out of me for you to keep calling them my 'stepdaughters,' Pauly."

Grimacing, Pauly clicked his pen. "Yes, sir."

"I've seen Kathleen Case exactly two times in my life."

Pauly fitted the pen untidily into his shirt pocket, which already bore an ink mark.

"The woman is only six or seven years younger than I am," Nathan insisted.

Pauly buttoned his tatty jacket.

"Besides, she despises me."

"No woman despises you, sir." Pauly gave one of his rare grins.

"Get the hell outta here, Escavito."

"I'll book you on a flight, sir."

Unruffled, Pauly marched to the door. With a twist of his mouth, Nathan waved him on, then thought better of it and bellowed to his back, "Hey, Escavito, reserve two seats."

Already in the newsroom, Pauly came to an abrupt stop.

When he looked back, Nathan wiggled two fingers and nodded evilly. *You got it—you're coming with me.*

Slumping, Pauly groped for his handkerchief and sneezed, so that the mail clerk made a wide detour as he collected outgoing correspondence. Returning to his office, Nathan smiled, then tipped back his head in a laugh so rousing that Rose rushed to his door.

Chapter 4

Funeral Set for Publisher. Lee Bradford Case Dead at Forty-one—Headline, *Washington Sentinel*. Seven years before.

Miss Case?''

At half past nine in the evening, Lillian Fornal unlocked the door of Kathleen's cell and stood between Kathleen and the stark corridor, her hulk defying refusal. She announced that Kathleen had a visitor.

''At this time of night?'' Kathleen said.

Kathleen sat on her cot, her legs clad in slim jeans and cross-legged, her oversize chambray shirt billowing about her like a tent and her morale suspended somewhere between the tangled cloud of her hair and her running shoes parked beneath the cot.

Case files lay in organized chaos around her, and law books spilled precedents that were blurring together. She hadn't been accomplishing much, her brain having reduced itself to reading the same meaningless words over and over again.

She inserted scraps of paper between the pages and slammed the books shut. "Why would a reporter from Washington want to talk to me?"

"I just call 'em like I see 'em, counselor. That's what he said. Washington."

"Well, there's been a mistake. I don't know any reporter from Washington."

Yet in a way she did. Nathan Cypress was in Washington. But the chances of him wanting to talk to her were so remote as to be impossible, thank heaven. Anyway, he had assumed the rank of executive editor after Lee's death, and an executive editor would drown himself in printer's ink before calling himself a reporter.

Lillian Fornal wheezed as she fished in the pocket over her formidable bosom. Finding a card, she squinted. "One... Paul Escavito, it says."

Kathleen tugged up her drooping cotton socks and located her shoes. One of the laces had frayed, and she stuffed it impatiently beneath the tongue.

"Never heard of him," she grumbled. "Besides, visiting hours are over. You know the rules."

"No need to quote the rules to me." Lillian motioned Kathleen out of the cell. "The orders came down from the warden himself. Pretty connected reporter if you ask me— waking the warden, getting special orders."

"The power of the pen, Ms. Fornal."

"Beg pardon?"

"Nothing."

Lillian Fornal passed her hand over the front of her girdled stomach. "This way, counselor."

Kathleen was only too glad to leave the collected smells of misery that had permeated the cement and the vomitus-colored paint and the stained mattresses and obscene pillows. She trudged behind the matron's churning hips and wondered again if Nathan Cypress actually had sent someone here. Maybe he wanted a headline for his precious *Sentinel*: Daughter of Deceased Publisher Rots in Jail.

As she tucked her shirt into her jeans and made an attempt to smooth her hair, they passed women in adjoining cells—prostitutes mainly, picked up the night before. Cheap perfume overpowered other smells, and Kathleen couldn't bring herself to look at the women. Some might have been old clients.

Matron Fornal led the way down a rank of hollow-sounding stairs, beyond which was a door opening onto men's detention.

Low, whistling suggestions followed them as they passed through. "Hey, mama, don't be in such a hurry."

"Would you look at that?" another voice rumbled huskily.

"Back it up, back it up."

"Back it up, nothin'. Take it off. Show us what you got, baby, and I'll show you what I got."

As toughened as Kathleen was by clients who were rejects of society, her cheeks burned, and she was grateful when Lillian Fornal turned and slammed meaty fists to her hips and bawled, "Knock it off, you perverts!"

The cell grew quiet as a monastery. A man would have had to be desperate or crazy to defy Lillian Fornal. Yet from somewhere in the shadows came the slurpy sound of a kiss.

"Filthy scum," Lillian grumbled, and waved Kathleen through a door. "This ain't no place to be, counselor. You'd better pray you're about to get sprung."

Behind the woman, Kathleen shrugged unhappily. "I wouldn't hold my breath, Ms. Fornal."

The visitors' area of the Philadelphia County Jail consisted of tables and chairs spread over an expanse the size of a basketball court. During the day the room was filled with people in all stages of trouble: lonely, defeated women to see their husbands and the fathers of their children, grieving mothers to see sons, lawyers to see clients and, sometimes, children to see parents.

Now the floor had been freshly mopped and reeked of pine disinfectant. The overhead lamps were turned off, and a fragile shaft of gold light streamed from an open door at one end, softening the ugliness. The room adjoined the warden's office, and voices drifted from inside—tense, argumentative.

Matron Fornal positioned herself outside the door and folded her arms. To let any intruder know from the outset what he would be up against, Kathleen thought. Just in case.

A short, shaggy young man was detaching himself from the wall. Kathleen watched him remove an all-weather coat as he approached. His trousers were too long and bunched ridiculously about the tops of his brogans. His sport jacket didn't fit well. His shirt appeared never to have seen an iron, but a tie was fitted beneath its collar.

Any person with the courage to put a tie about the neck of such a shirt had to be likable, she decided, and smiled.

She called out, "You wanted to see me?"

"You're Miss Case?"

"Almost all the time."

As he reached her, he shifted his coat to the opposite arm. His grip was bone crushing, his small palm rough and reassuring.

"I'm Paul Escavito, Miss Case." His eyes had away of stripping away externals. "From the *Sentinel*."

"The matron told me. How can I help you, Mr. Escavito?"

"We're here to talk about your father."

The mention of William Case made Kathleen's stomach tighten, but she tried to make her reply broad-minded and neutral. "I see. What's happened?"

"Nothing." He held up his hand. "I mean, obviously we have a problem for us to come in the middle of the night like this, but your father's perfectly fine."

"You keep saying 'we.' Who is 'we'?"

"I was getting to that."

With an intuition that almost never failed her, Kathleen tried to imagine the connection between Nathan Cypress and this reporter. She was surprised how little she honestly knew about Lee's husband.

"He sent you here for a story, didn't he? Nathan Cypress? About Lee's daughter who got herself thrown in jail."

"Oh, no, ma'am."

"Well, you've come to the wrong person, in any case. I haven't seen my father in two weeks. He's in Washington visiting his daughters. I'm surprised you don't know that. Isn't Carl Berstein your brother?"

Paul Escavito didn't find a great deal of humor in that remark.

"We know your father's in Washington, Miss Case, but it really wouldn't be ethical for us to talk to him, not under the circumstances, you understand."

Kathleen's arching brows implied the next logical question: What circumstances?

"Your father's filing suit against us," he explained. "Against Mr. Cypress, actually. He says he wants the *Sentinel*. Pardon me, ma'am, but your shoelace has come undone."

As she stared blindly at the flyaway lace Kathleen thought that the news of her father's lawsuit didn't come as a great surprise. William's depressions were like a virus looking for someone to infect. "Writer's block," he called it, but no one had writer's block for ten years. In her opinion, William was having a very quiet, very private breakdown, and her role had somehow reversed: she was now the parent and he was the child.

She moved closer and touched Escavito's wilted cuff, frowning. "What's really going on, Mr. Escavito? Your exec down there, your Nathan Cypress, what has he done that would drive my father so crazy?"

The rule was that inmates were not allowed physical contact with visitors. Kathleen knew the rule well. She also knew that the approaching footsteps would be Matron Fornal to remind her.

Stepping back, she dropped to one knee and twirled the frayed lace in her fingers, attempting unsuccessfully to thread it into the small eyelet.

Paul Escavito bent over her like a solicitous traveler over a highway casualty. "Miss Case?"

The sound of walking stopped, and Kathleen wanted to spin around and scream at the matron to back off and leave her alone.

But she compelled herself to work the lace into its hole. From an oblique angle of vision, she observed a trousered leg slip into view, a resilient leather shoe.

Trousers? Her jaw sagged, and she looked up.

"That'll be all, Pauly," Nathan Cypress said as he bent to one knee and faced Kathleen at her level.

With a quick smile, he plucked the shoelace from her frozen hands and ignored her stunned surprise as he threaded it and tied it into a perfect bow. Then he gave her foot a pat that was about as casual, Kathleen thought, as stripping her stark naked in the lobby of the Plaza Hotel.

With a fingertip beneath her chin, he closed her mouth and added pleasantly to Pauly, "I'll explain everything to Kathleen myself."

* * *

The moment was unfettered by all the natural laws of seconds and minutes.

From where she knelt on the floor, Kathleen could only stare at Nathan Cypress's topcoat, which he let spill over the floor with the negligence a man assumes naturally when he's accustomed to having nothing but the best. His nails weren't professionally manicured but were neat and trim; his teeth were well cared for; his eyes-steady, intelligent, the color of deep water off Bermuda—were Superman eyes. They saw everything.

He had kept the mustache. Its sun-bronzed frame made his mouth appear even wider and more sensual. His curls were as untouched by gray as a boy's, and the glasses, a new addition, enhanced his masculinity rather than detracted from it. Yet time had touched him in its way. Lines were tracked between his brows and at the sides of his eyes. Slashes were chiseled from the sides of his nostrils to the corners of his smile. There was also a resignation in his look that hadn't been there before.

Well, Nathan Cypress, life has gotten to you, too, hasn't it?

Her heart jerked as if she had missed a step. The past superimposed itself upon the present, and she could have been the awkward young woman with Lee on her wedding day, surrounded by three younger girls who were little more than laughing strangers to Kathleen—pretty pastels smeared upon a canvas.

In a few stolen seconds after the ceremony, as Nathan was momentarily deserted by groomsmen and bride, Kathleen had seized the instant. He was standing on the steps of the church—a long leg braced on a step above. The sun dazzled his curls. The wind caught the tails of his tuxedo, whipping them back to reveal a physique so perfectly articulated, it took her breath away.

"Kathleen," he exclaimed with the bow of a man who is cockily proud of himself.

She made herself immune to his charm. "Don't waste that on me."

His eyes widened in surprise. "I beg your pardon?":

"Oh, you may have everyone else fooled, Mr. Cypress—" she was forced to shade her face from the sun, or was it from the brilliant blue of his eyes? "—but I want you to know that I'm perfectly aware of why you married my mother."

At first he didn't reply. He peered at her with an uncertain smile tipping the sides of his mouth.

Presently he chuckled. "Oh, you do, do you?" he teased, and lifted a shoulder. "Tell me then, pretty Kathleen. Tell me why I married your mother."

How brave a woman is when she is midway through a university, how quick to judge and come up with solutions before life has taught her its lessons in humility.

Her words dripped venom. "Do you think that because you have a pretty face we will accept you, Mr. Cypress? Do you think that this town won't find you out?"

"Now wait just a—"

"My mother is forty years old, Mr. Cypress. She can trace her roots to one of the oldest families in this country. And who are you? Hmm? I'll tell you who you are—you're a thirty-year-old opportunist and a gold digger, Mr. Cypress, and if Washington doesn't know it now, it soon will."

Their anger was ghastly as they faced each other down. His lips drew back over his teeth in a deadly smile, and she threw back her head in scorn.

"I'd be very careful if I were you, Kathleen," he said through gritted teeth.

Careful? Her fury was like wildfire. "Tell me, Mr. Cypress, how long do you plan to stay married before you file for the divorce? A year? And the divorce. Will it, when it comes, be on grounds of mental cruelty? For a healthy fifty percent?''

He was shaking with bitter rage. ''You don't know what you're talking about, so shut up.''

''Oh, you're not the usual caliber of con artists, I give you that. You're smoother, more clever. I'll lay money down that you didn't sign a prenuptial agreement, did you, Mr. Cypress?''

In the end, his need for her blood had been as desperate as her own for his. And his was a weapon she was not skilled at using. With an insolence that missed nothing, not her bitten nails or her fear of people, which no one else suspected except her dry cleaner, he panned her, looking her up and down with a callously mocking stare that would have made a statue turn away. His brows were those of a street hustler considering a mark but letting her know she fell considerably short of his high standards.

To remain standing before such an indignity was impossible. Tears welled in her eyes, and her lips quivered. How could Lee have married this man?

But then his lashes had come to rest upon his handsome cheeks, and when he looked at her again, his mouth wasn't sneering or condemning. He showed her nothing, not even his contempt. Her attack was thwarted as surely as if he'd gagged her.

Less than a year later she had seen that same sensual mouth bleakened with pain. Lee's coffin was being lowered into the ground. His stunning looks had not changed in that year; he was just as tall, and his curls caught the sunshine in the same fetching way. He had grown a mustache and was a bit thinner, paler, perhaps, but even so, his paleness was infinitely attractive.

They were together for only a moment after the funeral. Her sisters had returned to the waiting limousine, and Kathleen watched the rest of the people leaving.

"I blame you for this," she told him cruelly.

He was no longer an ill-fated son of Zeus, fallen from grace and doomed to earth for a time. He was no longer insolent and arrogant and cocky. For an instant she was confused and strangely ashamed. Some eerie tenderness made her want to rise up on her toes and touch the gauntness of his cheekbones, to whisper, to placate him and draw his head to her breast and croon that everything was going to be all right.

But she refused to feel a shred of pity. "I'm going to make you pay," she said.

He didn't look at her, but at some place in the distance she couldn't see. "I've already paid."

Her laughter was ugly and awkward and not like her at all. "Oh, Mr. Cypress, you haven't begun to pay."

She hadn't seen him again after that. Over seven years had passed, and she had made certain that whenever she visited her sisters, Nathan Cypress was nowhere around.

Now not the slightest trace of vulnerability lay couched in his voice. It was the sound of authority, richly underscored with a sense of itself, a voice textured with cynicism and disillusionment. It was the voice of a man with a strong hand, a man who made his own rules as he went along and if there were prices to pay, he paid with his own money, free and clear and owing no one.

He drew her lightly to her feet and smiled down at her stunned face. "You're looking good, Kathleen," he drawled. "The years have been kind. I've come to do a little plea bargaining, counselor. Let's make a deal."

Chapter 5

Sentinel Takes New Executive Editor and Publisher—
Headline, *Washington Sentinel*, seven years before.

The moment he peered down into Kathleen's face, Nathan knew his own future was about to transpose, to change key. He was also struck by the realization that in the past his way of thinking about Kathleen had been all wrong. When he'd thought of her at all, that is, which was as infrequently as possible.

"What deal?" she said as she got her balance and pulled herself carefully out of touching distance. "What're you doing here? I don't have anything to say to you."

Now that he was actually facing her, Nathan wasn't sure what he'd expected to find in this Pennsylvania jail. The intriguing creature on the church steps who took herself so seriously? The poor little rich girl who had been raised by governesses and tutors and maids and who had made such an admirable determination never to need anyone's sympathy?

Physically she was an amazing replica of Lee, much more so than the other three girls. Where they had inherited William Case's square jaw and sturdy Scandinavian features, Lee's fastidious slimness, porcelain complexion and firestruck hair were Kathleen's.

Her figure was actually better than Lee's, her hips riper, her waist smaller, her breasts more feminine. She would have that smooth, freckled skin beneath her jeans, he was sure, and the firm inner thighs with that patch of rusty curls.

At the moment, she wore no makeup and her freckles glowed. Her nose, one that some might say was too large or a bit too pug, was as shiny as a new silver dollar. Her lower lip was also a tad too pouty to be classed as glamorous, and somewhere along the way she had inherited an overbite—small, to be sure, but one that would surely keep her off the list of the world's most beautiful women.

Yet there was something about her that was magnetic. She radiated a presence, and now she braced her fists on her sides and unwittingly caused the shirt to strain over her breasts—a posture that would have gone unnoticed for most women but one he found deeply erotic and disturbing for her.

He glanced self-consciously from the matron to the open door of the office. Inside was a man who was waiting to complete the arrangements with Helen Mason. A few paces away, his usual sense of order frustrated, Pauly was shifting his weight from foot to foot.

"If you'll excuse me, sir..." Escavito said, stepping toward them.

With a slash of her hand, Kathleen raised her voice and ordered, "You stay right where you are, Mr. Escavito. I want you to hear this."

The room was abruptly too warm. Nathan shrugged out of his coat and tossed it to a nearby table.

"Sit, Pauly," he growled. Then he turned to Kathleen. "Would you like to walk around while we talk? That woman—" he wryly indicated the matron "—scares the hell out of me."

For a split second a smile tugged promisingly at her lips, and an unexpected elation lifted Nathan's spirits. She quickly recovered, however, and pressed her lips together.

She folded her arms. "No, I would not like to 'walk around,' Mr. Cypress. Please say what you came to say and get done with it. I assume, of course, that you brought Mr. Escavito along to run interference?"

"That . . ." Nathan's temper was more than apparent as he threw his weight to the opposite hip. "That is *precisely* why I brought Pauly."

"Oh? You find me a threat, do you?"

He glared at her as hotly as she at him. "I don't wonder that you drove Helen to distraction, madam! It's a miracle she didn't gag you before she threw you in the damn jail!"

"I knew you came for a story!"

"Well, it wasn't my intention, but now that you mention it—"

"Sir." Pauly stepped forward and tapped the face of his wristwatch in a reminder. "Our flight . . ."

With a lift of his hand, Nathan let out his breath in a sigh and stood watching the pulse throb in Kathleen's neck. He had to stop losing his cool every time he was around this woman.

In his best country-gentleman drawl, he said, "Hell, Miss Scarlett, I don't want a story. I don't even want to be here. I only came—"

"Then don't let me keep you!"

So much for country gentlemen. "Look, Kathleen . . ." He lifted his eyes to the ceiling as if to pray, and thought it wasn't a bad idea. "I'm just trying to be civil about this. There's no need to make a federal case. Do you want out of here or not?"

Before she could hide her surprise with her tough-attorney facade, a quick, energetic young woman emerged, one who hadn't been jaded by too many years of disappointment, one whose delight with the challenge of life was a glow that was as perfect as a mother's with an infant at her breast. A genuine woman, no tricks, no gimmicks, no aces up the sleeve.

Nathan's nerves suddenly uncoiled and stretched until he feared he would make some stupid slip that would leave him looking like a fool. He swiped nervously at his mustache.

Kathleen, too, regained her aloofness, and finger-combed her hair from her face. "What are you trying to say, Mr. Cypress?"

"I thought it was clear."

"That you can get me out?"

"That's about it."

With a practicality that Nathan found fascinating, she stood rubbing the back of her neck, thinking.

"I appreciate your concern," she said at length. "I really do. But you've wasted a trip. Helen Mason cited me with contempt, and she isn't about to recant. Unless I grovel—which I have no intentions of doing. It's a matter of principle. I know—I know Tortorelli did it . . ." She turned up her hand. "We all know he *did* it, but the police and the prosecuting attorney made some incredibly stupid mistakes. The system, well . . ."

She sighed with a resignation that Nathan understood only too well. They were more alike than she knew.

"It's the only system we have," she said. "So unless you have some special 'in' with the judge—"

Nathan's smile was that of a chess player who knows he's just made a great move. "You were saying?"

The statement percolated, its message hot.

"Ahh." Clearing her throat, she moved aimlessly about the room. "I'm really in no mood to play games with you about this."

"If I were inclined to play with you, pretty lady..."

She stopped him with a look.

"Not that I am inclined." He grinned and held up an arm as if to ward off a blow. "No, no, I wouldn't be caught dead doing that. And, by the way, the name's Nathan."

From afar, Lillian Fornal was watching them for a false move. They both looked over their shoulders at her.

Kathleen said quickly, "You used the word 'deal' before. What do you expect in return? Gratuitous sex?"

He refused to smile; she couldn't know how close she had come to the truth. She reddened.

"All you have to do is talk to your father."

"That's it?"

"Knowing your father's present state of mind, it's enough."

With a minimum of words, he described the disturbing scene William Case had created in the newsroom of the *Sentinel*.

"I knew Daddy had been depressed lately," Kathleen said. "But he told me he was going to visit a friend in New York. Aunt Elsa and I were so worn out with his moods, I didn't question him."

"Aunt Elsa?"

"Daddy's sister. My aunt. She lives with us."

"Oh."

"Actually, I thought he had a woman. I really hoped he did." She looked up, found his eyes. "All right. I'll talk to him, but over the phone. It isn't necessary for me to come to Washington."

The truth was, she *could* do it over the phone, and Nathan warned himself it would save a lot of confusion if she did. Especially as he was having a bit of difficulty remembering who was making the deal, him or her.

"Actually, it's William's attorney who concerns me most." Without barring an eyelash, Nathan let the lie fall from his lips.

She laughed incredulously. "David Richardson? Are you serious?"

"Considering William's state of mind and how delicate this situation is, it's imperative that you be there. I'm afraid I really have to insist, Kathleen."

When she hesitated, Nathan added before he thought, "You do think the *Sentinel*'s better off with me, don't you?"

Her half smile lost its whimsy, and her eyes, a mixture of green and brown, darkened until Nathan wasn't sure what color they were.

"Ah, so good old American capitalism is at the root of this, after all," she purred caustically. "I see."

Nathan wanted to bite his tongue. "You don't see anything, Kathleen."

"But I do. I see that you, my stepfather—"

"Hey!"

"Oh, you'd rather I called you 'Daddy'?"

Feeling more and more like an infantryman sent into battle without knowing whose side he was on, he strode to the table and snatched up his coat in an angry fist. "Take the offer or leave it, Kathleen," he said in a clipped tone. "I haven't got all night."

"Mr. Cypress, I hope this doesn't come as a shock to your nervous system—" she raised her voice as he walked away "—but maybe William's doing the world a favor."

When he wheeled hard about, she in turn spun around like a spiteful child, giving him a splendid view of her derriere. Bizarrely Nathan saw himself dragging her to the ground and hushing the mouth that uttered such hurtful things. He felt his own mouth wet upon her breast, his own relentless drive into her, and finally he heard the whisper of his own name as she twined her arms about his neck in loving surrender.

The strange violence of the fantasy made sweat stream down his sides. With a burst of intensity, he gripped her by the shoulders, turning her and lifting her so that she was all but standing on her toes.

With a thud Lillian Fornal lunged from the wall, and Nathan hurled her a warning over his shoulder.

"Look, Kathleen," he said grittily, "I've got a lot of things at stake here besides a seven-year-old quarrel I didn't even start. Now, I've been watching people get swindled out of their money where I come from, and I've had the guts to say something about it. Only I can't get anyone to listen. I've inherited three teenage girls who think Bloomingdale's is their home away from home. And now I've got a half-crazed man who should be taking an interest in Bloomingdale's but who's trying to dance on my grave, instead. What I don't need is a woman looking a gift horse in the mouth, especially when it's the only horse in town. Do you understand what I'm talking about?"

As he waited for her to reply, he held his breath, trying to second-guess her and wishing he'd said nothing, wishing he'd said how he really felt, realizing that he didn't even *know* what he felt whenever he was around her.

He slowly released her. "I shouldn't have said that."

An unhappy smile shaped her lips as she moved away and gathered the shreds of her lost poise. "On the contrary, you were very eloquent."

He looked at his feet briefly, embarrassed.

"I don't know what you and Helen Mason discussed," she said more calmly, "but I won't change my position with her, Mr. Cypress. I didn't want to defend Tortorelli, but I didn't have a choice. I didn't want him to go free, but neither could I cheat him of a defense. I won't crawl to Helen Mason. I'll rot here first.''

Nathan knew she would do exactly that. And he wished that at her age he had possessed such admirable conviction. His whole life might have been different. He wouldn't have married Lee. He wouldn't . . .

A muscle bunched in his jaw, for he couldn't bear to think about what might have been. ''Then we have no problem. Helen will let you save your skin for the price of a fine.''

''A fine?''

''Fifteen hundred dollars.''

Disappointment showed briefly on her face, and Nathan wanted to smash Helen Mason's head with a brick. Or perhaps his own—he wasn't sure.

''I'll pay it,'' he said, and grimaced.

''There's no need. I'll—''

''I'll pay it.''

''No.''

''Yes, damn it!''

She opened her mouth, then closed it and rubbed her lips with her fingers, until Nathan's conscience was shouting. She didn't deserve to be placed in this position; it wasn't fair, not when thousands of lawyers who didn't have a fraction of her skill or integrity were walking off with million-dollar plums and she was left with defending a gangster.

And he, if he wasn't careful, could end up making a very large mistake with this woman.

''All right,'' she was saying with a sigh that made him want to take her into his arms.

''All right,'' he echoed, and stepped closer.

''All right,'' she whispered, and moved away as if she had only just now discovered that she'd sold her soul to the devil.

Feeling hurt and unappreciated and unfairly accused, Nathan picked up his coat and began walking doggedly toward the matron.

"But this is an even trade," she assured him as she hurried to keep up. "Please don't think my feelings have changed, Mr. Cypress. I still consider you—"

"An opportunist and a gold digger." Nathan bleakly dared the matron to say a word as they entered the door of the office to finalize the release. "Don't worry, my dear. I couldn't possibly forget."

Chapter 6

Small-time Bust Unearths Big-time Racketeer John
Tortorelli—Headline, page one, *Philadelphia Reporter*, morning edition.

Kathleen wasn't surprised when her nerve failed at the last
moment. Ever since watching her fingertips being pressed to
the police blotter, part of her had marveled that she'd held
it together as long as she had. As they approached the outer
doors of the jail, however, and she tasted freedom, she no
longer cared what the two men thought about her.

She lunged, breaking from between them into a run as if
wild dogs snapped at her heels. With a gasp, she burst
through the doors and darted into the misty night, running
the length of the promenade to rain-slickened steps. She
skittered down them and was brought to a stop just as she
was about to charge pell-mell into the street.

"Hey, hey," Nathan Cypress said, laughing as he circled her waist with his arm and reeled her back. "I'm all for jaywalking, but I draw the line at suicide."

Dazed, Kathleen found her face stuffed into the reassuring thickness of his coat and didn't mind one bit.

"It was a nightmare," she confessed as she clung to him. "I can't believe I'm out."

He tucked her head beneath his chin with a chuckle. "Well, you are, Miss Case. Right out here in the toxic emissions with the rest of us." Tipping up her chin, he winked. "Let the good times roll, eh?"

Kathleen couldn't help smiling. He was actually a very charming man, and she didn't see how a woman could resist him for long. Not many did, she figured.

She moved to a more modest distance. "I thought I knew how they felt," she said as they waited to cross the street. "I don't think I could ever be a very good criminal."

"Wow, am I relieved to hear that."

"Laugh if you want to, but just take my advice and don't ever cross a judge."

"Not even if they're wrong?"

Was he actually saying he approved of what she'd done?

"Well, well." She kept her surprise to herself, and taking a fresh grip on her briefcase, she stepped off the curb.

A limousine was parked on the other side. Kathleen knew intuitively that it waited for them: black, shiny and sleek. She disliked limousines. They had been forever carrying people away when she needed them or bringing people into her life and complicating it beyond her ability to cope. How fitting that Nathan Cypress should have come in one.

"Would you have done it?" They dodged traffic to get across. "Stood up to a judge?"

"Oh, I don't know. I may have grown up on the wrong side of the Delaware, but there's nothing wrong with my sense of decency."

"Where in Delaware?"

His hand found the curve of her spine in that second-nature kind of way that some men had of caring for their women. "The Delaware *River*, Miss Perry Mason, not Delaware."

In disbelief, Kathleen stopped in the middle of the street.

"You're from Philadelphia? I don't believe it. You're making that up."

"Darling, no one makes up having come from Philadelphia." He grinned. "I swear on a stack of the *New York Times*."

Kathleen wished he wouldn't call her "darling." She tended to take such things much too seriously. "Where did you live? Maybe I know the place."

"I doubt it."

"It can't be that bad."

"You think not? The days I spent in there—" he jabbed his thumb over his shoulder to indicate the jail "—were like a weekend at the Holiday Inn. The kids on my block looked forward to going to jail."

"Jail!"

"The food was better."

For once his handsomeness wasn't obscuring the man behind it, and Kathleen glimpsed a disturbingly complex personality lurking there, one with a lot of scar tissue behind the smiles. That he was like herself in that way troubled her.

A car approached, and its hissing tires spattered dirty droplets upon their feet and seemed to whisper a warning as its red eyes winked at them on down the street.

She asked quickly, "Do you ever come back?"

"Well, I'm hardly into the possession of marijuana anymore, if that's what you mean."

"Not to jail, idiot."

They hurried across the street, and he grabbed her hand the way a lover would do—lightheartedly, without self-consciousness. It was all happening too easily—the tiny lowerings of barriers and slow openings of private doors, the subtle interweavings that were the warp and woof of any lasting relationship.

"My parents are still here," he said. "My visits home are made by way of a check—a thing they would much rather see than my face, believe me. And don't say it's sad, because it isn't. They weren't good parents, and I wasn't a good son. It kind of evened itself out in the end."

She was tempted to ask why he continued sending them money if he was such a bad son, but she wasn't sure she wanted to understand. Once a person started understanding, they invariably started liking. Liking Nathan Cypress could be extremely dangerous business.

The driver had climbed out and opened the door. He waited respectfully at attention while Paul Escavito trotted around to the other side of the car and prepared to take his seat on the passenger side in the front.

"We can go to the airport from here," Nathan told the man, and urged Kathleen inside.

Half in, half out, she realized what he'd said and stopped in dismay. "Oh, I'm sorry."

Turning, she attempted to stop him from climbing in, but succeeded only in throwing him off balance and sending his face slamming against the frame of the door. He gave a small grunt of pain.

"Oh, I *am* sorry!" she wailed, and tried to see the damage she'd caused.

"I'm all right. I'm all right."

He brushed away her concern and made a ginger inspection of his nose and his forehead. When he saw no blood on his fingers, he cleared his head with a wry shake. "Don't they call this assault?"

"Your glasses . . ."

They perched at a crazy angle upon his face; one of the ear pieces had lost its screw and was poking into his curls. As he removed them, Kathleen plucked the ear piece free and sheepishly handed it over. Grimacing, he stuffed everything into his pocket and wiped tears of pain from his eyes.

Kathleen felt like a fool, but the driver and Paul Escavito were finding it all highly entertaining. From the side of her mouth, she told Nathan, "I can't go to any airport with you tonight. I never dreamed that you assumed I would."

"Well, I can't stay here." Sniffing, checking his nose again for blood, he tossed her briefcase into the limo. "I've got meetings tomorrow that can't be postponed."

He gave her a high-voltage scowl. "I'm an important man, you see. The wheels of government might very well grind to a halt without me. You wouldn't want that on your conscience, would you?"

The reflection of the streetlights danced in the blue of his eyes, and one side of his mouth was curled in mockery, both at himself and at her. Though he wasn't touching her at all, she had the wildest impulse to fight herself free.

"And you think I can leave at a moment's notice?"

"What're you talking about? You'd still be in jail if not for me."

"Life doesn't stop just because the lawyer does, Mr. Cypress! People have been filling in for me. Everyone's overworked in this business. I'm causing a hardship."

"Well—" he sloughed the remark off "—life is cruel."

Kathleen balled her hands into fists and closed her eyes. "I'm going to be calm about this," she promised the street and the curb. "I'm not going to lose my temper. I'm going to be rational, and you, Nathan Cypress—" she lost it "—are going to realize that you're a hateful, rotten, pigheaded chauvinist who ought to be *strung up by his thumbs*!'' She shrank into her coat, exasperated.

"I see." He smiled benevolently. "You're welshing on the deal."

"I am *not* welshing on the deal!"

"I have a sensitivity to these things."

She drilled him with her eyes. "If you had the sensitivity of a rubber duck, you . . . you'd know that—"

The silence possessed its own voice. Kathleen refused to flinch as Nathan did an up-and-down survey of her stance—one that made his consideration upon the steps of the church quite ordinary and polite.

"I'd know what, my sweet?" he drawled, and gave the toe of her shoe a nudge that had to be the most bald, blatant sexual proposition she had ever received in her life.

Oh, what was the use? She had done more than go through a jail door with this man. She was tired, she was cold and she wanted only to go home.

"I am not getting on a plane when I look like this," she vowed, and brushed him off with a flop of her hand. "I—I smell bad. Okay? I stink like a jail, and I hope you sleep well, knowing you forced me to say it."

He sniffed as he handed her into the car. "Halston, if I'm not mistaken. If you smelled any better, they'd have to put *me* in jail."

Trying to argue when one's backside is where one's head should be was a hopeless feat. As he swung his length in beside hers while the driver shut the door and Paul Escavito settled in, Kathleen dropped her head against the seat and closed her eyes. At that moment she could have drunk hemlock.

"Look, Mr. Cypress—"

"Don't you think a discussion of personal hygiene calls for a first-name basis?"

She pried open her left eye with great effort. What magic spell did he weave so that every word, every smile, every innuendo placed more distance between what she wanted to feel about him and what was actually taking place inside her own body—that mellowing, feminine softening?

"I can't help it if I like Halston," he blithely explained, and stretched his arm along the back of the seat so that his hand grazed her hair. "I have excellent taste."

Turning away and pretending to stare into the darkness that was flying past, Kathleen saw her own reflection and imagined Nathan's charm as a tangible entity—something dangerous and deadly with notches carved in it, trophies on a gunslinger's glittering revolver.

And she wondered if there was still time to prevent her own initials from being the next.

The mist rising off the Delaware and the Schuylkill rivers had covered the city like a lace napkin. The usual turmoil and dirty streets and sidewalks had been transformed into sheer ribbons and pearl-strung arteries. Skyscrapers brooded darkly over the bridges and moody rivers. The people who were outside huddled together beneath umbrellas. Headlights flared in the drizzle, and the droplets that collected on the windows of the limousine ran together.

Nathan didn't begrudge a few moments of calm. He'd traveled much farther with Kathleen Case than he'd expected to, and in a very short time.

He wasn't sure he liked it. In fact, he was positive he didn't like it. Now it wasn't a simple matter of having gotten her to agree to talk William out of suing the paper; he was groping with some inner urgency he hadn't experienced since he was a young man. How much simpler it would have been if he'd shaken her hand on the steps of the jail, thanked her kindly and said he'd see her in Washington. Even simpler would have been his detachment if she'd been like everyone else and been infatuated with his face.

But she didn't appear even to notice how good-looking he was. So now he was hooked. He was sitting beside her and trying to pretend that his unconsummated marriage with Lee made Kathleen fair game.

No way! Kathleen hadn't known his marriage had been a sham, and he was honor bound not to tell. What a mess! Nathan Cypress, big man about town, put out of commission by the very thing that had put him in commission in the first place.

Kathleen was giving the driver more details about her address.

"Pauly—" Nathan caught Paul Escavito's attention "—I want you to go on back to Washington tonight. I'll stay here and drive Kathleen down myself first thing tomorrow morning. If I'm a few minutes late, tell Rose not to panic. And I want Jerry to follow through with the SEC. He'll know what I'm talking about."

"What?"

Kathleen swung around, her knee cracking Nathan's and her coat bunching against his thigh. She blinked at him and shook her head. "Wait a minute. I thought—"

Grinning, Nathan held up a hand and flicked his fingers at the driver. "Would you please shut the slide?"

"But it wasn't in the deal for you to drive me to Washington."

"I don't recall that the mode of transportation even entered into it. What's the problem?"

Glaring, Kathleen wanted to tell Nathan exactly what the problem was, but he would have laughed at her if she'd tried.

So she snatched her coat and her knee back onto her side of the car, hunkered against the door and thought about the aging Vega sitting in her garage at home. A wretched little machine, in her opinion, infected with more maladies than she knew the names for. It was bad enough for Nathan to see how simply she lived with William and Elsa, but to see the Vega...

"You can sleep in the car," he was saying mildly as he loosened his tie and sprawled back in his corner of the back seat. "We'll be in Georgetown in time for breakfast."

She snorted. "I wouldn't sleep a wink."

"Then you can stay awake, and we'll still be back in time for breakfast."

Kathleen braced her chin on a fist. All the advantages were so definitely on his side. He knew so much about her, and she knew almost nothing about him. He and Lee had to have talked about her. He had to have looked at her childhood photographs in the family albums and seen that one where she was standing on her head in her Easter dress so that one of the girls, she couldn't remember who, could snap a shot of her panties that were embroidered with "Whiskey-bent and Hell-bound."

It was a crime, anyway. No man should have a mouth like Nathan Cypress. No man should have that face. Had Lee run her fingers through those curls? Of course she had. And Lee had drawn her beautiful long nails down Nathan's bare back.

Get out of my life, Nathan Cypress, and out of my head! You keep coming back. What does it take to get you out and make you stay out?

Her breath caught with a painful knotting, and she lurched forward as if someone had delivered a sharp blow across her shoulders. Blindly she stared at a sparkling ashtray not six inches from her nose.

Was that why she'd done it? Attacked Nathan so long ago at the wedding?

All these years she had never understood that terrible day. She'd blamed it upon natural causes, the normal resentment any daughter would have for a mother who allowed one of her lovers to scar her child.

But now, in the warm, sensual darkness of this car, with the powerful engine throbbing beneath them and Nathan Cypress sprawled broodingly nearby, probing her thoughts as he weighed her in the scales of his mind, she felt as if she were teetering upon a high and killing precipice.

It was possible—remotely, *remotely* possible—that she had looked at her mother's bridegroom and wanted him for herself.

Chapter 7

Decision to Dismiss New Orleans Gangster Held Over, Pending New Counsel—Headline, page one, *Philadelphia Reporter*, morning edition.

Some people called Philadelphia an elegant but jaded great lady. Others considered her a sick, mean-tempered old woman.

There were two cities, actually: old Philadelphia with its substandard housing, crime and drug abuse, and the vigorous New Philly. To get to Kathleen's house, which was in the better part of the old, the driver took the Benjamin Franklin Parkway.

Tucked into the narrow valley of Wissahickon Creek, the place had once been the stable for a mansion that had fallen upon hard times and sold off its adjoining land. Remodeled, conveniences added, faced with biscuit-brown stone and overgrown with English ivy that graciously hid sins, it provided the mansion with enough income to offset the taxes.

When Kathleen tapped on the slide as the driver stopped at the front of the big house, she could feel Nathan's respect for the charming old property.

It galled Kathleen to tell the driver he must now go to the back like a deliveryman bringing frozen fish. With a touch of his cap, he nosed the big car into the driveway that led to the back, the headlights, slashing this way and that through the shivering trees.

"It occurs to me, Kathleen," Nathan said as the beams found the stable through the fog, "that I might have been remiss in coming here."

"What?" Kathleen nervously mimicked shock. "You're admitting to a mistake? Let's alert the press."

He didn't retort that he was the press, but took her hand and caressed her knuckles with his thumb so that she lost her train of thought.

"A number of those mistakes have been made with you," he said. "What I'm asking is if you're engaged? Is there a man in your life? I should've asked before, I realize, but you weren't wearing a ring and I couldn't imagine a husband letting a woman like you sit in a jail."

The implications of his questions were worse than the innocent violence of his touch. "Don't you think that's a bit personal?"

"No more personal than asking me if I signed a prenuptial agreement," he said.

The car came to a gliding stop. Kathleen wanted to pull herself free, but she was as powerless to move as a doe freezing at the sound of a hunter in the woods.

"I'm not married," she told him quietly. "I'm not engaged. I'm not anything." Before the driver could get out, she opened the door and stepped onto the dripping grass.

The grounds of the mansion were tended by a gardener, but the grass around the stable was her own responsibility. It had been left too tall from the onset of winter. The wind was rustling the weeds grown up near the hedge. A loose sheaf of newsprint was blown across the lawn. A garbage can had tipped over, and one of the garage doors drooped crazily by one hinge. How many times had she intended to fix the damn thing?

"We're downwardly mobile around here," she said bleakly.

At the sound of the car, a golden retriever had bounded down the steps of the porch and was streaking across the lawn. Kneeling, Kathleen wrapped her arms about his beautiful neck while the animal thrashed his tail from side to side.

"Oh, Dusty," she whispered lovingly, "I think my life is going down the tubes."

Nathan tipped the driver, said goodbye to Pauly and fetched Kathleen's case while she walked on ahead. The house was locked and barred and shuttered. Elsa was a firm believer in "early to bed" and would have been asleep long before the ten o'clock news.

Hardly had Kathleen opened the screen, however, holding it propped with her knee while she rifled noisily through her bag for keys, than the porch light blazed to life like a prison spotlight.

A long, thin finger warily drew the curtain aside. An unblinking eye peeped from behind it.

Kathleen laughed more easily than she'd expected to. "Aunt Elsa's convinced she'll be murdered in her sleep," she told Nathan, who had leaned against the house to wait. "It's in the stars, she says."

"At least she doesn't intend to go easily," he quipped.

"Aunt Elsa never does anything easily."

Kathleen made a face at the eye behind the curtain, while at her feet Dusty waited expectantly, his tail thrumming a happy percussion. "Would you hurry, Aunt Elsa? It's freezing out here."

Then why was he sweating? Nathan wondered.

Five dead-bolt locks lined the side of the door, and metal scraped metal with each one being thrown.

"Actually, Elsa isn't positive about the stars, either," Kathleen said. "The courthouse where her birth certificate was kept burned to the ground."

"Like I always say, one can never be too careful."

"I should warn you—Elsa despises all men except William. And there are times when I'm not sure she likes *him* all that much."

Nathan chuckled. Neither did he.

A woman stepped into the shaft of spilling light. She had once been beautiful. Her gray bun was undone so that a thin shank of hair dropped to her waist, and she was reed slim, like a dancer. A flannel nightgown peeked from beneath a light, graceful robe, but upon her feet were scuffed army-surplus boots, their trailing laces as worn as if they had survived a stint in a prison camp.

"Kathleen!" Elsa's masculine voice was sandpapery from years of chain smoking. "They've pardoned you. Well, come in before you catch your death or I catch mine."

Before Kathleen could explain that she wasn't alone, Nathan stepped from the side of the house, and Elsa's brows were suddenly those of a hawk that had just spied a rat.

She pointed a nicotine-stained finger and demanded, "Who's he?"

"The warden." Kathleen held up her hand. "Just kidding. He's a friend. Sort of. I mean, not actually. This is my—"

"Kathleen and I have known each other for years, Miss Case," Nathan finished, and gave Elsa a brilliant smile as he clapped one of his arms about Kathleen's shoulders in an embrace that sent her stumbling in surprise. The other hand he extended to Elsa. "I'm very pleased to meet you. Kathleen talks about you all the time."

Apparently fearing he might try to hug her, too, Elsa stepped back inside and tucked her chin reproachfully in the lace of her flannel nightgown.

"Yes, well," she said after a calculating pause, and touched her fingers briefly to his, "won't you come in?"

"Thank you very much, Miss Case."

It occurred to Nathan, as Kathleen wriggled free and swept inside, that not hearing Elsa's reply was probably a blessing. William and his sister were obviously a matched set, geniuses whose talents were equaled only by their crusty eccentricity. Evenings, they probably sat around discussing Roosevelt and the New Deal as if the fireside chats were ongoing events and Eleanor might come to town any day.

He deposited Kathleen's briefcase on the floor. The building, large enough to be a skating rink, was in the shape of a hexagon, supported by pillars that were positioned throughout. The furniture supplied the partitions. Art canvases on easels stood around in various stages of completion. Upon several tables sat an untidy collection of paints and jars and brushes and cleaners and rags.

At one end William's writing nook had been set up with an attractive desk and typewriter and floor-to-ceiling bookshelves. In another grouping were a glossy grand piano and a harp. Bedrooms and a bath had been partitioned off in the perimeter, and the kitchen occupied a single wall, its appliances lined up like sentinels side by side, with a table marooned upon a rug that probably cost more than everything else combined.

It wasn't without charm. It could easily have been a scene in any loft in Greenwich Village. But where was Kathleen in all this art and music and writing?

"I'm impressed," he told Kathleen, who had placed as much distance as possible between Nathan and Elsa and was thumbing through a huge collection of unopened mail, hardly looking at it.

"What did you expect?" she said as she dumped the whole lot of it into her briefcase. "Dry rot and dirty underwear piled in the corners?"

From his perch on a coffee table, a monstrous yellow cat dropped to the floor with a thud. He padded toward them, and Kathleen scooped him up in her arms and kissed his head.

Lucky fellow, Nathan thought dryly.

Elsa had clomped to a stop before the refrigerator. With her hand on the door, she squinted from the backwash of cigarette smoke that wafted into her face and asked, "Have you had dinner?"

"Yes," Kathleen said quickly.

"No, ma'am," Nathan said politely at the same time, looking at Kathleen.

Their looks dueled briefly, but Elsa didn't appear to notice. Ash spilled to the floor. "I'll fix sandwiches."

"We're *not* hungry, Aunt Elsa. It's midnight." She turned. "Don't encourage her," Kathleen told Nathan.

But he said blissfully, "I'd love a sandwich, Miss Case," and lifted his shoulders at Kathleen in an innocent shrug.

Dropping the cat, she snapped something about Nathan's parentage and shrugged out of her coat. On her way to a closet, she passed an étagère and caught sight of her reflection. Pausing, she laid down her coat to fluff her hair with a feminine absorption that Nathan responded to deep in his groin. She located some hairpins and gathered the mass of it in both hands, swirling and twisting it into an artlessly lovely frame for her face.

The sight of her engaged in such a task—her gracefully uplifted arms, the tempting curve of her breast, the slope of her side, the image of himself walking up behind her, drawing her shoulders back against him, folding his forearms lovingly over her bosom and burying his face in that fragrant tangle of hair—made him unexpectedly rewrite history.

He had married Kathleen instead of Lee, and the three girls were their children. This was but an informal, late-night visit to her eccentric aunt's, and they were having a small husband-and-wife tiff, having settled into that comfortable mode where minor conflicts are taken in stride and settled much more enjoyably in bed.

He moved behind her, and when she glimpsed his reflection blending with her own, they both trembled at the memories, memories they had never truly shared but had participated in mutually.

Without planning to, or considering the consequences, Nathan drew the back of his hand along her jaw. She followed its path, and her breasts lifted with a quick breath.

"Something is happening here," he said quietly, needing her acknowledgment of it in a way that frightened him.

They exchanged moments when nothing else existed except their mute regard. Slowly then, she moved her head from side to side, and stepped away so that they were no longer connected.

"But it can't," she whispered tremulously. "I won't let it. You . . . we can't let it."

"It already has."

"Then make it stop," she said, and walked unsteadily to a closet and opened the door.

Elsa was rattling noisily in a drawer, and she drew out a butcher knife as large as a scimitar. Flourishing it like a ninja about to decapitate an enemy, and making Nathan dryly wonder at his timing, she asked, "Are you the policeman Kathleen keeps telling me about?"

* * *

It was one of those freeze-frame moments when an entire lifetime can be lived in the spaces between the seconds.

Nathan looked up.

From the closet, Kathleen swung around.

Elsa looked at Kathleen, then at Nathan.

Kathleen looked at Elsa and wanted to shake the woman for speaking so out of turn. Peter Brooks was but a brief, desperate attempt at a relationship that never came about. How could he have been resurrected suddenly from the entombed failures of her life?

Her shame was that she would have slept with Peter. Not that she loved him, but she was so heartbreakingly lonely.

After a long and complicated strategy, she had actually gotten the circumstances arranged, but the trepidation at stepping so far out of character had taken its toll—all that giddiness, the nerve-racking purchasing and placing of condoms in the glove compartment of her car, trying to get a tan, grieving over her nails, worrying about her underthings, her hair, her makeup, never knowing how to conduct herself, never knowing when or what and afraid to ask. In hindsight, it wasn't difficult to see why she had failed so miserably. She hadn't really thought past the relationship ending, only to the possibility of a few memories, even the chance of being pregnant. Maybe if she had a baby, life would have some purpose.

She just hadn't counted on Peter's refusal. Oh, it was all very polite. But what did a rebuffed heart care about courtesy? Crushed, her spirit mangled, she'd concocted a lie even when there had been no need to. It was something William and Elsa had wanted to hear, so she deliberately let them believe she was dating Peter long after things were over, and when they'd asked to meet him, vague excuses had been easy to invent. Then, much too late, there had been no good way to end it; the lie kept swallowing its own tail.

So now she had brought this unnamed man into the house at midnight, and all the stupid mistakes of her life had just been dredged up—much from the bottom of a lake, swirling to the surface from a swimmer's careless kick.

"A policeman?" Nathan was murmuring as he shrugged out of his coat, dropping it to a chair and stuffing his hands into his pockets to stroll nearer. "Why, I do believe you've been holding out on me, darling."

"No, Miss Case," he said over his shoulder to Elsa as he braced a shoulder upon one of the posts and stared relentlessly at Kathleen, "I'm not the policeman. My name is Cypress. Nathan Cypress."

To Kathleen, Elsa's dawning was as painful to watch as Nathan's assumption that she was playing him for a fool. Now Elsa would make the connection that Nathan was Lee's husband, that Nathan was her sisters' stepfather. That dawning would topple the domino that would topple another domino, and another, and on and on and on.

Jerking a garment bag from the closet and several items of clothing that she hardly looked at. Kathleen strode across the room to a sofa and worked the zipper with a harsh rasp.

"I have to go to Washington tonight, Aunt Elsa," she announced tartly as she commenced stuffing clothes inside.

Not understanding, Elsa slapped the slices of bread on the tops of the sandwiches with dull finality. Slash, slash went the great knife.

"I've got to talk to Daddy," Kathleen added.

Elsa didn't look up. "He's making a nuisance of himself again."

Kathleen stared at her aunt.

"The stars," Elsa explained with a shrug. The sandwiches finished, she pointed to the cutting board and took a final drag from her cigarette. "They're done. Now if you'll excuse me, I'm going back to bed. Tell William when you see him to stop behaving like his father and get home where he belongs.''

Without another word, Elsa walked across the expansive interior, her boots ponderous, and opened the bedroom door and disappeared.

Now they were alone.

Nathan looked around at the easels and pedestals and musical instruments and could find nothing to remark to Kathleen about, nothing safe and casual that would fill the silence.

Outside, thunder rumbled with disapproval. Dusty scratched at the door, and Nathan's thoughts leaped crazily from one scene to another. For the millionth time he saw the wind tossing Kathleen's skirt and snatching at her wide-brimmed hat. He didn't know why she had attacked him that day any more than he understood now why she had lied.

But how could he understand, then or now? He who had been so selfishly absorbed in wondering what she thought about *him* whether or not she fancied *him* or noticed how handsome *he* was. He who had been so very clever to have married Lee that he had never once seen the girl who had had a reason to behave the way she had.

Now that girl was gone. The woman before him was still making no excuses, still giving no explanations. The tiny lines framing her eyes bespoke her tension, but she asked for nothing. God, what *was* her mystery? Why couldn't he throw it off and get on with his life?

"Why?" he said at last as she leaned against one of the posts and let her lashes drop with silky exhaustion to her cheeks.

She held up her hand as if warding off a blow. "Don't."

"Ah. Head-in-the-sand time, is it?"

"Oh, Nathan, is your life so perfect?"

"I don't lie about it."

"Really?"

"Come one. Can't you admit that you're hurting? Can't you come off that perfect pedestal of yours for one minute and talk to me?"

The green of her eyes went dark as color pulsed in her face. "Everybody hurts," she said in a voice dry as sand. "And if you think it's perfect where I am, think again."

"Then there's no need to be afraid of the truth."

"Don't speak about the truth to me! I know the truth about *you*, remember?"

"About Lee and me? I doubt that. But we're not talking about my marriage here. We're talking about us."

"Are you insane?"

"Maybe."

"There is no 'us.' You are your marriage, and I'm—"

"The policeman?"

"No, damn it!"

She choked on the word, and two glistening tears collected upon her lashes. With her fingers she pressed her eyelids hard and made a swipe at her forehead, then rubbed and rubbed at its center.

Never had Nathan wanted to hold a woman so badly. Never had he felt himself so capable of comforting, of making all the pain disappear.

And he had the impression that something in her would have welcomed his embrace. But he waited that millisecond too long, until she was grappling inside for a means to survive. She was assuming her old and reliable facade of toughness, and to have held and kissed her now would have been to hold and kiss the young woman upon the steps of the church.

"I don't know what I am," she said. With a poise that lent her jeans and shirt a queenly dignity, she drew herself tall. She lifted her head. "But, unlike you, Nathan, I accept that. Whatever I am, I live my life based on law. And the law is that a woman doesn't become an 'us' item with her stepfather.''

"For God's sake, have you ever asked yourself who made that law, Kathleen?''

"Leave God out of this one, Nathan.''

Her forehead was as high and queenly as ever and her jaw as bold, but the past seemed to have been chipped away from her eyes until their lively green was lost. With a gesture as closed as a book, she moved toward her room and turned at the door.

The air between them quivered with an unexplainable misery.

"I'll keep the bargain we made, Nathan,'' she said, "but I can't take being in your life.''

Nathan lost track of exactly how long he stared at the place where she'd been. Long after she had gone, he realized, to his amazement, that his fists were clenched and every muscle in his arms and shoulders was rigid with rage.

He picked up his coat. He would trade everything he possessed simply to retract his oath to Lee that he would never betray their secret. But clocks didn't run backward, and he went out into the cold, wet night.

Chapter 8

While Washington Presses Roll, Curtis Sterling Talks about Wall Street and his Critics—Life-style/Entertainment, page three, *New York Journal*.

It was too bad, Kathleen thought as she walked into the garage—all showered, shampooed, dressed in gray sweats, heavy socks, leg warmers and sneakers, plus a coat guaranteed to keep out all kinds of weather—that she couldn't keep out the one-o'clock-in-the-morning blues that made her long to go to Nathan and wrap him around her, to hide in him and to say that she didn't know what was happening.

His upper half was hidden beneath the hood of the Vega. At her step, he straightened. Though he contemplated her with hunger, he smiled pleasantly, neutrally.

He had dialed an old David Gates ballad on the radio, and the singer always had been able to melt the bones right out of her body. Raindrops were drumming a soft percussion upon the sheet-metal roof, and the mist lent the dirt floor a musky smell. The wind was flirting moodily with the eaves, and water sluiced gently down the guttering.

Far in the distance, a train wailed its melancholy plaint. They were literally cocooned by the blues. Kathleen tossed her garment bag into the back seat, along with a stack of case files that she was rarely without.

"You'll forgive me for saying this," he began as he emerged, wiping his hands on his handkerchief, "but this automobile and your Aunt Elsa suffer from some of the same maladies."

Kathleen was grateful one of them could still play the chitchat game. "And Elsa isn't senile." She cautiously returned his smile. "A bit strange, perhaps, but not senile."

"That's what I said. This car suffers from strangeness."

"You can always take American Airlines."

"And leave you with General Motors? Forget it."

Kathleen wandered nearer, her hands plunged anxiously into her pockets. "Where'd you find the flashlight?"

Grinning, he teased her face with the light. "In the glove compartment. Why?"

Kathleen's face burned. For so many long months the little packet from the drugstore had lain there undisturbed. Now it was a ghost come back to haunt her. Had he seen?

"No reason." She nervously pretended to be interested in a dent on the door.

His silence was obvious and uncomfortable. He had no intention of letting her off the hook. Finally, she shrugged and said, "I'm sorry about what happened. Before. In the house, I mean. It isn't like me to just fly off like that."

The beam flickered across the stone walls when he balanced the flashlight on the radiator. Walking nearer, he shrugged out of his coat and thrust it at her.

"No, you were right." He rolled up his cuffs to reveal forearms corded with ropes of hard muscle.

Kathleen deliberately kept herself from burying her face in the jacket. The scent of him was just as incongruous as his personality—not flashy or overpowering, considering its handsome packing, but rather elusive, musky, daring her to move closer.

"Hell, what can I say?" He stripped his tie from about his neck and handed it, along with the jacket to her. "I'm a brute. I'm a monster, a dinosaur. I'm a—"

Laughing breathlessly, Kathleen flagged him down with his tie. "Okay, okay. You made your point."

"Don't stop me now. I'm on a roll." The blue of his eyes sparked with amusement.

Sighing, she placed his jacket in the back seat, then remembered the safety pin. She fished it from the pocket of her coat and found his glasses in the pocket of his.

"I was trying to apologize," she said as she struggled to align the pieces of his glasses and pin them. "You don't make it easy."

The amusement was abruptly gone. "Nothing is easy."

She looked up from the broken glasses. Oh, he was a smoothie! She cleared her throat and said with an attorney's verbalese, "I'd say you have to define the word 'easy,' Mr. Cypress."

So long did he inspect her, and so warmly, Kathleen wouldn't have been surprised to see her buttons melt off her coat. When she slid a look sideways, he smiled beneath his mustache and returned to ponder the mysteries of the machine.

Pressing her lips together, Kathleen forced her breathing to steady. She moved around for a moment, kicking restlessly at the dirt and, finally, placing herself in the light to repair his glasses. At last she fitted the hinges and fastened the pin with a click.

"Actually, Elsa is an excellent artiste," she said over her shoulder, though they had stopped talking about her. "The critics love her. She's doing her own show in the spring."

"Good for Aunt Elsa."

She inched closer until she could lean upon the fender. Curls awry, he leaned nearer to sniff at the troubled set of her jaw. "Mmm. Halston again?"

Kathleen ground her teeth in consternation, and she colored hotly, thrusting her jaw at the light when he aimed it at her.

"Get that thing out of my face."

Chuckling, he walked to the rear bumper, where he ran his finger along the inside of the exhaust pipe. Trudging after him like a pouting child, Kathleen braced her hands on her knees.

"All right . . ." She sighed. "So it burns a little oil sometimes."

"Do yourself and the ozone a favor, Kath—" his hips were balanced on his heels as he stooped "—trade this thing in."

"That's easy for you to say with a Lambourghini sitting in your garage."

"Give me a break."

"Excuse me. A Rolls-Royce."

Standing, he made as if to wipe the greasy finger over the tip of her nose, and both of them understood that the skirmish was a necessary part of whatever existed between them. It was a dangerous sign, Kathleen thought, when two people couldn't be casual. Very dangerous.

She pushed the glasses toward him, and he considered her with fresh surprise. Then he jutted his chin toward her like a child expecting a kiss on the cheek, his breath frighteningly warm on her own cheek.

"D'you mind putting them on? My hands are greasy."

She minded very much! She minded almost everything about him! "I'll bet you don't even need these."

"Terrible astigmatism."

Kathleen closed an eye, then peered through the lenses at his face. His smile was as flawless, and maddeningly innocent.

"A strange prescription, if you ask me." She raised skeptical brows and pushed the glasses onto his face, feeling in his curls behind his ears to make sure they fitted comfortably, a process he seemed to enjoy as much as a lazy tomcat would.

"There are stranger things," he murmured.

Second meanings hung in the air: ambiguities and forbidden perceptions. He could have kissed her, and Kathleen wished, as her heart thumped painfully, that she hadn't made such a production of her ultimatum before.

Taking the light, he disappeared beneath the hood and left her to ponder her reaction to the sight of his frame in the shadows—his firm, spare hips and thighs, graceful, articulate legs, his white shirt accentuating the strain of muscular shoulders and his waist swiveling each time he moved. He represented man in its most perfect form. He awakened the homing instinct in her, the deep, aching readiness inside that she'd futilely hoped Peter would arouse.

"What's wrong with my car?" She sidled apprehensively nearer. "It'll make the trip, won't it?"

He tested a spark plug wire here and the distributor cap there. He moved around to open the radiator and peer inside. Returning, he tested the belts of the alternator and air compressor—each examination either passing or failing a specific test.

"Faith is a virtue, Kathleen—" he wiped his hands on his handkerchief "—but don't you think you're taking it a little too far." He gestured to a grime-covered, boxy affair.

"What is it?"

"That, my precious child, is the manifold. And at the risk of sounding unduly critical, if those bolts aren't tightened, very soon you'll being driving around Penn Square and half your engine will fall out. Then you'll get fined for defacing public property, a fine you won't be able to pay, of course, and I'll have to make another trip up here to get you out of jail again."

His face had migrated so near to hers that their noses could have Eskimo-kissed, and Kathleen felt as if she were teetering over a precipice.

"All in all," he murmured, "it's much easier on my checking account if I simply tighten them now."

Remember who this man is. Remember who you are. Kathleen couldn't catch her breath.

"Do you have an end wrench?" he asked. "A piece of metal about this long with thingamajigs on each end. You know, for nuts and bolts. In case you don't know what nuts and bolts are—"

"I *know* what nuts and bolts are." Her voice was thin as paper.

Quickly, before she did something stupid like reach up and place her fingers into his hair, Kathleen fetched a toolbox that sat primly upon a crossbeam. Her instincts warned her to give him the tools and run.

As far and as fast as you can, Kathleen Case. Run, run.

But she placed the box upon the fender with a clatter. Flicking the clasp free, she swung it open. "You should find anything you need in there."

"I doubt that."

Even as the words slipped past his lips, Nathan cursed himself. She was trying very hard to keep things on a tolerable level, when everything he said, everything he did, was guaranteed to lose ten steps for every one they had gained.

He aimed the light into the box and found an assortment of tools, all neatly arranged. "Now this is what I call user-friendly," he said, trying to joke.

In an attempt to help, she lifted the tray and removed a claw hammer and a small crescent wrench. The closeness between Nathan and her was of the most innocent kind—the unplanned, ordinary kind of contact no one ever notices or takes exception to.

But whatever the factor was in their lives that had brought them this far, they had dispensed with anything remotely ordinary and casual. In the same instant, both of them looked up and, startled, stepped back as if a bullet had just ricocheted past their faces.

Nathan felt himself abruptly searching for words, but there were none. She opened her mouth, then swallowed, unable to speak. She licked her lips until they were pink and glistening.

Be wise, Nathan warned himself. *Don't hurt this woman. She isn't like the rest, and at this moment, neither are you.*

But wisdom had never been a good bet against desire. The music and the night and the gods conspired. He honestly didn't know who moved first, only that the flashlight was falling and painting the rough walls with its beam, glancing off glass and chrome and the buckles of her coat, and in trying to catch it, she was stumbling and striking the tools with her arm, sending wrenches, screwdrivers, pliers, nuts and bolts flying in every direction with a horrific clatter.

"Oh!" she wailed softly as she dropped to her knees.

Consumed by adrenaline, Nathan rushed to catch her frenzied hands. "I'll get them," he blurted, shaking her frozen fingers. "Kathleen, lost them ... it's my fault."

"No, no." She shook her head in an attempt to put him off, warning him to keep his distance.

"Kathleen." He struggled to see past the waves of tumbling hair, but she kept shaking her head, clawing up the tools and dumping them into the apron of her coat, mumbling earfully about her clumsiness, how she was tired, how she didn't care about the old car, let it fall apart in Penn Square for all the good it was.

Nathan felt as if he were at the wrong end of a flame thrower.

As a wild creature knows when trouble stalks the forest, Kathleen raised her head and gave a small gasp. She scuttled backward, waiting, poised on her hands and knees, her face so white Nathan was certain it would shatter like bone china if he touched it.

She started to say something, then stopped. He tried to speak and couldn't. Rising, he reached for her, but she jumped back and lunged to her feet.

Both of them watched as he closed his hands upon her shoulders. It was as if a spell had been cast, the lodestone of its power being the center of the earth itself. She was powerless to resist. Her jaw slackened as he moved his fingers upon her arms. He traced a wisp of hair that had snagged on her cheek. The past remained very much between them— double-edged and sharp, glittering, murderous.

Then, somehow they were melting against each other as the music played and the rain spattered against the biscuit-brown stones outside. She pressed her hips to his, and her eyes lost their focus. He moved his lips soundlessly above hers, then fastened, fearfully at first, then with the consuming burn of man's unfathomable hunger. Deeper, deeper they kissed until, she was both fighting and surrendering at the same time.

To Kathleen, the violence of sensations was not to be believed. He was holding her head between his palms, his lips parting hers and his breath struggling, his tongue searching for a quick response. The first kiss did not end before another began. Even as she cried out in frustration and dismay, she rose on her toes and shook her head no and wrapped her arms about his neck. Warm blood raced through her belly and her groin. Heat suffused her limbs.

"God, you taste good," he moaned as he swung her around and began pulling her into the seat of the car, setting her on top of him.

Kathleen couldn't bear to think about what would happen if she surrendered to his searching hands, to the ways in which he was making it so easy for her to love him.

She pushed weakly against his chest. "Nathan, this can't happen. This isn't real."

His kisses were veering off course as he found the seat, tasting her skin wherever he could pull her coat free, drinking her in, breathing her in as if he must hoard enough of her to last the rest of his life.

"Sweet, so sweet," he muttered thickly. "I never thought anything would be so sweet again."

They were the wrong words for him to say. Kathleen wanted to tell him so, but when she attempted to summon her voice, it was gone, along with the rest of her logic and control. Gasping, she pulled her lips free of his.

Nathan felt her withdrawal, and he saw his hands shaking as they had the very first time he had ever touched a woman. In some some strange and untutored part of himself, he knew that what was happening was not casual. They weren't faces passing each other in the darkness. This thing between them, it nurtured, would blossom into that elusive thing called love. If he never touched her again, the residue of this lost opportunity would remain with him the rest of his life and would, in all probability, never be matched again in quite the same way.

He considered telling her the truth. Now, while she was gazing up at him in stunned wonder. What would it matter now? Lee was dead; she couldn't be hurt anymore.

Yet if he confessed to Kathleen now, and she knew that he was violating an honor he had held sacred all these years, would she believe he would honor any other kind of vow? Would it change anything if she did know? Would she return his love?

"You're right," he whispered roughly. "We shouldn't be . . . only fools would—"

Now was the moment to stop. He tried to. He gathered the strength to, and he felt the same happening in her. They sat up and drew back, not touching, not speaking.

Did she move first? Or did he? It didn't matter, for as the flames closed over them, setting them ablaze, her mouth was suddenly on his. Then she was clinging as he had not dared hope she would. He tried to touch her everywhere, and her lips rained kisses he greedily captured, accepting them, missing them, trying to find them as she fumbled to help him.

All the demons of hell could not have stopped them. He took the brunt of the hard seat and fitted her into the urgency of his own body, conforming himself to the willingness of hers and moving against her in the oldest invitation known to man.

"But this isn't free," she warned with a ragged whisper into his mouth.

"I'm willing to pay."

And Kathleen knew, even as Nathan was pulling her down into the burning malestrom with him, that she would never look back upon this moment and think she couldn't have stopped it. However out of bounds their desire was, however more desperate its forbidden catalyst, she could have stopped him.

But her eyes closed, and with full knowledge of what she was doing, she surrendered. When he sought her waist with his firm touch and moved lower to the warmth she no longer denied, they knew they weren't children; their hunger was very adult. Reaching between them, she found the proof of his desire, and he fumbled for the catch to the glove compartment and groped inside. So, he *had* seen!

While she could still speak, Kathleen lifted her head. "But you used her, Nathan," she gasped, voicing the truth as she had always believed it. "You used her."

He was possessing her now. He was finding her with his fingers and searching her sleek heat.

"I didn't use her," he argued brokenly. "I got used."

She didn't believe him, and she didn't understand. The lie was only more fuel to their forbidden ecstasy.

In the end, she was certain she didn't feel as much as he, for hers was not so much the need of that sharp filling of herself as the hunger to be wanted so terribly. He was out of control, and that knowledge was a balm to her wounded heart.

Guiding him, helping him, locking her ankles at the small of his back, she lifted herself, impaling herself upon him as deeply as it was possible to do.

Their primal madness ended almost as quickly as it had begun. In that moment he was at her mercy, and he trembled as he spilled into her. For moments afterward, he held her and they drifted to the cold, cold reality of earth, awed by the enormity of what they had done.

Gradually reason returned with all its icy certainty. Nathan's thoughts were drawn to the parents of all men and how they must have looked at their deed before the very eye of God.

"Ohh."

The fragility of her regret was as a dagger twisting in Nathan's heart.

"Shh, my darling," he whispered, and kissed her with a desperation that bordered on reverence. "It's all right, my sweet, sweet love. It's all right."

Slowly, slowly, he eased himself from her, his eyes never leaving her face as that moment of parting came. He kissed her and stroked her and bore the ghastly way she had of grieving—wracked with sorrow, her hands upon his shirt opening and closing.

He waited until she was calm, and as he smoothed her hair from her face, he said against her ear, "There's something I have to explain, Kathleen."

The greatest sadness he had ever known was when she turned her face away. "You don't owe me any explanations."

"It isn't what you think. *I'm* not what you think. There are things you don't know, my love, things you don't understand."

She didn't reply, but went unhappily about her dressing. Keeping her head bent, she placed the curtain of her hair between them. Nathan lifted a tress.

Without accusation, she shook her head and said, "I don't want to hear about my mother, Nathan. I don't blame you for any of this. I could have stopped you, and we both know that. I just...didn't...I wanted you. I wanted...something. But I don't want to hear about my mother."

Despising himself now, Nathan repaired his own clothes, and as he kissed her a final time, he wanted to kneel at her feet and say he wouldn't blame her if she never trusted him again. Then, like a craven coward, he busied himself with finishing the repair of the car. He was reminded of Faust. Had he, when he entered into an agreement with Lee Bradford Case, sold his soul to the devil?

On the other side of Philadelphia, in the penthouse suite of the Downtown Hilton, John Tortorelli picked up the telephone receiver in the middle of the second ring.

Tortorelli was by habit a light sleeper. On a number of occasions the trait had literally saved his life, and life, to

Tortorelli, was an "iffy" affair at best. One wrong move and it could be over.

Even now the room wasn't entirely dark. At fifty, Tortorelli still had a phobia about the night, a reality he was not prone to discuss with anyone.

"Yeah," he said hoarsely.

A reedy voice punched out words. "She walked."

"When?" Tortorelli turned abruptly onto his side, every nerve on shrilling alert.

"Tonight."

"Then she did spill her guts to the judge."

"I don't know anything about that. I just know a limousine left the county jail with her in it, and two men."

"Feds?"

He was suddenly chilled, but all he could think of was the hierarchy of the world in which he lived. Men like Carboni survived because they were well insulated within a hierarchy, each level depending upon the one below for protection against the danger of exposure. Now Carboni saw him, Tortorelli, as a channel through which the media could reach him, and he in turn saw Kathleen Case as the same channel.

"I don't think so," his informant was saying. "They didn't have the look."

Tortorelli began to sweat. "Carboni?"

"I don't know, Johnny. I swear I don't."

"Keep in touch," growled Tortorelli. "And let me know every freakin' move that woman makes. If my face is in the papers one more time, I've had it."

Then Tortorelli slammed down the receiver with a bitter oath, amazed at how a series of seemingly inconsequential events were pivoting on something so volatile as one small public defender from Philadelphia, Pennsylvania.

Chapter 9

Sterling Ethics to be Target of SEC Probe, Says Commission—Headline, page one, *Washington Sentinel*, morning edition.

Sunshine streaming through sheerly draped windows, ivory paneling blurring with silver-leaf paper, lustrous cherry bedposts supporting a canopy of white eyelet, shelves of books, a desk, a vanity, bottles of perfume, a powder puff, ribbon streamers from a corsage on a mirror, photographs in silver frames on top of a walnut bookcase.

Kathleen was wrapped in the diaphanous pastels of morning—a girl again, having gone to sleep with *The Three Musketeers* open upon her pillow. Daydreams were a cloud upon which she floated to vague worlds where she was never unwanted, where the ribbons were new and the perfume was always sweet.

With sleepy yawns, she skimmed her hands down her flanks. She drifted with a self-created illusion of Prince

Charming with curly brown hair and pansy-blue eyes, a mustache framing a mouth that laughed down at her.

Her eyes snapped open, and she remembered Nathan Cypress and what they had done.

She pulled the covers over her head, Oh, God, she didn't want this. She didn't want this day, and she didn't want to face Nathan. She had betrayed everything she believed in, and now it would be between them forever, a worse memory than the one before.

She lay very still and slowly peered out from her cave with the eyes of a realist—at the canopy above her head that was yellowing with age, at her worn books, at the desk with its sad, empty drawers, empty perfume bottles, desiccating ribbons from a long-forgotten event, a tarnishing silver frame. One could never go back.

But if she had been one to go back, she would be dead by now. She threw back the covers. Life was now. *Be brave, Kathleen. Be stouthearted. Be Helen Gurley Brown!*

"I'm home," she announced to the room. "The sinner has arrived. Do your worst."

She showered and shampooed her hair, though she found the sight of her breasts disgusting and her waist totally unsatisfactory, her hips beyond redemption. If only Nathan could have seen her somewhere besides a jail or on the damned seat of a car. If only he could have seen her dripping in silks or an ivory satin peignoir or black lace...if only...

"For pity's sake, Kathleen!"

The loose-fitting slacks and voluminous pink sweater in her bag had to be symptoms of some terrible Freudian complex; they hid her breasts and her waist and her hips. But she pulled them on, anyway, and yanked on a pair of heavy wool socks. She was about to tromp shoeless to the door, when a soft rap sounded outside.

Her first impulse was to wonder if she looked as guilty as she was. She flung open the door and blinked at the black woman who had been more of a mother to her than Lee. In Frannie's hands was a silver coffee service on a tray.

"Frannie!" she squealed, laughing, then playfully stomped her foot and braced a fist on the side of her hip. "Get in here this very minute," she pretended to scold. "The very idea."

As Frannie placed the tray upon the desk, Kathleen couldn't wait to be engulfed by the woman, and fell into her arms. For a moment their laughter was smothered in purring hugs that turned the hands of the clock backward.

"When I made this coffee," Frannie said at length as she stepped back to give Kathleen an affectionate, love-is-blind inspection, "I told Simon that nobody, but nobody, got to bring it up but me. 'After all that child's been through,' I said 'all that wicked judge put her through, my honey deserves to be carried around on a silk pillow for a few days.' Welcome home, Miss Kathleen. Like I told Simon, no jail's big enough to hold my girl, no sir!"

Kathleen could have stood forever, breathing in the wonderful scent of starch in Frannie's crisp uniform and her apron, which was ironed so perfectly it crunched when touched, like gift wrapping from Saks.

"You mean Simon's still around?" She pretended surprise. "Haven't you run that man off yet, Frannie?"

Laughing, Frannie commenced to make the bed with fresh linens from a pantry, snapping sheets so tightly a dime would have balanced on its edge.

"That white man? Simon says he'll be here till the day he dies," Frannie said. "And I told him, 'Simon, if you don't learn to mind your manners, that day'll be a lot sooner than you think.'"

One of the family's favorite pastimes had been to place bets on who would win, the British Simon Larchmont or the

Georgia-born-and-bred Frances Jones. Frances had always been the louder, but Simon had phenomenal lasting power. It was generally a toss-up.

They laughed again simply because it felt so good to do it. Stripping off a pillowcase, Kathleen pinched the pillow beneath her chin while drawing on the fresh case. Her hands were as quick and efficient as Frannie's.

"You really know how to put the fear in a person, Frannie," she teased.

"Honey—" Frannie flicked her fingers in an imitation of a swoony Southern belle "—they don't come any better. After breakfast we'll have ourselves a little chat, but right now I've got to get down to Miss Annalee. You heard about her foot, didn't you?"

"The cast?"

Deft hands put the finishing touches on the bedspread. "I moved that child into one of the bedrooms downstairs, and bless you me if she hasn't run my legs into the ground already. I bring clothes, and she wants something different. I bring socks, and she has to have a special color to stretch over her chest. Then hair clips to match the sock."

After scooping up the old linens, Frannie patted her uniform pocket for the morsel of peppermint candy with which she rewarded herself.

"Hey, what about me?" Kathleen said with a crinkling grin.

Locating another candy, Frannie gave Kathleen's cheek a pat of affection. "Like I told Simon, it's a good thing you're here, Miss Kathleen. We need a firm hand around this place. Yes, we do."

Kathleen made sure her expression was as clean and blank as a new window. "Really? I would've thought that Nathan Cypress's hand was very firm."

"That man? Why, honey, he spoils those girls something rotten. I told Simon that if it wasn't for me, Miss Lee would come back to haunt us sure as taxes. Then we'd all be in the stew pot. You're just what Annalee needs, honey, and I expect you to do your duty.'"

Looking about to make sure she hadn't left anything, Frannie stepped into the corridor. Kathleen stood a moment, crinkling the candy wrapper and envying Frannie's confident saunter down the hall.

"Now I'm beginning to figure out why you brought me a whole pot of coffee, Frannie," she called, when what she meant to say was *I desperately need someone to talk to, Frannie. I need to tell someone what I've done.*

Laughter trailed in Frannie's wake. "Does Mr. Nathan have a firm hand?" she muttered, chatting happily with herself. "Land sakes, will Simon ever get a charge out of that one."

When Kathleen stepped back into her room to consider the pot of coffee, she imagined Nathan downstairs having breakfast, all properly suited and bespectacled and shaved and ready to get in the limousine and be driven by Simon to the *Sentinel*, where he would turn women's heads.

Damn the man!

Rubbing the back of her neck, which was suddenly ablaze with tension, she poured herself a cup of Frannie's strong coffee and drained it. Jerking open the door, she swept out into the hall. She might as well go downstairs and cast her bread upon the waters.

Leonard Bradford had made one of his fortunes in the manufacture of Teletypes, but upon the advice of an up-and-coming young man who later had an investment publication named after him, he'd gotten into the computer business before they were hot. By the time Leonard had retired to Miami Beach, no one knew exactly how much he really was worth.

Having sired only one daughter, Lee, and having been left a widower young in life, he had amused himself by designing the Georgetown mansion in his free moments, Palladian structure. A balcony ran the entire width. U-shaped, its twin wings had their own stairs. The upper story opened upon a loggia facing the front, from which one could look out over the spires of Georgetown and the high-rise building opposite them, the lush foliage of Roosevelt Island and the handsome bridges, the alabaster beauty of the Lincoln Memorial far beyond.

At each end of the wings were two matching staircases—light and airy stairs railed with sleek curving banisters of high-gloss mahogany.

As Kathleen traversed the length of the corridor toward the stairs, she wondered anew at the lavish tables that had been placed at intervals against the walls, fresh flowers spilling from their vases. She could hardly appreciate their beauty for wondering how some could afford the luxury of fresh daisies and roses and cornflowers when millions of others were homeless. And she could hardly remember Grandpa Lenno.

At a sound she turned. A television was playing in one of the bedrooms—a small guest suite she couldn't recall being used very much. Her first thought was that William had come during the night, but that was ridiculous. William wouldn't be here even if he hadn't threatened to take Nathan to court.

She tapped lightly on the door. When no one answered, she shrugged and padded in stocking feet toward the stairs. Belatedly the door swung open. She looked back, expecting to find Polly with her shoe laces dangling, or Victoria with her hair crimped.

Her jaw dropped. Nathan stood in the opening, wearing nothing but flimsy cotton putter pants and shaving foam.

All the senses Kathleen had worked hard to discipline tripped over themselves. She blinked at age-stretched elastic drooping low on his hipbones. Soft brown curls defined a wedge across his chest. The hair on his head, tightly, tightly curled, dripped water onto his shoulders. In his navel, a single jewel trembled, and the soaked pants, paper thin, adhered to his groin in ways he couldn't possibly be aware of.

A trail of wet footprints was visible behind him. The sun was beating relentlessly against the closed blinds. The *Today Show* was playing silently on the television; he had turned down the volume on his way to the door, as evidenced by the telltale footprints.

"You knocked?" he drawled as his Adam's apple rose up, then down, punctuated with a comma of foam.

Kathleen looked guiltily over her shoulder. She felt like a spy caught selling information to the enemy. "You're the last person I expected to see."

"Well—" he lifted his arms with a total lack of inhibition "—you're seeing just about all there is."

Oh, murder! She rolled her eyes toward the chandelier in the hall.

He invited her to enter, and Kathleen gaped at the open door as if the earth had suddenly split in half and she was teetering over the abyss. There was no way on God's good earth that she was going into that bedroom!

Smiling tensely, she flicked her tongue over dry lips and began inching back to the stairs, groping behind her for the railing.

"I really should be getting down, Nathan," she babbled nervously. "I've gotten a late start myself, and I'll probably have an attack of hypoglycemia if I don't eat. I mean, I haven't even put on shoes. I mean, I've obviously interrupted your . . . shaving."

"No, you didn't."

He took an inordinate amount of time assessing her sweater, picking up on all the inadequacies, no doubt.

She added swiftly, "And Frannie's getting breakfast."

"Frannie always gets breakfast."

"What I mean is, I don't think it would be smart—"

"After last night, darling—" his unexpected laughter made the muscles banding his chest tighten and stretch "—I don't think either one of us is in a position to use the *S* word, do you?"

Kathleen snapped her mouth shut, then said before she had time to think, "So, now I guess you're going to tell me that I've ruined you for all other women." She blanched in horror, unable to believe the words had come out of her mouth.

Moving toward her, he didn't stop until they were so close that she could have counted every whisker. She could have touched every spiked eyelash, and she saw two little Kathleens superimposed upon his blue irises.

"Would you believe me if I did?" he murmured, and leaned so near that she had to tip back at a perilous angle.

"No," she whispered in a thin, child's voice.

"Do I make you nervous, Kathleen?"

"What do you think?"

Laughter tugged at the corners of his mouth. "I think I'm a breakthrough kind of guy."

"Somehow this conversation isn't going the way I thought it would," she said lamely.

"Then you did think about us?"

"*It*. Not us."

"You thought about *it*."

Kathleen had the most irresistible urge to wipe a dollop of shaving cream from the lobe of his ear. "You obviously did," she whispered, "with no self-remorse."

"Hell—" he grinned "—I'm riddled with self-remorse."

As she bridled, meaning to tell him that until he could take the event seriously she had no intention of prolonging the conversation, all the tease left his face.

"Look," he said honestly, "I have about forty-five minutes before I leave. I'd like to talk to you about William without the lawyers present. I want this meeting to be as easy for everyone as possible." He spread his hands wide. "I'll be good."

Good? she wanted to shriek. But she entered and said softly, "You can leave the door open."

"Not on your life." He chuckled. "I'm a modest man."

The room was simpler than Kathleen remembered. The fabric on the chairs was a bit outdated now, and the rug not nearly as nice as the ones in the hall. The draperies had been taken down, and only the narrow blinds left in place. Except for the books—walls and walls of them, tall stacks in the corner and many of them with wilting bookmarks sticking from between pages, fiction and nonfiction, bestsellers and biographies, histories and commentaries, some open on a desk, some open on his chest of drawers—the suite would have lacked any stamp of personality whatsoever.

His closet was open. Inside was a contradictorily sparse collection of suits, all of them the best that money could buy, and their neatness as precise as a photograph. But remarkably unelaborate.

How strange. She wouldn't imagine Nathan choosing such a room when others were so much better.

With a boyishness that she found endearing, he moved through the room ahead of her, scooping up dirty clothes. Just as she was about to take a chair, he swept up behind her, his arms spilling underwear and shirts, and reached swiftly between her bottom and the cushion.

Her gasp was loud as she jumped a foot.

"Easy, easy." Laughing, he caught her arm to prevent her from toppling over. Then, as if to prove his innocence, he dangled a culprit sock.

"You," she said when she had recaptured enough breath to speak, "are a dangerous man, Nathan Cypress."

"I can't fool you, can I?"

Glowering, she warily eased herself onto the arm of the chair. He dumped his dirty laundry into a pile for Frannie and returned to the bathroom, where he raised his voice above the hiss of the water running into the sink.

"What *are* you going to say to your father, Kathleen? I need to know."

"I won't really know what I'll say until I say it. I'm not sure I should be talking to you about it, anyway."

Trying not to watch him shave was as futile as demanding that her heart stop racing. He lathered his jaw and spread his feet as he leaned nearer the mirror to rearrange the planes of his cheeks and deftly ply the razor. Lean, roped muscles flexed in his buttocks and along the backs of his thighs.

How many woman had he had in his lifetime? she wondered. Had he made love to Lee in this room? On the floor? No way. They did it on the bed on Lee's gorgeous suite.

Over the sound of the water, he asked, "Are you legal representation for your father?"

"Of course not."

"Then you can talk to me."

"Don't tell me the law, Nathan."

The water had stopped running. He was blotting his face. His bare feet made no sound when he walked from the bathroom and searched in a bureau drawer.

They could have been old marrieds the way he was behaving. Flushing, she gave him her back.

"You know, don't you," she said as the sounds of his dressing amplified to deafening decibels in her ears, "that Lee once promised William he could have the *Sentinel*."

She could hear him shrug out of his cotton pants and pull on Jockey shorts, could hear the removal of trousers from a rack and his feet sliding into them, the rasp of a zipper and the soft whisper of a leather belt being drawn through its loops.

"She changed her will," he said. "People do it all the time."

"The man paid his dues, Nathan!" Wired enough to detonate, Kathleen plucked distractedly at a hangnail. "You'll never know how much. He took things from Lee..."

He was rummaging in his drawer for a dress shirt. She could turn her head slightly and watch him unbutton it as he talked and removed the cardboard. A line of darker hair divided his body into two perfect halves as he shrugged into the shirt and fitted cuff links into the cuffs.

Oh, Lord! She nibbled urgently at the cuticle.

"I don't argue with that," he said, placing straight pins on the bureau. "Look, when Polly comes of age, you four girls have the option to buy my shares. If you feel so strongly about William having the paper, buy me out. Hell, buy me out now."

"With *what*?"

She threw her hands into the air, whether at his insufferable male force overpowering the room or her inevitable reply, she did not know.

Tension sparked between them, and she spun to face him as he closed the distance, the tails of his shirt flapping about his hips.

"Your million-dollar trust, Kathleen," he said. "You know, the one in the bank drawing interest? The one that you could have had years ago but have never touched? Ring any bells? Hmm, sweetie?''

She wanted to hit him with her fist. She wanted to reach up and take a handful of those curls and pull them out by the roots. "I'll never touch a penny of that money."

"Then someone ought to put you under lock and key."

"Not one red cent until the day I die."

"Dying's a long time off, babe."

"Then throw me a great funeral!"

Communication was as effectively broken as if she had derailed and he had stalled on the track. Kathleen struggled to anticipate his next move, but her senses were too enthralled with the spicy musk on his jaw, and his soap, the bleach in his shirt. She could have pinched the skin at his waist and not found a millimeter of fat there. Why did he have to be so perfect? Why did he have to be Lee's husband?

He caught the edge of his mustache between his teeth and started to speak, his eyes burning into hers as if she were a locked safe he could not break into.

"And I don't understand it!" He chopped the air with his hand. "Not in a thousand years will I ever understand it."

It wasn't his fault that he didn't. It was Lee's fault. And *that man's*—that tall, good-looking stranger who had one day walked across the living room of this very house and when she was six years old, and had stooped so that his face was level with hers, and had taken her face into his hands and, over Lee's cry of horror, had said, "Kathleen, I'm your father."

Until Lee had died, the secret had hung between them like an unburied corpse, rotting, until finally, when the divorce had come, Kathleen had chosen the man who had been more her father than any blood parent. Maybe that's why she'd gone into law. It was justice. Going to live with William was justice.

She'd never told William her secret. And only since seeing Nathan again was she certain that she had never forgiven Lee for putting a six-year-old in such a horrible position.

Her pain must have showed, for his gaze softened, and he lowered his accusing finger and reached out and pulled her nearer.

"Well," he said gently as he cupped her face, "it really doesn't matter whether I understand or not, does it?"

With a sigh, Kathleen went into his arms. It was so blessedly wonderful just to be held. To know that someone cared enough to put his arms around her.

"Why are we doing this to each other?" he whispered against her hair.

The poignancy in his voice made Kathleen's throat ache. She closed her eyes. "I don't know."

"I don't want to go after your father, Kathleen. I don't want to hurt him, but he isn't capable of running the paper. You know he isn't."

She leaned back until their waists were touching, the softness of her melting into the hardness of him. They each took in the rapt expression of the other.

She knew he meant to kiss her, and without her knowing, her head tipped as their lips met and blurred the pain of so many memories. She moved her fingertips lightly over his chest and found the crisp curls. He shifted her in his arms and sought an even deeper taste.

Again they were lost in the exchange of tastes and textures and willingness. Kathleen tried to keep her eyes open, but she couldn't, and his were closing, too.

"It won't stop, will it?" he whispered into her mouth.

"Let me go," she begged, and prayed he would have the strength to do it for her.

"Why?"

"There are terrible names for this. Don't pretend you don't know it's wrong."

It was, Nathan wanted to tell her, the most unwrong thing that had ever happened to either of them. To hell with honor, to hell with deathbed promises. If Lee were in his place, she wouldn't think twice before betraying a vow.

The question was, when? And how? He would resolve the issues between them first. He would go the third and fourth mile with William Case if he had to. He would be magnanimous; he would be trustworthy; he would make peace. Then, when he had won her trust, when she would believe in him no matter what, he would tell her.

With an exertion of will that took much more out of him than he'd counted on, he released her. Then he touched his lips, savoring the taste of her that lingered. He even managed a lame smile as he began buttoning his shirt.

Presently she said, with a cough into her fist as she kept her head bent, "I know Daddy couldn't run the paper, Nathan. He knows that. He just needs to feel he has the right to say you're not doing all that good of a job. You can understand that, can't you?"

The groove between Nathan's brows deepened. "But what are *you* saying, Kathleen? How do you feel about my having the paper? You told me years ago, well, you sort of told me, but how do you feel now?"

At first he thought she would not address herself to something so important. Then she said, "It doesn't really matter in the final analysis."

Nathan frowned. How could she hold him so passionately and deny him this one claim? "You know damn well it does."

Stung, Nathan moved to a mirror and unzipped his pants, making an adjustment to his crotch and tucking in his shirt. Blast, how he resented her ability to get to him!

After putting on a tie and knotting it, he took a brush to his hair, but he had waited too long, and the curls were a hopeless mess. He tossed a pair of shoes to the floor and slipped a socked foot into one, then the other. Placing a foot on the rung of the chair, he tied a lace.

"Well?" he prompted, looking up.

Her lips were pink with the fullness of having been thoroughly kissed, and her cheeks were flushed. "I think you're in trouble at the paper," she said reluctantly.

"Oh?"

"I think . . ."

"Well—" his voice cracked as he finished tying his shoe and waited with his fingers upon the lace "—you started it, finish it."

Her manner was so painfully honest that now Nathan wished she had lied to him.

"I think," she said, carefully smoothing her sweater repeatedly, "that you probably had good reason to question the ethics of the Sterling operation, Nathan. But I also think you were a bit naive." She slowly confronted him. "The Sterlings evidently have powerful friends in powerful places, a number of them in the FBI. You played your hand too soon, and now you're caught with your pants down."

Resentment consumed Nathan with a galling bitterness. Who was she to judge? Had she done so much better in the area of expertise? She'd gotten herself thrown in jail, that was for damn sure!

"With my pants down!" he exclaimed, throwing out a hand. "That's just great. You know, Gloria and Curtis Stern are con artists, Kathleen, high-class swindlers. And they didn't just luck into it. They planned it out as calculatingly as Jesse James. They're taking this town for a ride, and they're getting rich doing it!"

She threw shoulders back, and her voice was low and so toneless that it slashed Nathan's dreams like a machete.

"Well—" she looked straight into his eyes "—I guess it takes one to know one, doesn't it, Nathan?"

Damn! Seven years before it had hurt, but seven years ago his ego had been so huge, it hadn't entered the realm of his comprehension that she could have been right.

Now blood roared in his ears. He stiffened down to his bone marrow. No man would take being accused of the same crime year after year after year after year. His life was different because of this woman. In the space of one night, she had spun him around like a top and made everything blur together. He could never pick it up as it had been before.

"So, it's honesty time, is it?" He was eager to get the fight out in the open at last. "Okay, Kathleen, darlin', I'll answer your question if you'll answer one for me."

She fretted with a nail. "What?"

He smiled nastily. "It wasn't really an accident that you knocked on that door this morning, was it?"

Confoundment loomed in her face, Nathan could feel the heat in his body, feel the sweat on his skin, feel his heartbeat increase. He could almost taste her.

"What?" she gasped, stumbling back. "You're crazy!"

"Am I? You want me, Kathleen, as much as I want you, but you can't admit it to yourself. You're so hung up on her outdated moralities, your pre-Victorian ideologies, that you can let a piece of paper between Lee and me tell your heart what it can feel. Except that it won't listen, will it? And that scares the hell out of you. So you come here, thinking that I'll take things out of your hands—what were the words?— yes, that I'll *have my way with you*, and then you can blame nasty old Nathan, lecherous old Nathan, incestuous old Nathan. That way you can still feel good about yourself, hmm, pretty lady? There are words for that, too, you know."

Her hand was uplifted to strike before she could think about it, and Nathan extended his palm. "Don't even consider it."

She was shaking all over, and tears of fury welled in her eyes and spilled over. She wiped them away with a savage swipe, and her voice was low and sharp as a razor. "You go to hell, Nathan Cypress."

"Hard words, counselor."

"There are harder."

"Are there?"

She came toward him, her jaw knotted and her teeth clenched. She flung her hand out in an outraged circle. "This room, for one."

Nathan looked around himself, seeing nothing to warrant such an accusation. "So?"

Her smile was as cruel as his own. "When I'm not here, Nathan, do you live in this room? Or do you live in my mother's rooms? Along with your Ralph Lauren suits and fancy wristwatches? Is all this Spartanism for my benefit? So I'll feel guilty for having misjudged the brilliant Nathan Cypress? You wonder about me? Well, I wonder about you, Nathan. Oh, I know why you went after my mother—because of your ambition. But why would you come after me? You say you brought me here to talk to William, but now I wonder if there isn't another reason. Something less obvious. You know, you've mentioned my trust two times. Should I be concerned about that? Should I, Mr. Cypress?"

Not in his wildest scenario had Nathan been so consumed with justice. He wanted to see her arrogant eyes glazed with repentance. He wanted to see her out of control. He wanted her mouth begging him—for forgiveness, for love, for sex, for her very life. All his life women had wanted him, damn it, and had come after him, and now this one wouldn't!

She was walking toward the door, as tall and as dignified as any queen would ever dare, even if her color had drained away, leaving her skin so translucent he could almost see through it. Her cheekbones seemed to shine and protrude through the tenseness of her expression. Her lips were white.

Cursing himself for a fool, he reached the door first and barred its exit with outstretched arms. "Wait," he whispered in repentant anguish. "Just wait."

Slowly she turned her head from side to side, her blurred eyes staring sightlessly into space. "We hurt each other too much, Nathan."

"Only because we keep fighting the truth."

"I don't know what the truth is anymore."

She tried to move past, and Nathan saw himself making the same mistake twice. He eased out his hands in a calming way and, praying that she would believe him, said, "Everything you've accused me of is true, Kathleen. I told you last night that I didn't use Lee, that I got used, and that's true."

She hugged herself, then slipped her hands beneath her folded arms. She stared at her feet.

He smiled an unhappy smile for them both. "But I did go into it, at the beginning, with the intention of using her. That day at the church I was using everything and everybody, Kathleen. I was so damn tired of having nothing. But I guess you can't understand that, can you? If you've ever gone without it was your own choice. Believe me, it's not the same. But I didn't end up being the one who did the using and the manipulating. There's no way I can prove that to you, Kathleen, because Lee isn't here to tell you. You'll just have to believe me."

So now it was a matter of trust.

The silence was a weighted stone sinking to the bottom of the ocean. Their need for understanding was far past the limits of sexuality. They had reached the basis of human compassion and soul-searching.

She lifted a shoulder, and when Nathan reached out and took her hand and placed a kiss in its palm, she didn't pull away, but left it cupped about his jaw for a moment.

He placed another kiss in her hand. "Do you have any idea what I thought when I saw you at the wedding?"

She shook her head.

"I think you do. I think you've kept it down inside you all these years, just as I have. How many people have come and gone in your life, Kathleen? I know how many have come and gone in mine."

She stepped back, as if she didn't want to add the sum of that list. She mumbled, "People pass through everyone's life."

"But how often does life double back upon itself? Tell me that? How many times does it give two people a chance to take a fresh perspective and start all over?"

Kathleen heard the words. She heard the ring of truth in them. But she covered her mouth and tried to think like a lawyer, from cause to effect. She tried to be logical and reasonable and see the end from the beginning and protect herself so she wouldn't regret her actions later on.

"I don't know, Nathan," she whispered her lie. "I've grown so used to hating you, to hating myself, I don't think I can learn another way."

He shared bitter laughter with the walls. "Hating is easy, Kathleen. You've never taken the easy way before."

She shook her head, and a tear spilled from its forlorn position upon the tip of an eyelash. "I have to go downstairs now, Nathan. Frannie will be expecting me."

Nathan knew he had no choice but to let her go. "Well, we wouldn't want to disappoint Frannie, would we? I'll see you this evening, then." He swallowed down an old familiar ache. "I hope your meeting with your father goes well."

Kathleen managed a frail smile. "At least the manifold won't fall out on the highway during the drive over there."

His smile flickered unhappily, and to her surprise, he reached into his pocket and tossed her a set of car keys and said, "Here, take my old Thunderbird."

Chapter 10

William Case's Prisoners of the Sea—a Story that's All Wet—*The New York Book Review*, Archives, three year before.

During the course of the day, Nathan came to the conclusion that the only worthwhile thing in life was getting Kathleen Case into bed.

As the day wore on, however, he would have settled for the mere sound of her voice. A dozen times he laid his hand on the telephone. A hundred times he looked at his watch and counted the minutes. Time moved with an exquisite futility, and he kept thinking to himself over and over that in a little while he would be with her...with her...with her...

His meeting with Abramson was a dismal failure. He learned more about the official's sick alternator on his Mercedes 300D than about Curtis Sterling's sale of commodities he'd never registered with the Securities Exchange Commission.

Rose appeared in his office door and eyed his scratch pad. Kathleen's name was scrawled several hundred times there in all shapes and forms.

Grimacing, Nathan ripped off the page and wadded it, then hurled it at the wastebasket, missing by a yard. He flushed. "Draft."

Picking up the paper, Rose dropped it in the wastebasket with a long-suffering sigh and placed two thousand milligrams of Vitamin C on his desk.

"You're coming down with a cold," she said.

"I'm fine."

"Yes, well...you look terrible. Take these before your immune system collapses. And get some sleep tonight."

He took the Vitamin C.

Kathleen's suggestion to William that they meet at the zoo in Rock Creek Park for a walk before lunch was greeted with considerably less enthusiasm than she'd hoped for. She dreaded seeing him and secretly hoped he would explain that he was too busy calling off the lawsuit of Nathan Cypress to join her. But he complained, instead, that it was too cold for a walk.

"Aw, you're such a lazy puss, Daddy," she teased wearily.

"And you, miss, are a fresh kid with no respect for old bones."

"See you at eleven then. At the park."

"Sadist."

"I inherited it."

At Chadwick's, their table overlooked the Potomac, and the crab cakes were exceptionally delicious. After William had been mellowed by a bottle of Chardonnay, Kathleen gently explained how she had become a liaison of sorts between Nathan and him.

"What I don't want," she said, "is for you to get embroiled in something that could just go on and on and on, Daddy. It's not worth it. Believe me, anything is better than a lawsuit, and a person never loses face by calling one off. In fact, to withdraw makes you very savvy."

"The last time anyone called me 'savvy,' they stole fifteen thousand dollars from me in royalties. You be careful of that man." He gestured with his glass. "Nathan Cypress is the devil in human flesh."

"I won't give the man an inch," she lied.

"Even if he weren't a home wrecker, I wouldn't trust him. Not with that face."

"What face?"

"Why, I wouldn't put it past him to try to make a move on you. That's the way his mind works."

"I'm sure Nathan Cypress wouldn't be that stupid, Daddy."

Feeling like a traitor, Kathleen persuaded William to agree to at least listen to what Nathan's attorney had to say.

"There's still some truth to the old adage about catching more flies with honey than vinegar," she quipped. "And don't tell me you haven't got a few sweet drops hidden away beneath that tough hide."

The smile he gave her was more like the gentle, loving smile she had grown up with. Then he stared sightlessly at the river rolling past.

"I promised myself I wouldn't think about her today," he whispered after a time. "And here I am doing it."

Kathleen pleated her napkin into accordion bellows. "Maybe human beings would never really grow up if they don't have their hearts broken. Maybe they're destined to love the wrong people. Who's to say?"

Yet what Kathleen truly wanted to say was that *she* was falling in love with the wrong person. And if that person hadn't been Nathan, William would probably have understood. Now her most faithful friend in all the world couldn't help her, and she couldn't help him.

She lifted his long slim fingers and touched her lips to them.

"There are times when I do things, Kathleen," he admitted brokenly. "And I don't understand where the ideas come from. From inside me." He tapped the center of his tie. "I do them, and I think, 'That wasn't me. I didn't do that.' Don't grow old alone, my dear. It's not worth the trouble."

It's not worth the trouble when you're young, Daddy, she wanted to whisper, but she only fixed her eyes on the river and followed its melancholy roll as it washed history farther and farther away.

Nathan had one arm in a sleeve when the telephone rang. Lifting the receiver, he stood hovering over his desk, half in, half out of the jacket to his suit.

A woman identified herself as Nancy Poole. "I'm a former employee of Sterling Interbank, Mr. Cypress," she said. "They told me I should talk to you."

Wedging the receiver between shoulder and chin, Nathan brushed the empty sleeve out of his way and searched for a notepad. He sank into his chair and began scribbling.

"I'm listening, Ms. Poole."

"I've been keeping up with what's been going on," she said. "When the *Sentinel* ran that first article, you know the one that raised so much ruckus—"

"I remember it well, Ms. Poole."

"Well, I told myself then that I would help you if I could."

"Why did you leave Sterling, Ms. Poole?"

"Well, it wasn't for incompetency on my part. No, no. The Sterlings only hired the best. Why, the sales force for that company was a bunch of barracudas like you've never seen. They didn't stop at anything, and that was part of the problem. But they brought in money like I've never seen before. That's what had me stymied, Mr. Cypress—that Sterling would try to arrange a loan with one of those mobster types in Las Vegas. The man has millions. Or at least, he did have. I saw briefcases filled to the brim with cash.''

Nathan was scribbling frantically. *Come on, lady. Come on.* "Do you think that Curtis Sterling was laundering drug money?"

"I wouldn't put it past him. I don't care what he looks like on television, Mr. Cypress. Curtis Sterling is slime. That company was a circus. Why, the whole time I was being interviewed, Gloria Sterling was talking to her decorator on one phone and her car dealer on the other! Can you imagine someone wanting to match the color of her Jaguar to the office carpet? And they spent millions in cash that they never gave us a receipt for. It was so frustrating. I was expected to keep up with all that, but how could I keep books with no receipts? And whenever I asked Curtis about it, he told me not to worry, to do the best I could. Well, I finally couldn't stand it anymore. I want you to know that there were three sets of books at Sterling Interbank—one for the IRS, one for the sales force and one for *them*."

"By 'them,' you mean Curtis and Gloria."

"Curtis Sterling is a bastard."

Sprawling in his chair, Nathan finished filling in blanks where he had written too fast. After thanking Nancy Poole, assuring her that someone would be contacting her again for a follow-up, he leaned back to steeple his fingers beneath his chin.

So Curtis had millions coming in, yet had approached a racketeer for a loan. And three sets of books? Nathan tapped his mustache, then told the entire conversation to Jerry Franks.

"Go with it," he said to Jerry. "Sterling may be hiding things from his people, but he has to pay his bills. Call the electric company and see if he's behind. Check out one of those jets he owns. See if he pays his fuel bills on time. Repair bills on equipment, anything. And call Children's Hospital. See if Gloria came through on those fantastic donations she crucified me with on television. Hell, go through the man's garbage."

Rose stopped Nathan on the way out, plucked a microscopic piece of lint from his topcoat and brushed its shoulders. Hesitating, she sniffed. And got a whiff of Kathleen's Halston, Nathan supposed. If she said a word, he swore he'd fire her on the spot.

The meeting with William Case was in neutral territory. The prestigious offices of Timble, Hoovey and Lichtenmeyer occupied an entire floor of the International Plaza.

By the time Nathan arrived, Jeff McBain was waiting for him in the lobby. Nathan had always liked Jeff, even if the man did read the rival *Informer* from cover to cover and mark the best parts with a yellow highlighter.

Together they stepped from the elevator onto the tenth floor and into a suite, where a receptionist rose from her desk, her gaze going immediately to the third fingers of their left hands. Dismissing Jeff on sight, she gave Nathan a greedy head-to-toe approval and reached for his topcoat.

Her voice dripped with promises of all things pleasurable. "Mr. Lichtenmeyer's expecting you, Mr. Cypress. My name is Renee. If there's *anything* you need, don't hesitate to ask."

With a sway of tightly skirted hips, she led the way along a corridor where a group of up-and-coming male assistant attorneys were huddling around a coffee machine, flirting with female secretaries on their coffee break.

What made Kathleen so different from those women? Nathan wondered. They dressed more modishly; they worked in better surroundings and made a hell of a lot more money. Yet no one could ever mistake Kathleen for a secretary. In a room packed with women, she was the one people would turn twice to see.

Jeff McBain made a production of clearing his throat. Looking up, Nathan found Jeff and Renee waiting beside a closed door.

"Are you going to sublet the spot where you're standing, Chief?" Jeff asked.

Nathan adjusted his cuff links and caught up. "Sorry."

From the corner of his mouth, Jeff asked, "What's the matter with you today?"

"Hell if I know," Nathan lied.

"Maybe you're coming down with a cold. Every try vitamin C?"

A tennis court would have fitted into Lichtenmeyer's conference room. Around the rosewood table were arranged twenty-four matching Louis XIV chairs, and on the walls were portraits of Aaron Lichtenmeyer's ancestors, all of them mirroring Aaron's elegant, silvering head.

At one end was a bar and an elaborate sideboard. The catered hospitality cart was manned by a wiry, white-coated waiter who looked as if he hated his job. William Case, having already made an entry, waited behind his chair. Dressed to the teeth in a gray suit with a light pink vest, he looked remarkably like Christopher Plummer at his most debonair best.

Beside William was his dottering attorney, David Richardson. Richardson's name, Nathan vaguely recalled, was on some of Lee's earlier legal papers. The man should have retired fifteen years ago.

Lichtenmeyer's silk-clad secretary was instructing the waiter to place glasses of ice water at each person's place.

"May I have the waiter bring you coffee, gentlemen?" she asked of Nathan and Jeff before returning to her desk outside.

Seeing William Case had already made the acidic level of Nathan's stomach potent enough to eat through steel. He shook his head. "No, thank you. Jeff?"

"I'd love some." Jeff was shamelessly propositioning Renee with his eyebrows.

"Cream and sugar?"

"Sweet." Jeff winked. "I take everything sweet."

Renee peered down at Jeff's wedding ring. "Which is undoubtedly your problem."

Gad, Nathan thought, the meeting had all the earmarks of becoming a bloodbath. He was in the process of sitting, when Kathleen stepped through the door. Every head turned as she moved across the carpet in her slim-heeled shoes.

"Who's she?" Jeff McBain asked.

She was hardly the blue-jeaned assistant defense attorney who had gone up against Helen Mason and lost, Nathan wanted to say. She was riveting. Her blouse was black, expensive and as chic as anything Lee Bradford Case had ever put on her body. The color was perfect beneath her slim-cut ivory suit. Her makeup was understated in the extreme, and her jewelry consisted of an uncomplicated onyx brooch bordered with gold, and gold earrings. Combined with the restraint of her hair, which was skimmed back in a twist, she was strikingly unelaborate; yet that was the touch of genius, for it allowed her femininity to come to the fore. Now he knew why people would look twice. Kathleen Case had quality—that rare essence no money could buy and no wardrobe could create.

Weariness slid from Nathan's shoulders, and his mind was as sharp as a diamond. He wanted to spring up to the tabletop, throw out his hands and shout, *this is the woman I love!*

With little more than a cool, professional smile for him, she moved to take a chair near her father. With a cross of her legs, she lowered her eyes to a neatly aligned sheaf of papers and picked up a pen, turning it idly, back and forth, back and forth.

Jeff McBain considered Nathan, then Kathleen again. When Nathan confronted him, Jeff raised his brows.

"I believe we all know one another," Lichtenmeyer was saying to everyone. "Please be seated anywhere you're comfortable."

Rather than correct him, Jeff extended his hand across the table to the woman. "Jeff McBain," he said with reserve. "Counsel for the *Sentinel*."

"Kathleen Case. In an advisory capacity only. William Case is my father."

"Ah." McBain's brain went on red alert, and he shot an accusing glare at Nathan and mumbled, "What's going on?"

"Nothing that concerns you," Nathan growled.

Kathleen had taken the chair beside Richard, who had placed himself between William and her. The receptionist was passing out coffee before returning to her desk, and she placed a cup in front of Jeff McBain.

Nathan absently reached out to slide the cup in front of himself. "Would you like me to bring you coffee, Mr. Cypress?" Renee asked as she hesitated to return the cup to Jeff.

Starting, Nathan tore his thoughts from Kathleen and smiled up at Renee. "I have some, Renee, thanks."

"That," Renee said with an impatient click of her fingernail on the rosewood table, "is Mr. McBain's."

Nathan was too absorbed with the memory of Kathleen's finger on his mouth. For endless moments he studied the way the light played on the tiny golden hairs that gleamed on her cheeks.

"I changed my mind, Renee," he said absently as a strand of fiery gold hair slid across Kathleen's forehead and she distractedly skimmed it back. "Thank you. It's delicious."

The woman turned up her palms to Jeff McBain, seeming to blame him. Jeff shook his head sorrowfully, as if he couldn't possibly tell the worst of it.

"I'll get you some more, sir," Renee murmured sourly, and marched from the room.

Timble, Hoovey and Lichtenmeyer rarely bothered representing anyone in Washington who was not famous and over fifty. Aaron stood proudly at the head of the table in his usual stately black, his inevitable vest and Rolex watch. His flowing silver hair matched that of William Case's and Richardson's. He smiled with benevolent paternity at Kathleen.

"Since the principals have all arrived and are now in place," he intoned like a cardinal giving the benediction, "without any objection I think we can commence."

Whereupon Aaron, David Richardson and Jeff McBain all removed cigars from their pockets.

Earlier in the afternoon, Kathleen had seriously considered having a root canal rather than attend the meeting. But when William turned his sad brown eyes on her and said he needed her there if she didn't mind coming, she said she was hoping he would ask.

Sitting in the same room with the two most significant men in her life, however, she felt like Benedict Arnold. However much she loved William, she could not side with him in this. And it wasn't as if anything could ever exist between Nathan and her; she accepted that. But her heart didn't know.

From beneath her lashes, as the men argued back and forth, she considered Nathan, his handsomeness, his sharp intuitions, his shrewd skill at survival. And how many women looked at him and had their hearts beat faster? How many were lured by that hint of the outlaw in a three-piece business suit?

"But that violates the terms of the trust as drawn up by Lee Case," Jeff McBain was protesting to Aaron Lichtenmeyer. "I'm sorry, gentlemen, but Mr. Case has no rights whatsoever concerning the *Sentinel*."

"I know the terms of my ex-wife's will, you condescending barrister!" William lashed out with a theatrical sweep of his arm that made Kathleen come forward in her chair and try to catch up on what she'd missed. "Can't you get it through your thick head? Lee's *first* will was the legitimate one. You think she was of sound mind when she wrote the second? She was dying, and she was under the influence of...*him*! Tell them, David."

The senile attorney shrugged. "William, I'm afraid they're right."

"You're afraid they're *right*?" William gaped at his attorney in disbelief. "What am I paying you for, man? We're talking about *decency* here, moral obligation. Whose side are you on?"

David Richardson wiped the sides of his mouth with the prissiness of a woman. Rising, he cleared his throat importantly. "Gentlemen, ladies, I believe the word here has to be decency. Wouldn't you agree, Kathleen? Decency and faith?"

Kathleen couldn't keep the astonishment off her face. She looked at Nathan, who was hiding a smile beneath his mustache.

To the naive old man, she said with a straight face, "They've always been two of my favorites, David."

"Have you lost your mind?" Jeff McBain exclaimed, lunging from his chair as if he could strangle Kathleen. "We're considering a lawsuit here worth many millions, and you're talking decency and faith?"

William sputtered something about leaving, and Kathleen reached behind Richard to touch his hand. "Daddy," she whispered, "Mother's will is legal. You know that. But Nathan Cypress will listen to reason. If you'll just talk to the man—"

"I have nothing to say to the almighty Mr. Cypress," William whispered rashly.

"Then may I?"

When William lowered his eyes in submission and everyone at the table looked to someone else for the next move, Kathleen folded her hands and sat very still. She willed Nathan to meet her halfway.

He understood. Kathleen slumped with relief as he spread his big golden hands on the surface of Aaron Lichtenmeyer's conference table.

"Gentlemen," he said, "if I might, I'd like a moment in private with Miss Case."

"I beg your pardon," Aaron said, surprised.

"Oh, brother," Jeff McBain groaned, and narrowed his eyes at Kathleen, then at William, who was gaping at his daughter.

Nathan shrugged as if it were the perfect, logical next move. "I was under the impression this was an informal consultation."

"It is," said Aaron.

"The purpose here is to avoid a courtroom hassle, isn't it?"

"Yes."

"Then I'd like to talk with Miss Case."

The chairman looked to Richardson for approval as a lock of silver hair fell across his forehead. The old man was more than happy to give it if it meant that Jeff McBain would stop snarling.

"The children of Lee Bradford Case have indisputable ownership of the newspaper, Miss Case," Jeff McBain reminded her, and tapped his fingers in a little cha-cha on the desk.

She made her smile sweetly polite. "I know, Mr. Mc-Bain. I'm one of the children. May we use that room, Mr. Lichtenmeyer?"

Jeff's lips were curled sourly as Kathleen walked across the room toward a door leading into a small inner office. She felt the thoughts of each occupant of the room like darts in her back.

When the door shut and she turned to face Nathan, he moved to take her into his arms. She shook her head violently. "No, please."

He leaned his weight against the door and drawled softly, "Are we going to play *Let's Make a Deal* again?"

"I think I've come up with a workable solution, Nathan."

"A church wedding," he murmured. "I love it."

Kathleen steeled herself against his formidable charm. She touched the brooch at her throat. "This is serious, Nathan."

"I know."

Kathleen twisted around and leaned her forehead against the wall so she could collect enough composure to speak. "Nathan," she said weakly, "my father is not a lunatic. He's not even unreasonable, if you'd stop fighting long enough to get past your own self-interests."

Moving beside her, he leaned a shoulder to the wall and ran a knuckle over the slope of her cheek. "I'm not fighting. I'm listening."

Though she didn't believe him in the slightest, she raised her eyes to meet his. "Publishing is a cruel business."

"I know that only too well."

"It uses people up and throws them away. It's changed faster than he has, that's all. Now this meeting can get nasty and long and drawn out, a thing I believe your Mr. McBain might relish.'' She faced him and balled her hands into fists to keep from touching his hair and his face. ''Can't you be generous, Nathan? It wouldn't cost you a thing. And maybe have a little decency and faith? Offer Daddy something at the paper that wouldn't insult his pride. I doubt that he would take it, but even if he did, would it be any worse than a costly legal war?''

Removing his glasses and a handkerchief from his suit, Nathan breathed on a lens and calmly proceeded to wipe it clean. But his palms tingled with the need to hold her. Inside he was aching for her.

''For someone who was supposed to talk to William in my behalf, sweetheart, I'd say you've done a little horse switching in midstream,'' he said.

''I choose to call it seeing both sides of the story. Compromise has always been the best way. Daddy's scared and afraid to lose. Do mankind a favor, Nathan, don't be like him.''

Nathan caught her hand as she reached for the knob. ''One thing before you go,'' he said.

Obediently she faced him. ''What?''

''Did you think about us today?''

In that moment his heart stopped beating. He swore.

''I've thought of nothing but you,'' she said softly, and opened the door.

Once they were seated, Nathan said politely, ''Mr. Case, gentlemen, Miss Case and I have discussed an arrangement that may interest you. In Lee's will she made no stipulations about your being an employee of the *Sentinel*. I find no problem with the paper offering you a position, sir, as a free-lance commentator, perhaps—a position you could tailor to your own style and taste. Should you wish to consider this offer, any recommendations you have regarding salary or terms of contract can be discussed at a later date.''

Kathleen was already leaning back in her chair, silently thanking him.

When William turned, his face was ashen with betrayal. "You asked this man for charity, Kathleen?"

She couldn't believe her ears. She came forward. "What?"

"A charity that's not even his to give? I should be offering *him* a position on the staff."

Felled with a single blow, Kathleen slowly closed her eyes. Whispers sounded around the table, and she said from behind her hand, "Daddy, you don't know what you're talking about."

Nathan cut in. "Kathleen, if I could say something—"

"Gentlemen," Aaron Lichtenmeyer interrupted, appalled by the lack of protocol.

"Nathan?" Straightening, Kathleen sought Nathan's support.

William leaned behind David Richardson to whisper loudly, "So, it's 'Nathan' now, is it? Nathan and Kathleen? Like mother, like daughter."

So swiftly did Nathan rise from his chair and lean across the table, his lips drawn back from his teeth in disgust, that his chair went crashing to the floor.

"Look, Mr. Case," he snarled, and slammed his hands on the rosewood surface.

Jeff McBain dropped his head. David Richardson sagged as if the whole incident were preordained and nothing would help. Aaron Lichtenmeyer consulted his pocket watch in disgust, while the poor waiter, about to refill the coffee cups, stood with his carafe poised and blinked at all of them.

"Not now, not now," Aaron said, and motioned the waiter away.

The man replaced the carafe and prepared to roll the cart out of the room.

Like a monarch who had discovered treachery in his court, William lunged to his feet and brought his cane down on the table with a shattering crash.

"I no longer wish to be part of this," he declared to Kathleen. "If you'll excuse me..."

"William!" Richardson attempted to placate his old client.

"Sit down, David," William ordered, and pointed the cane at Kathleen. "My God, daughter, he must be irresistible."

Kathleen felt as if she had been stripped naked in front of the entire world. Nathan was coming around the table with long strides, and she knew he wouldn't allow anyone to treat her with such disrespect, especially not her own father.

In the height of the confusion, no one noticed that the waiter had deserted his hospitality cart at the door and was returning. In his hand was a camera, and as the participants of the meeting whirled around to gape at him, he lifted it to his face.

Click-click-click. The high-speed shutter echoed through the room like the chatter of a submachine gun.

Chapter 11

Grand Jury Convenes to Consider Possible Indict-
ments of Sterling Hierarchy—Headline, page one,
Washington Sentinel, evening edition.

Get that son of a bitch!" Aaron Lichthenmeyer screamed,
and clapped a hand over his mouth in horror at his own in-
delicacy.

"Head him off!" yelled Jeff McBain as he flung his cigar away and jumped to his feet, but made no move to do
more.

William Case and David Richardson looked at each other
in stunned surprise and sank into their chairs. Nathan,
Kathleen thought, was the only one with the presence of
mind to react.

"Call the police!" he ordered Lichthenmeyer as he
sprinted across the room with lightning reflexes.

The intruding waiter—Kathleen had to give the man
credit for nerve—snapped the shutter as long as he dared

before making his escape. But he had not counted on Nathan Cypress, and when he whirled nimbly around and headed for the door, he instantly realized to his dismay that the tall, curly-headed man possessed every chance of reaching it before he did.

Two steps did nothing to change his mind, and in panic he skidded to a stop and scuttled as agilely as a crab on a sandy beach in the opposite direction toward the table. The seated men rose in unison and hurried out of harm's way.

With his suit jacket open and his necktie flying, Nathan was grateful for all the running he did. The waiter hesitated where he stood and considered their equal distance to the door.

"Okay, you bastard," Nathan snapped. "Who are you? Who sent you here? What d'you want?"

The photographer was heaving to breathe. Not deigning to reply, he moved to his right. Nathan mirrored the move and snatched a look at Kathleen, who was hanging up the phone. Working on the same wavelength, she nodded that the police were on their way.

The intruder darted to the left, clutching his camera.

Nathan kept him at bay. "Who's paying you?" he demanded again. "Who's paying you to do this? William Case?"

"Damn you!" shouted William.

A blank look swept over the man's face, and Nathan was certain Kathleen's father had had nothing to do with it.

"You might as well tell us," he barked. "The police are on their way. D'you work for some magazine?"

The smaller man's eyes were wild and wide, and Kathleen feared he might be more dangerous than Nathan realized. She moved cautiously from the table, not wanting to alarm him more. "There's no need for this," she said soothingly. "Nathan, back off. We can work this out."

Nathan was willing to allow Kathleen a chance, but the moment he gave the intruder an inch, he lunged for the table. With a shocking burst of agility, he bounded to its top in one tremendous, clattering leap. Jeff McBain made a wild grab at his legs, but the man was too quick and scampered along the rich gleaming surface.

In another time and place, Kathleen thought with growing hysteria, the man could have been Gene Kelly tap-dancing his way off the screen. But he didn't dance away, and each time Nathan or Jeff McBain made a move toward him, he skipped easily out of their way.

From his vantage, Nathan stood in a crouch in an attempt to second-guess the man's intentions. He forced himself to sound passably calm when he spoke.

"The Sterlings sent you here, didn't they?" he said. "They paid you to take some incriminating pictures they could have on hand, just in case. Is that it?"

"If I came to do that," the man sneered, "I certainly wouldn't be fool enough to confess it, would I?"

"You're a fool if you don't. There's no possible way you're going to get out of here. She's called the police. Why don't you save us all a lot of trouble and just hand over the camera. If Mr. Lichtenmeyer doesn't want to press charges for trespassing, we'll call it even."

For a brief second, Kathleen thought that Nathan's tactic would work. The muscles in the man's face tightened as he juggled evils in his mind. How had he possibly believed he could get away with such a crazed scheme?

He hadn't counted on Nathan, that was how.

An ugly snarl curled his lip. "Up yours, mister."

With a sudden yell, Nathan made a half-running jump onto the table and sent the waiter, yelping, to the other end in a hair-raising skid. Just before toppling off the end, he leaped to the floor and fell briefly to his knees.

Up in a flash, he whirled around with nothing to prevent him from reaching the door except Jeff McBain, and Kathleen doubted the attorney would risk involving himself in a hand-to-hand scuffle with the man.

The intruder flipped a mocking salute and waved with his camera. "Thank you, gentlemen, ladies. I bid you good-day." He raced at top speed for the door.

But Nathan had not grown up on the rough streets of Philadelphia ghetto for nothing. With a quick-footed skid, he leaped from the table with the grace of Baryshnikov and kept his balance. As the man reached the door, he hurled himself forward and caught him about the knees.

With a stream of curses the man fell, and they rolled, a medley of arms and legs. The door swept open, and two attorneys rushed in, Renee behind them.

"Someone call the police!" screamed Renee. "Call 911!"

Small as he was, the photographer nevertheless landed a wild blow to Nathan's face, opening the flesh over his cheekbone.

Aghast, Kathleen ran toward them. "Aren't you going to do something?" she cried to Jeff McBain.

The attorney lifted his arms in a shrug. "What?"

Over and over they tumbled, and it was difficult to tell who was winning. Harsh breaths and the dull sounds of blows filled the room. Fabrics ripped, and pocket change spilled to the floor. The older men watched as if they were spectators at a boxing tournament.

In the past, whenever Kathleen had watched staged fights in the movies, she'd found it phenomenally stupid for people to stand around with their mouths open. Why didn't they rush in with a chair, or a heavy book, and slam it against the bad guy's head?

To her dismay, she found out, for as she rushed up, demanding that the grotesque scuffle stop at once, the intruder managed to swing around and land a blow on her shoulder that all but toppled her.

With a bitter oath, Nathan hauled the man to his feet and shoved him against the wall, his fist drawn back in search of its target.

"No, no!" the man cried, and crumpled, covering his head with his hands. "A minute, a minute!"

"Ten seconds better be enough," Nathan rasped, "'cause it's all you got before you stop breathing! Now who sent you here?"

Shuddering, the man screwed up his face and refused to confess. With a viciousness that took Kathleen's breath, Nathan slammed the man against the wall again. The man's head rolled pitifully from side to side.

"You can kill me," he wailed, "but I won't tell. I'd rather be killed by you . . . than him."

"'Him' who?"

"No."

"Curtis Sterling?"

"I can't . . . tell you."

Nathan lowered the man to the floor, and Kathleen picked up Nathan's glasses, which lay in pieces a distance away. The sleeve was partially ripped out of Nathan's suit, and the tail of his shirt hung beneath the jacket's hem. A pocket was dangling, and his tie lay over his shoulder. His shoulders and his hands seemed capable of tearing the world apart.

"Let him go, Nathan," she begged, not daring to get too close. "Let the police handle this."

Hardly had she spoken than a commotion sounded from somewhere outside in the hall. Presently two uniformed officers appeared in the door, and while Nathan kept the man on his feet, Aaron Lichthenmeyer hurried up to the police to explain what had happened.

Jeff McBain was taking Renee aside, describing everything blow by blow.

Before anyone could deal with the issue of the camera, Nathan wiped the blood from his lip and walked to where it lay on the floor. Stooping, he opened it and stripped out the film, then thrust it at the man.

"Tell Curtis Sterling for me," he said as he looked over his shoulder for Kathleen and extended his hand, "that if he's trying to stop me from exposing him, he's going to have to send about a hundred like you." He ignored the officer's nervous attempt to keep him at bay, and aimed a meaningful finger. "And if you ever, *ever* come near this woman again, you'll need the police to protect you from me."

As he took her hand, Kathleen was both proud and embarrassed. With the possessiveness of a man who has every right to claim his woman, he moved his eyes up and down her, seeing to her well-being while blood oozed from his own cheek.

"You have the right to remain silent," an officer was saying as he slipped handcuffs on the man.

William had sunk into his chair in abject defeat, and David Richardson was bending over him, patting his hand. "Take Mr. Case up on his offer, old friend," he was saying. "It's the best way."

The sight of her father's bowed head broke Kathleen's heart. She touched Nathan's arm, and Nathan met the older man's bitter scowl—their understanding that of time-ordered standing, of the reigning patriarch forced to concede his reign to a younger, more powerful generation.

To her, Nathan said softly, "Are you coming with me, counselor?"

It wasn't fair, Kathleen wanted to tell him, that Nathan had taken two women from William. She could hardly bear to go, but did she have a choice? She didn't even know how things would end with Nathan. Or where. Only that they would end, and she would, in the final analysis, be hurt.

Yet she still didn't have a choice. Her answer was in the trembling compression of her lips and her stoop over her father as she placed a kiss into his silvery hair.

With a hasty clearing of his throat, Aaron Lichthenmeyer made a note to himself to fire the entire security force of the building and replace them by morning.

"The meeting, gentlemen," he said with a squeaky retrieval of his parliamentary skills, "is over."

Chapter 12

FBI Pressured to Investigate Sterling Interbank's Compliance with Federal Law—Headline, page one, *Washington Sentinel*, evening edition.

Kathleen not only didn't protest when Nathan took her by the shoulders and planted her on the carpet outside Aaron Lichthenmeyer's office, she was grateful.

"I'll get us a cab," he said as he proceeded to remove a handkerchief and blot his cheek, gazing at his own blood with a look of wonderment. "We'll have dinner someplace."

"If you don't mind, Nathan," she argued, sighing, "I'm in somewhat of a hurry to get home."

His cheek ceased to interest him, and he looked up at her. "So you can go back to Philadelphia?"

Kathleen pursed her lips. "Not everyone has your staying power, Nathan. I'm dead on my feet."

Yes, become a Silhouette subscriber and the celebration goes on forever.

To begin with we'll send you:

4 new Silhouette Intimate Moments® novels — FREE

a lovely 20k gold electroplated chain—FREE

an exciting mystery bonus—FREE

And that's not all! Special extras— Three more reasons to celebrate.

4. FREE Home Delivery! That's right! We'll send you 4 FREE books, and you'll be under no obligation to purchase any in the future. You may keep the books and return the accompanying statement marked cancel.

If we don't hear from you, about a month later we'll send you four additional novels to read and enjoy. If you decide to keep them, you'll pay the low members only discount price of just $2.74* each — that's 21 cents less than the cover price — AND there's no extra charge for delivery! There are no hidden extras! You may cancel at any time! But as long as you wish to continue, every month we'll send you four more books, which you can purchase or return at our cost, cancelling your subscription.

5. Free Monthly Newsletter! It's the indispensable insiders' look at our most popular writers and their upcoming novels. Now you can have a behind-the-scenes look at the fascinating world of Silhouette! It's an added bonus you'll look forward to every month!

6. More Surprise Gifts! Because our home subscribers are our most valued readers, we'll be sending you additional free gifts from time to time — as a token of our appreciation.

FREE! 20k GOLD ELECTROPLATED CHAIN!

You'll love this 20k gold electroplated chain! The necklace is finely crafted with 160 double-soldered links, and is electroplate finished in genuine 20k gold. It's nearly 1/8" wide, fully 20" long — and has the look and feel of the real thing. "Glamorous" is the perfect word for it, and it can be yours FREE in this amazing Silhouette celebration!

SILHOUETTE INTIMATE MOMENTS®

FREE OFFER CARD

4 FREE BOOKS

20k GOLD ELECTROPLATED CHAIN—FREE

FREE MYSTERY BONUS

PLACE YOUR BALLOON STICKER HERE!

FREE HOME DELIVERY

FREE FACT-FILLED NEWSLETTER

MORE SURPRISE GIFTS THROUGHOUT THE YEAR—FREE

YES! Please send me my four Silhouette Intimate Moments® novels **FREE**, along with my 20k Electroplated Gold Chain and my free mystery gift, as explained on the opposite page. I understand that accepting these books and gifts places me under no obligation ever to buy any books. I may cancel at any time for any reason, and the free books and gifts will be mine to keep!   240 CIS YAET (U-S-IM-02/90)

NAME
(PLEASE PRINT)

ADDRESS   APT

CITY   STATE

ZIP

Offer limited to one per household and not valid to current Silhouette Intimate Moments subscribers. Terms and prices subject to change without notice. All orders subject to approval.

© 1989 HARLEQUIN ENTERPRISES LTD.

SILHOUETTE "NO RISK GUARANTEE"
- There's no obligation to buy — the free books and gifts remain yours to keep.
- You receive books before they're available in stores.
- You may end your subscription anytime — just by letting us know.

PRINTED IN U.S.A

Postage will be paid by addressee

BUSINESS REPLY CARD
FIRST CLASS   PERMIT NO. 717   BUFFALO, N.Y.

SILHOUETTE BOOKS®

901 Fuhrmann Blvd.,
P.O. Box 1867
Buffalo, N.Y. 14240-9952

FILL OUT THIS POSTPAID CARD AND MAIL TODAY!

NO POSTAGE
NECESSARY
IF MAILED
IN THE
UNITED STATES

His perusal was on the mistrustful side. "All right, I'll call Simon, but—" with an appallingly bad imitation of John Wayne, he hooked his thumbs in his belt and spread his legs wide "—this is a warnin', li'l lady, if you're not here when I get back, I'll hunt you down like a desperado."

Kathleen swore that if she cracked a smile, she would never forgive herself. "Now, hon, this may come as a surprise to you," she said oversweetly, "but the police are already here."

Frowning, he dispensed with John Wayne and jabbed his thumb at the officers. "Not them. The ones with big guns. You know the kind. They dangle one of those lights over your head and are fond of strip searches."

She whispered wryly, "I'll let you in on a little secret, Nathan. They wouldn't find much."

He frowned, his sun-streaked brows drawing together over his handsome nose. "Is that a fact?"

"Yes," she said, not batting an eye.

With unruffled calm, he patted his pockets for his glasses, and she reached into his bag and handed him the pieces.

"I'll be damned," he said, and leaned so near she could count his eyelashes. "Don't go away."

William had been right; Nathan was irresistible. And Kathleen prayed he wouldn't read the truth in her eyes, because if he had asked anything in that moment, she would have given it to him.

Her voice was husky. "I won't move from this spot."

His grin was a startling flash of white. "Good girl. Oh, I mean—" he anchored his thumbs in his belt again and threw out a John Wayne chest "—that's usin' your noggin, li'l lady."

He tipped an imaginary Stetson and walked away. After she watched him go, Kathleen closed her eyes and sank weakly against the wall. "Irresistible" wasn't strong enough. Nathan Cypress had a way of going through her like a tornado tearing up the countryside.

She looked up to find David Richardson and her father leaving. So beaten was William, she went into his arms and hugged him and kissed him and reassured him that things would be all right now. He appeared to be encouraged, but when he stepped into the elevator and turned to face her, she saw the same defeat as when Lee had divorced him.

The unfairness was an outrage. Why must she be the perfect little girl he could always count on? Could she not, just once, go where her heart dictated without being damned?

Nathan returned, having, unknown to her, jokingly chartered a helicopter. A terrible sense of failure weighted Kathleen down. The sting of unshed tears burned beneath her eyelids.

"What a disaster," she said as he struck the elevator button with a fist.

"Your father's okay, Kathleen. You did him a service, and in time he'll see that."

She doubted that very much.

"And you also performed a great one for the paper," he added. "You know that, don't you?"

At the moment, she hardly knew her own name.

The elevator came to a whispery stop and opened its doors, then closed them on Nathan and her inside. As they leaned against opposite walls and played hide-and-seek with their eyes, Kathleen had difficulty linking Nathan's lanky slouch with the tough-fisted street fighter. One minute he was the sophisticated publisher and she was matching wits with him. Then he was rolling up his sleeves and fixing her car. He was a brawler and a brain all in one, and now he was a plain, ordinary man, watching her as if he could devour her in one hungry bite.

Sweat drizzled down her spine beneath her coat. Her pulse was slamming in her wrists.

"You're wasted in Philadelphia," he said bluntly. "You have about as much business being in the public defender's office as I would working at the *Informer*."

"Yes, well, that's where I am, and I'll make the best of it." She snapped open her case and pulled out a white silk scarf longer than she was tall. She flung it about her neck. "I do wish you'd stop that."

"Stop what?" He grinned lazily.

"You know exactly what."

His laughter was soft. "I just know what I like, and I like you, Miss Kathleen Case. Yes, I do."

By the time the door opened, Kathleen couldn't have put two logical thoughts together if her life had depended on it. She stepped out with an urgent click of her heels. Once in the corridor, she looked about.

Well, great! Turning, she motioned him back inside. "We're on the wrong floor," she said, and tried to keep the door from shutting.

Chuckling, he spun her around by her shoulders and propelled her toward double steel doors where an Exit sign glowed in red.

"We're on the roof," he announced. "Come on, beautiful."

Kathleen bridled. "Despite what you may think, Nathan—" she lowered her voice a meaningful octave "—pushing me over the edge isn't going to change a thing."

"I was thinking more in terms of myself." He laughed as he pulled on his gloves and nodded to hers, peeping from one of her pockets. "I suggest you do the same. It'll be cold out there."

"Good. Maybe it'll cool that temper of yours."

"That isn't what needs cooling, my sweet."

He made a bridge of his arm after he opened the door, and Kathleen, feeling way in over her head, marched through.

Immediately the wind took her hair, loosening her chignon. It hoisted the skirt of her coat like a sail and threatened to blow her away like Mary Poppins.

An early dusk was darkening the vaulted sky. Far below, Washington's rush-hour traffic was inching slowly to the suburbs. The view was spectacular.

A helicopter was taking off from the heliport on the roof, and its blades slowly gathered speed, turning faster and faster until the machine bounced slightly, collected its power and lifted off, its running lights flashing and its blades beating the dusk.

"Okay," she yelled over the deafening noise, "you can tell me why we're here now."

"You said you were in a hurry to get home." He threw out his arm to include the whole sky. *"Voilà!"*

Laughing in disbelief, Kathleen twirled around in a circle and tipped back her head to squint at the underbelly of the chopper. Her case bounced against her knees as she stumbled back and forth, and she clawed strands of hair from her eyes and her mouth.

"You chartered a helicopter just to take us back to Georgetown?" she cried.

He would have chartered the Concord if it would have ensured her being his, Nathan wanted to tell her, wishing for the words that could express how much pleasure she brought him with her stubborn little smile and her feisty ways.

He was at a loss to remember how many years he'd been without the anticipation he felt now, the elation that makes every act in life an opportunity to give. He hadn't been sure he'd ever wanted to live that much outside himself. But now he was content to relate everything in his life to her.

"You're crazy," she declared, and was suddenly an irresistible combination of girl and woman. "Certifiable, Nathan Cypress."

"And you're perfect." Taking the case from her hands, he captured a long tress of hair and drew it across her upper lip to form a mustache. "A little rude, but otherwise..."

"A cultivated trait."

"I can live with that."

Abruptly she turned and walked to one of several parapets at the edge of the roof opposite the heliport. He moved to stand beside her. They made no attempt to fill the silence with conversation but looked out at freeways furling from the city in silver-white ribbons, at the Potomac River dotted with boats that were headed for their moorings.

At length, as their sides touched for warmth and comfort, she said softly, "He isn't really like you saw him today, Nathan. I wish..." She closed her eyes briefly. "I wish you could see the good part of him. I wish that you could like him."

"I understand where he's coming from, Kathleen. He thinks I took something from him. And I guess I have."

She shrugged. "In the back of his mind, I don't think he's ever accepted the fact that it was over between them. Certainly not that it was over long before you ever came on the scene."

"Lee once told me that she hurt him. She said she regretted it very much. Especially because of you."

Surprised, Kathleen smiled up at him, at the curls ruffling about his head in boyish, wind-whipped abandon. He was silhouetted against the city that she had once predicted would never allow him to find his place, and he had done everything he'd set out to do. He'd done it better than most.

Memories flashed vividly through her mind, of his weight pressing her down into the car seat, of his soft, hungry moans when he kissed her.

"What else did she say?" she asked.

"What would you like her to have said?"

"It's not polite to answer a question with another question, Mr. Cypress."

"That's because I'm not a polite man."

"Then why did you offer William a job? Not many would have." She shoved her hands deep into her pockets. "Which doesn't make my position any easier, does it?"

"I might be able to answer if I knew what your position was."

She looked blindly into the dusk. "You know, when I was a little girl, William was more of a mother to me than Lee was. Sometimes after the car had taken her away to work, he would pick out one of my pretty dresses and help me get dressed. He must have taken me through those buildings down there fifty times or more. I once stood in the top of the Washington Monument and dropped bullet casings that we'd gotten at the FBI Building." She laughed. "I suspect that somewhere this very minute a car has a dent in it from one of those casings."

He didn't reply but caught her hand and concentrated on her knuckles encased inside her gloves, the way her fingers were not as long as his.

"We'd often catch the shuttle up to New York," she said. "You know, I didn't think a thing about going to Harper and Row or to the Russian Tea Room. Most of the time he would meet another writer at the Algonquin, and while they talked books I would gorge on ice cream." She sighed. "I still do on occasion."

His grin relieved the hard edges of his mouth. "Oh, I don't think you're any worse for the calories."

"I'm good at camouflage." Laughing, she gave her hip a slap.

He pretended to examine the evidence in the rear and clucked sadly to himself. "Ah, I see what you mean. The wages of sin, my dear Kathleen."

With a playful fist, Kathleen laughingly struck his shoulder, and he just as quickly dropped her case at their feet and caught her waist and drew her close.

"The helicopter is taking a long time, Nathan," she said with a lightness that didn't come easily. "I'm having second thoughts about letting you push me off the roof."

He swung her around in the circle of his arm and pushed her gently back against a parapet. "Nathan..." she protested.

But he wrapped them both in his coat until she was cocooned in the satiny lining. He wasn't smiling, and the warmth of his breath on her cheeks triggered wave after wave of shivers.

He drew the scent of her into his lungs and spread his hands upon her sides. He pressed his lips into the hair over her ear.

"I want you to stay in Washington," he whispered, and burrowed until he found the sensitive shell where his breath did electrifying things to her senses. "I don't want you to go back. You don't need to go back. There's nothing there for you."

"What's for me here?" Kathleen asked, not even wanting an answer.

"The paper. It's perfect for you, and you'd be perfect for it."

"Oh, Nathan..."

He gave her a shake as he reached for her lips, then drew back. "*I'm* here, Kathleen."

How could she tell him no when she wanted to say yes? Their stolen intimacy would be with her a long, long time as it was. And even if he could go about life as usual, she couldn't. She leaned her weight against him and felt the deep shudder of need inside him.

"If there were just the two of us," she grieved, "it might be different. But you know it's impossible."

"I don't know anything except that you're here, touching me, close enough to make love to. I want you, and I've made no pretenses about that."

"Don't say that, Nathan."

"Yes, I'll say it. Look at me."

She couldn't, but he forced up her head, and with brimming eyes, Kathleen found the face that was a part of her now. His hands were trembling as they blotted the moistness on her cheeks.

"When I say I want you, I want *you*. I want inside this pretty head of yours." He kissed her lips softly, then her spilling eyes. His thighs strained against hers. "I want your thoughts, my love. I want your feelings. I want your heart. I want . . . you."

She was trembling, and when he dipped his head in search of her lips, she thrust her fingers between them, pushing his mouth away.

"Don't put me in this position," she begged. "Do you think this is easy? Saying no to you?"

Though he didn't move, Kathleen felt distance between them.

"Did you say no to him?"

"Him?" Kathleen's lips parted in bafflement.

"The policeman?"

How could he? How dared he? Kathleen attempted to strike his chest with her fist. "That's beneath you, Nathan!"

"Is that a no?"

"Look—" she threw back her head "—I don't pry into your relationship with my mother, do I? Do I ask you what it felt like to kiss her?" She was desperate to wound him. "Did my mother close her eyes, Nathan? Did you like her breasts as well as mine, Nathan? Was she different inside? Did she groan? Did she scream?"

Only once before had she seen him so angry. And now, when he locked his fingers about her thrashing hands and reached for her mouth with his, she made no attempt to hold back her own anger. Before he had come into her life, *uninvited*, she'd been reasonably happy. Now she was ruined. She could never go back to what she'd been. She would never be happy again, not for the rest of her life.

He lowered his mouth, and as she jerked away, he moved to capture her pulsing lips. All her twisting and turning could not elude him, and his tongue made fearful demands of hers. His hands beneath her coat held her pinned fast to him, and he was hard against her. He clasped her hips beneath the coat and pulled her upward so there would be no doubts.

From the back of Kathleen's throat came tiny tortured sounds. Over and over he kissed her, as if he could never slake the thirst, until, with the strength left her, she forced her hands between them in a last stanchion of refusal, barring him from that triangled juncture.

Releasing her, he leaned back on the parapet, his breaths coming hard and his eyes closing in disappointment at himself.

"I'm losing my mind," he said with a shake of his head. "I'm going insane. I don't do this to women. I've never done this to a woman."

Kathleen was so drained of strength, she could but hug herself to keep from shuddering. Misunderstanding, he braced a shoulder on the concrete and pulled her around so that they faced each other. He pushed back her hair.

"Do you hate her so much that you must punish me?" he asked.

Kathleen looked down at the concrete surface. "I don't hate Lee. I mean, I didn't hate her."

"You didn't love her."

"I may not have liked her sometimes, but I loved her. Of course I loved her."

"Then why did you leave?"

"Didn't she tell you?" Kathleen threw him an accusing look. "I thought you two shared everything."

Nathan knew, as he watched Kathleen drawing deep into herself, that he couldn't have it both ways any longer. He could either tell her the whole truth now about his marriage, or he could lose her.

At the sound of an approaching helicopter, Kathleen looked up, then back at Nathan. "Child abuse doesn't always take the form we expect it to, Nathan," she said woodenly.

"What're you talking about? That Lee beat you? Locked you in a closet? What?"

Kathleen slipped her thumbnail between her teeth, then lowered it quickly, only to nibble at the cuticle of another finger. Time was running out. The helicopter was gaining on them, and she had the feeling that if she didn't get the words said now, she would never find the courage again.

In disjointed sentences, she told him about the man who had knelt before her and told her he was her father. "I've looked back on that day a million times and tried to make it worth the pain, Nathan. And one day it hit me, that Guy Whoever-he-was wasn't the cause of the hurt."

"Lee was only a human being, Kathleen."

"It wasn't because she had a lover. I could have gotten over that, and I think Daddy could have forgiven her that. No, it was that *I* was made the weapon. I was made her leverage, Nathan. She made me promise never to tell Daddy. She told me—and I was only six years old at the time—she told me that if I betrayed our secret William would divorce her. And that years later I would look back and see what I had caused, and it would be too late then to do anything, and I would carry that guilt around with me all my life."

The helicopter was hovering above their heads. The vibration rattled Kathleen's bones.

Even without the ending of the story, Nathan thought he understood, and he drew her into his arms and rocked her back and forth as a father would comfort a frightened child who had been lost.

"Oh, baby," he whispered, "I'm so sorry. I'm so sorry. It's all right now, I promise."

But it wasn't all right, and he couldn't promise anything.

As the great machine above them settled onto its pad, Nathan placed his mouth to her ear. "You have a trust of nearly a million dollars. Is that why you've never touched it?"

The pilot was waiting for them. They could not ask him to wait.

Taking up her case, Nathan grabbed her hand and ran with her to the open door. The rotor wash threatened to tear off their clothes, and instinctively they ducked.

Handing in her case, which the pilot took and placed on the floor beside a seat, Nathan drew Kathleen to the entrance, and the look they shared was one that time could never touch, one that no words could ever be invented for.

As Kathleen gazed up and let him see the full impact of her awakening to him, the time for deceptions and half-truths was past. She had the feeling she would look back upon this moment as a dividing of roads in her life, for there was no doubt in her mind that once she said the words aloud, nothing would ever be the same again.

"No," she cried. "That wasn't the reason."

"Why?"

"You! You were the reason!"

Nathan didn't understand. He signaled the pilot with a distracted motion of his hand. "Me? I—"

"Jealousy, Nathan."

"Jealousy?"

Kathleen closed her eyes in a search for the courage to finish. She drew in her breath and spoke quickly before she could change her mind. She didn't quite manage enough bravery to meet his eyes, and turned slightly away.

"Because she had you," she cried into the deafening throb. "And I wished I were her."

Chapter 13

Philadelphians Speak Out on Tortorelli Release—Headline, page three, *Philadelphia Reporter*, evening edition.

Watching Simon Larchmont fuss over three buoyant girls as they spilled out of the limousine and dashed across the street toward the helipad was like observing a mother hen go slightly berserk over chicks flying the coop.

"Oh, dear, Miss Annalee!" Simon hustled around the car, his rotund stomach vibrating in time to his tiny feet. He shut doors and dodged puddles of rain, only to discover that by the time he reached Annalee, the thirteen-year-old was making better time with her sticks than he was without.

"Dear-oh-dear-oh-dear. I advise against going out there, miss. By the time you reach them, they'll be here."

"Piddle-de-squat, Simon," Annalee yelled as she chugged stoutly after her sisters. "Nathan'll probably take them up.

I've never gotten to ride in a helicopter and Polly's been up three times!''

"Yes..." Simon's voice was as thin as he was round. "And she's thrown up three times, miss!"

"Wait for me, you heathens!" Annalee was a blur of bright blue windbreaker, white cast, faded jeans and crimped blond hair filled with as assorted color of grippers. She thumped through slush without a care. "Kathleen, don't you *dare* let them go without me!"

Kathleen laughed as she and Nathan were overrun.

Georgetown was now a twinkle with streetlights and Christmas glitter. The private heliport was deserted except for them—a good thing, to Kathleen's mind, for Polly threw her arms around Nathan's neck like a banshee and climbed his leg, wailing for him to hire the pilot for just one ride, please, please, *pleeease*.

"Not on your life, youngster," he growled, and placed the eleven-year-old firmly on the ground. "I'm still cleaning the stain out of the upholstery from the last time you went up."

By the time Annalee huffed and puffed her way up, the helicopter was swinging out into the night. "Well, heck." She thumped her crutch on the ground in a manner that Nathan thought was remarkably like her father.

"Oh, do take it down a thousand, Annalee," Victoria declared presently in one of her cool, chic, practiced voices.

Annalee pulled a face at her sister. "Like, gag with a spoon, sis."

Polly looped her arm through Kathleen's as if Kathleen had been in their young lives forever. "Simon let Victoria drive all the way to the airport," she cheerfully informed them. "And she doesn't even have a driver's permit yet. Nathan, can I drive on the way back?"

Over all their heads, Nathan's smile embraced Kathleen's.

"Ah, Simon, my man—" Nathan elongated the words as if contemplating deep and abiding tortures "—I see it's your intention to depart this life in your prime."

Poor Simon could but give a repentant tug to the bill of his cap. "You know Miss Victoria, sir," he wheezed, as if that were the definitive statement on the subject of Victoria.

Nathan nodded sympathetically. He sighed. "Yes, yes, I do know Victoria."

"Please let me drive back, Nathan," the girl cajoled, and turned to Kathleen for sisterly backup. "You're always telling me how I should be more mature, Kath, and here I'm trying to do just that. Make Nathan let me drive back."

"Hey..." Kathleen, having had her briefcase pilfered by Polly, who was staggering beneath its weight, raised both hands in neutrality. "Leave me out of this. Nathan's the boss."

"Nathan Cypress is a tyrant." Victoria traipsed on ahead and spoke over her shoulder as they walked. "Nothing but rules, rules, rules." She mimicked Nathan in a singsong voice. "You can't go out with boys, Victoria. You can't stay out past ten o'clock, Victoria. No shaving your legs until you're fifteen, Victoria."

"*I* like you, Nathan," Annalee assured with a no-nonsense practicality.

Polly chimed in supportively, "So do I, Nathan. I love you. I'm gonna marry you."

"Don't be silly, runt," huffed Victoria. "You can't marry your guardian."

Inwardly Kathleen winced. *Out of the mouths of babes!*

"Nathan," Polly said as she deftly inserted herself between Kathleen and him, "we have to go out for pizza. Frannie put garbonza beans in the salad again."

"Garbonza beans are good for you," Nathan countered.

"With lentil soup?"

"Bitch, bitch, bitch," Nathan said, laughing.

Kathleen felt shortchanged by her memories. How good Nathan was with them, how they adored him. There was no way on earth he could be the things she had once accused him of. And he could not know how starved she was for the very thing he instinctively gave her sisters. He could not know that even the inflections in his voice and his playful gruffness opened doors to empty rooms inside her.

"Watch your language, Nathan," Victoria was chiding him. "You're supposed to set us a good example."

"Good example, my foot."

Victoria turned so that she was walking backward to the car. "If you let me drive home, I promise I'll never use your razor again, Nathan. I'll never argue with you as long as I live, and I'll iron all your shirts so you don't have to send them out to the laundry to get messed up."

"I wouldn't make too many rash promises, sis," Nathan advised, and found the small of Kathleen's back in a way that seemed nonchalant to everyone but Kathleen.

"Kathleen's a witness to all these vows," he added, and moved his hand over the span of her ribs, causing her to catch her lip between her teeth.

"Yes, but she's going home," Annalee said.

"Maybe," he murmured, and Kathleen twisted around to see if he was serious.

He was. But before she could protest, the girls were scraping their shoes and climbing into the car. She cleaned her own shoes, and Simon opened the trunk of the car and placed her briefcase there.

Victoria had already usurped the driver's seat and was demonstrating how perfectly her tall frame fitted the spacing of the seat and the tilt of the wheel.

"I'm ready," she chirped brightly, and indicated that Nathan must sit next to her just in case she got into trouble. Then Kathleen must sit on the other side of him. Simon and her two sisters could sit in the back.

"If the police stop us," she added as she made the shifting of the gear a momentous occasion, "Kathleen can tell them she's a lawyer."

"I'm sure they would be greatly impressed," Kathleen said with wry irony.

"Well, I know I am," Nathan quipped.

"What you are is in trouble."

Kathleen gave him a sharp elbow in his ribs, which made him howl with pretended agony and playfully grab her arm for a tussle, much to the delight of the girls.

Polly was so excited that she tumbled over the seat and slid into the small space between them. She hugged Kathleen's arm with sweet innocence and flashed a toothy grin. "I like to snuggle," she said.

With a roll of his eyes, Nathan slid his hand along the back of the seat and found Kathleen's nape beneath her hair. "So do I."

"It's hot up here." Polly was oblivious to the two adults, who were caught in the undertow of double entendres.

"It is that," Nathan said, and toyed with the lobe of Kathleen's ear in an alarming way.

If he could have guessed even *part* of the storm that his touch incited, Kathleen knew she would have been at his mercy forever. She was grateful for the ridiculous lengths Victoria went to in starting the car, for a roar deafened them as she revved the motor.

From the back seat, Simon pulled his cap down and slid as low on his spine as his fine breeding and girth would allow.

"Are you ready?" Victoria asked everyone, looking around.

Coughing gently, Nathan maintained a smile. "Yes, dear. Anytime you are."

The girl removed her foot from the brake and began to jerk forward, two feet at a spurt. Polly snuggled happily in her safe nest between the two adults.

"Kathleen is going to stay for a long, long time, isn't she, Nathan?" she said.

Nathan's caress of Kathleen's cheek with his thumb was seen only by Annalee, for Simon had his eyes closed.

"Definitely." He smiled into Kathleen's horrified eyes. "No doubt about it."

Kathleen was of no mind to go jogging with Nathan Cypress at six in the morning when he banged at her door. So she did not understand how she wound up trotting alongside him as he made his usual circuit around the Water Gardens Retirement Center two blocks from the house.

Nathan took his running very seriously. She was more inclined to begin at a plodding pace and work it up to a chug and hold it there. At first Nathan held himself in check, trotting along at a leisurely jaunt and making ribald remarks about how she was operating on kerosene and had to get some stamina. After he found himself passed by several of the elderly set, his pride compelled him to stretch out and make three circuits to her one.

Kathleen didn't mind. She rather enjoyed watching him run past, reveled in the easy strength of his stride. His headband was already soaked, and he squinted against the rising sun as his muscles flexed inside his gray sweat pants. She imagined the wet hair matting his body. None of the other men were as interesting, though a group of the younger crowd had arrived and streamed past in their racing Pumas, their breaths pluming in the cold morning.

Eventually Nathan fell back into step and danced a few feet beyond her, running backward, sparring playfully, feinting and jabbing and skipping back.

"Great tush you got there, Miz Case," he huffed. "Just thought I'd throw that in."

"Great feet, too," she puffed, "so get out of my way before I kick you with one of them."

"Do the words 'bad sport' mean anything to you?"

"Yes. And so do 'felonious assault,' so move. Unless you want to call the paramedics."

"For you or me?"

She laughed. "At the moment it could go either way."

Nathan chuckled, loving the way the sun held on her, the way her hair trailed her head in a glistening mane. He loved the way she leaned upon the chain-link fence when they'd finished running. She hooked her fingers into its squares and trotted in place, letting her shoulder blades collapse and her neck drop. Then she eased into a walk along the path to cool down. He hadn't known it was possible to love anyone so much.

"I need to use the telephone," she told him as she glanced at her wristwatch and blotted her face on the sleeve of her sweater.

She had borrowed a pair of his old navy sweats that had shrunk in the dryer. They were drooping comically about the tops of her socks. She pulled them up and looked around the complex.

The running path circumvented a luxurious retirement center, veering past neatly clipped grounds and waterworks copied after those at Versailles. They were near the recreational center, where, in warm weather, outdoor dances were held beneath the huge canopy. On Sunday afternoons during the off-season, the neighborhood children came to roller-skate.

Picnic tables and park benches were scattered among the trees, and along the outer rail of the dance floor was a kiosk with an old-fashioned jukebox tucked inside and a trio of telephones, a concession stand with its window closed for the winter.

Nathan indicated the phones. "But we have a few in working order at the house, you know."

"Farrell's in his office now. That one is fine. Do you have a quarter?"

"And you call me a gold digger."

Nathan doled her out a coin from the few that Frannie insisted he carry on him when he jogged, just in case he had a heart attack and needed to call an ambulance, she teased.

Kathleen dropped the coin into the slot and danced lightly to keep from getting chilled. When Farell Mulhaney, Philadelphia County's public defender, came on the line, she smiled at Nathan while she talked.

"Farrell," she said brightly, "guess who's checking in late."

"Well, now, jailbird," Farrell said, "I heard it was a toss-up between releasing you and the Boston Strangler, and Boston was the lucky winner."

Farrell Mulhaney was one of the least handsome men Kathleen had ever known. Small and balding, he looked like a beaver, his face destined to be the butt of lifelong jokes. But he was unlike most of her colleagues in that he truly cared about the people he defended. She adored him. She had even tried to feel for him the sexual interest she had felt for Peter. But Farrell was like the brother she'd never had.

"Are you kidding?" She laughed. "I nearly got carried off to one of those medical experimentation labs. You know the kind."

"Shades of Stephen King. Do you have all your organs?"

"Everything but my heart, Farrell."

"I knew you'd lose it one day. Who's the lucky fella?"

She'd asked for that one, hadn't she?

Kathleen slapped at Nathan's hand, which was errantly tracing the shape of her bra. She turned her shoulder into his side so his warmth would protect her from the wind.

"Farrell—" her tone grew serious "—I need you to do something for me."

"Ask away."

"Would you take care of Duane Stuart? Nothing big, petty theft, a probation thing, but a petition has to be filed before Heiliger in ten days."

"Consider it done."

"I have everything else pretty well under control. I've been doing some work by phone."

"Anything else?"

Kathleen hesitated, having stayed awake half the night debating the wisdom of what she was about to do. Holding Nathan at bay as he persisted in nibbling the lobe of her ear and strewing kisses beneath her hair, she said, "I'd like to stay here until after Thanksgiving, Farrell. Things will hold together there, won't they?"

Farrell's hesitation weighed a ton. Kathleen strained to read its reason and slapped at Nathan, pressing her ear more tightly to the receiver. "What's happened?"

At her tone Nathan stiffened and fixed her with a frown.

"Oh, you never know about the ranting of lunatics, Kath," Farrell said guardedly. "Mike stood in for you with Tortorelli when he appeared before Mason, otherwise I wouldn't have heard anything about it."

"Heard what, Farrell?" The hair on the back of Kathleen's neck was rising, and when Nathan pulled her more tightly into his arms, she didn't resist. "Go on. You're scaring me."

"You were released from jail, kiddo. Tortorelli thinks you bought your way out."

"You mean—"

"He thinks you ratted on him to Helen. He told Mike he was going to get you. But you can't pay any attention to that, Kath. You know how they rant and rave. It's nothing but wild talk. I wouldn't have said anything except to let you know that I think it would be a good idea if you did stay there a few days."

Kathleen's heart ceased to beat for a few moments. "Yeah, I know," she said softly, trying to figure out how things had gotten so out of her control. "Well, look, thank Mike for me, will you, Farrell? And I'll see you soon."

"Your case was brilliant, kiddo. I would've made the same defense."

Kathleen's facade slipped a notch. "Oh, sure, Farrell. And now a murderer has gone scot-free."

"That's the system, Kath."

"Yeah, that's the system, all right."

By the time she hung up the phone, Kathleen was shivering, and she turned her face into the side of the kiosk and squeezed her eyes tightly shut.

"What was it?" Nathan demanded. "What did he say?"

She didn't want Nathan to know. She didn't want him to worry.

Summoning strength she would have sworn was not left in her, she arranged her expression to one of a mild pique. "He's out, that's all. Tortorelli's walking the streets. I guess I was hoping something would happen at the last minute and send him to Devil's Island."

Nathan leaned back to study her, one arm about her shoulders, the other resting on the top of the phone. Kathleen pretended to take an interest in the joggers.

His hand found her back. "Come here," he said.

With a small sound, she pressed her head into the hollow of his shoulder and was grateful for the steady assurance of his arms around her, of his muscles surrounding and protecting her from the world.

Presently, though, a more carnal assurance asserted itself against her belly, and she leaned back to blink chidingly at him.

"Come with me," he murmured, "before I embarrass us."

She moved numbly beside him, only vaguely aware that he had stopped before the old jukebox and plugged it in. As he inserted a coin into the slot, she inspected the antiquated machine. "What're you doing?"

With a facetious charm and self-mockery, he bowed from his waist as the record dropped into place on the turntable, and he purred, "Madam, may I have this dance?"

The sound of Glenn Miller drifted through the bare trees, the speakers raspy from remaining outside too long.

"Are you crazy?" In disbelief, Kathleen twirled around to see if the whole world was observing.

"Absolutely." He caught her into his arms as lightly as thistledown and twirled her out in a series of turns until they were on the floor of the pavilion.

No matter what happened to her in the years to come, Kathleen thought as she melted in his arms, that she would never forget this moment. She looked up to see his slow smile finding her just when she needed it, and moved in sync with the saxophones and clarinets that couples had danced to during wartime and peace. Her small hand was nestled in his large one as their running shoes skimmed the cold, weathered floor.

When the music stopped and the needle continued to ride the scored path with a swish, swish, swish, she realized that they had stopped dancing and were already involved in the wordless language of lovers. The silence that said I'm so glad you're you, the touch that expected to find a murmur, a smile, a sigh.

Deadly, deadly things. As were his lips reaching for her with such poignant gentleness that it broke her heart.

Kathleen pressed her face into his sweatshirt and held him tightly so he would not see her tears.

"I love you, Kathleen Case," he whispered into her hair. "God, how I love you."

Four days until Thanksgiving.

Then three.

Every minute was crammed with memories to take back to Philadelphia—the combination of odors, the tones of voices, the inflections, the gestures, the special haze of light. The way Nathan would grope in his pocket for his car keys, the way he would bring his elbows to the center of his back to pop out the kinks, his pretense of toughness with Polly, which the child adored, his head dipping as he thought a thing over and changed his mind, his arm draped about Frannie as he teased her mercilessly, his Adam's apple when he killed a soft drink in one gulp, and the wistful way his eyes would mellow when Kathleen would turn suddenly and find him studying her. All her life these things would be part of her.

On Wednesday, Kathleen went last-minute grocery shopping with Frannie, and the two of them spent all one afternoon baking.

Pastry had a way of making all things seem possible. Into the dough, Kathleen kneaded her dreams. The laughter she and Frannie shared was as delicious as the sweet filling of the pies.

When the telephone rang, Kathleen was shelling pecans, and Frannie answered. "Cypress residence . . . Miss Case?" Frannie threw a look at Kathleen. "May I say who's calling?"

"Keep your fingers out of that." Kathleen was playfully slapping at Polly, who had come home from school and was systematically robbing her of pecans like a squirrel.

Polly ran squealing from the room, and Frannie shrugged and handed Kathleen the receiver. "'For Miss Case,' the man said. Wouldn't give his name."

Kathleen dumped shells into the wastebasket and said, laughing, "All right, Nathan Cypress, this is beneath even you. Prince Albert's in the can. I know that old joke."

She could hear him breathing. The quickening of Kathleen's body was the same as when she knew she had lost a jury. It was the pulsating pressure of certainty.

Farrell's words about Tortorelli came rushing back. "Who is this?" she sharply demanded, and cupped the receiver.

Frannie glanced around. Kathleen avoided her.

She waited. Nothing. No voice, no message. Then, *click*.

A person could kid themselves just so long, and Kathleen had never been one to cheat herself at Solitaire. When she slammed down the phone, she knew she had been tricked by the smell of pumpkin pies and the jingle of Nathan groping in a pocket for small change. This could not last. She couldn't do this to her family.

It didn't happen again that day, but the next day it did. Twice.

But this time the caller asked specifically for *Kathleen* Case, and though Kathleen refused to admit she was Kathleen, the truth was like flashing red neon.

Later, when she stood at the window of her bedroom upstairs and studied the long, tree-studded street, she guessed that the blue sedan parked at the end of the block didn't go with the neighborhood. All the baked pies and daydreams in the world wouldn't alter that.

The question was, how did she protect Nathan? That her own heart would be broken was a given, and when it came to a choice between Nathan's heart and his safety and that of the family, there was no contest. Was she strong enough to do what must be done?

Love was a Goliath when it had to be. Her leave-taking would be done in such a way that he wouldn't worry. He might despise her, but he wouldn't worry.

Life was as suddenly cold and fragile as the icicles hanging from the roof outside her window. Kathleen felt very old and tired. Sometimes life wasn't worth the trouble.

After Thanksgiving dinner, Nathan drove Frannie to visit her sister's and dropped the girls at the football game at Lockesbury. He'd had it! He loved the girls and Frannie dearly, but he couldn't wait to be rid of them!

On the drive home, he planned his afternoon alone with Kathleen, the fire he would build, the wine he had secretly chilling, the music he would put on the stereo. He was past playing around with this woman. He wanted it all: the ring, the wedding, the baby, in any order she would have them.

But several mountains stood between that and now, and he would climb them all or die in the process. He glanced in the rearview mirror and bared his teeth, inspecting them for whiteness. He gave his hair a once-over and looked down to see that his nails were okay. He could have used a shave, but that would have been a little obvious.

If only his heart would stop thudding in his ears. By the time he pulled into the garage, it hadn't. Inside the front door, he stamped his boots and pulled off his gloves, only to see that his hands were sweating.

Taking a deep breath, glancing at his wristwatch and giving himself five hours before she broke down and agreed to marry him, he wet his lips, gave his sweater a jerk and walked into the living room.

Kathleen's suitcase and briefcase were parked neatly beside the grand piano. Sitting on the piano bench, her ankles and knees primly aligned, her coat draped beside her, Kathleen looked up at him with watery, green-brown eyes. She was wearing a pair of knee socks and sneakers. A swirling wool skirt reached her ankles, and her familiar pink sweater was pulled to her knees and made the skirt flare beneath it. Her hair tumbled down her back in a loose, single braid, caught midway with a bow tied from a narrow scarf.

A pose, Nathan thought as he dug his nails into the cup of a fist, needing something painful to clear his head of the raging voices of betrayal. She was leaving him!

"What's going on?" he asked with a voice that sounded like a rasp drilling through stone.

The room was chilled.

"You knew I couldn't stay forever, Nathan."

She concentrated on her knees with such a solemnity that Nathan wanted to smash everything in sight.

"When?"

"As soon as possible. Today. Now."

"The taxi's on its way?" He raked his fingers through his hair and said to the walls and unseen demons.

"No. I wouldn't go without saying goodbye."

"Great." Then to her he added, "I was under the impression you were going with me to Senator Packford's reception tomorrow night."

With the long slim fingers that he adored, she nervously flicked at a tooth. "I can't. I have to go back."

"I see."

But Nathan didn't see anything except that she was bound to have her own way. He had waited thirty-eight years to fall in love like this. Some people waited all their lives. And now she was saying she must leave. Was her life so fulfilled that she could retreat into herself, could dismiss so dryly the way they combined into one whole, could turn her back on the infinite paths left to explore?

He wanted to roar with outrage. He wanted to destroy the walls, to destroy her, to bring her to her knees and make her sorry.

She swiveled on the bench so that she faced the keyboard and not the room, not him. Leaning an elbow on the music rack, she seemed to collapse upon the support, and let her hand come to rest upon random keys, striking one here, one there in a plaintive, meaningless melody.

He strode to the sideboard, where Frannie kept decanters of liquor and glasses, and he sloshed two fingers of Irish whiskey into a glass and tossed the alcohol down. After the burn had subsided, he licked the residue from his mustache.

"Well, we mustn't keep your criminals waiting," he said testily. "Back to the glorious future in Philadelphia."

"That's not fair, Nathan."

"I don't want to be fair. I want to kill something."

"You have to accept it. I've done my best. Things are like they are."

"Things are never like they are!"

Not knowing he was capable of it, he spun around and, with a sound that was more animal than human, picked up a piece of Lee's priceless Steuben glass and hurled it at the fireplace, where it struck the bricks with a earsplitting impact and shattered into thousands of pieces.

She screamed and clapped her hands over her mouth, her eyes wide with disbelief as she jerked about to view the sparkling shards.

Slumping, Nathan lifted a hand to his temple, pressed hard with his thumb. What kind of a fool was he? Kathleen didn't belong to him, and she wasn't his to lose. What did he have, really, besides a stolen moment of bliss and a few kisses and whispered words?

She opened her mouth to speak, then clamped it shut.

"What?" he demanded, stepping toward her.

Her eyes had all but lost their greenness. A fine line of perspiration beaded her upper lip, accentuating the microscopic golden down.

"Tortorelli was released," she said at last.

Nathan rubbed his palms together, then dropped his hands uselessly. "That's not why you're going back."

"Yes, it is."

"You're not to blame for Tortorelli."

"Nathan, you know I am, and I know I am. Blame . . . whatever, but we know. Philadelphia knows."

She made a determined effort to immerse herself in anger, but Nathan knew she was hurting as badly as he. He wanted terribly to hold her, but all he could do was mutter, "You know that neither of us will ever feel this way about anyone again, don't you? Not ever, Kathleen. Don't take that away."

Nathan wasn't sure how to interpret the raggedness of her sigh when she turned. Her hand fell limply to the keys, sounding a harsh dissonance, and her head dropped against the music book.

Standing at her back, he reached out for her, but clenched his hands into fists. She wasn't a woman who could be forced. The decision would have to be hers.

With the slowness of a man in pain, he carefully lowered himself to the bench, and his inquiry was as hesitant and breathless as a boy's. "Do you play this thing?"

She didn't seem able to answer.

"I play," he said, and managed to construe something resembling a chuckle. "I taught myself in the rec hall at Camp Pendleton. Not Beethoven, though. More . . . Stephen Foster."

Inching her to one side, he began, quite tortuously, to read the complex array of notes on the page of music. Not even a tone-deaf mutant could have borne the cacophony.

She had no choice but to shake her head and catch his hands.

"Do yourself a favor, Nathan," she said with a breathy tenderness that had nothing to do with his playing of the piano, "don't tell anyone ever again that you play."

Ever so lovingly, Nathan reversed her grip until he was holding her. He met her gaze. "You play, don't you?"

One side of her mouth curled suspiciously. "Is this an invitation, Mr. Cypress?"

Dear God, his heart was breaking! He tried to swallow the knot in his throat. "If you can play, it's an invitation."

To the room, she said shakily, "*If* I can play, he says."

With very little embellishment, she began to play the sonata where the book was open, her touch upon the keys an artistry that Nathan had known, intuitively, that she would possess. Enthralled, he thought he could still smell the stench of the ghetto clinging to his past, and he realized he had no right to claim her. It had been a dream. He was a fool.

"Oh, God, enough of this!" He lunged from the bench, starting to leave. Then he swiveled back and pulled her to her feet—awkwardly, because the bench was between them now.

She blanched, and did not say the words he'd hoped for: *You're right. I love you so much, I could never be parted from you.*

"Don't leave," he begged, and dipped his head, kissing her hard and bitterly.

She didn't resist, but neither did she kiss him back, as if by refusing to respond she was proving a point, compelling him to admit it would not work between them.

He lifted his head, his eyes burning as they searched her face for answers, his whisper harsh. "Say you'll stay."

Her lower lip began to tremble.

"Damnation, Kathleen!" He caught her by the shoulders and dragged her up onto the bench. "Then I'll say it for both of us. You run, if that's what you've got to do, but it won't change the truth. You'll never get away from me, do you hear? You'll never look at another man and not see my face in his. You'll never speak another man's name without mine echoing in your ears. Are you listening? I'll haunt you till the day you die. I'll never set you free!"

As a man would scoop up a child, he swept her into his arms, overturning the bench with a splintering kick of his boot, catching his hip against the piano. Her head had dropped back over his arm, and the scarf was slithering loose from her braid. Her eyes were closed, and she was shaking all over.

But her voice was a stropped razor, slashing him to the bone. "Let me go."

But he could not have released her if a knife had been at his throat. Turning, her skirt swirling about his legs, he spoke through gritted teeth.

"When I let you go, my love," he grated, "you will have at least told me the truth."

"I won't tell you anything."

"Oh, but you will, my darling." Passion was a roar in Nathan's ears like the deadliness of a hurricane. "I promise, you will."

Chapter 14

Big-Name Celebs Expected to Attend AIDS Fund-Raiser—Headline, page three, *Washington Sentinel*, morning edition.

It was hardly Rhett Butler carrying Scarlett O'Hara up the stairs of Tara, Kathleen thought in the dazed recesses of her mind.

They did make it to the bottom step before she gave up her struggle. What did the human heart know about reason, anyway? What did the heart know about logic and precaution and common sense?

With the sound of surrender, she wrapped her arms about Nathan's neck as he carried her, and fastened her lips ravenously to his.

"I don't care anymore," she gasped.

He leaned their weight against the banister, letting them both sink to the step as their kisses and touches became too much to bear.

"Just do it," she whispered to the base of his throat. "Anything, I don't care. Maybe I'll die—maybe I won't."

At that moment, with his hands starving for the touch of her and his mouth taking everything before she could give it, she truly did not care. If this was the last time she would have Nathan, she wanted to taste as deeply as her hunger drove her to taste. She wanted to be honest, and she would not worry what she looked like, she would not worry about foolish things, she would not worry about tomorrow. She would let him do as he would, and she would forget, for this one mindless afternoon, that this man had been her mother's lover.

Theirs was a mad thing, thoughtless and wild. Their clothes hardly entered into it, becoming a strewn tangle upon the steps, as they tried to progress up the stairs. Stubborn buttons gave way as they tried to say the unsayable despite kisses and yearning flesh. They wrestled with shoes. "Help me . . . no, ah, yes. Ahhh."

Belts were flung aside and socks were torn free. Zippers were wrecked and catches cursed, and still they could not bear the separation of an instant.

"Not here," Kathleen tried to say as they finally crawled to the landing and he was dragging her skirt to her knees, pressing her back.

"Yes." He stripped her panties away, sleeking his tongue eagerly from her navel to groin. "I've waited all my life...I want . . . everything."

Kathleen feared being seen in such an incrimination, but she was paralyzed by his hands and her own heat. His worshiping was burning her skin. His fingers were tangled in the carmine curls that cloaked the place he sought. He was lifting her up, adoring her, drawing her to his quick and eager torture, tasting until she was half-blind with the thrill of it.

"Nathan, Nathan." She was lost.

Reaching, she clasped his curly head and drew him closer, closer, ever closer. She tried to say his name. She tried to breathe, but she could only surrender—dizzying heights, blood-red sunbursts when she reached the pinnacle and slowly, ever so slowly, fell to earth again, spent as a summer storm, drenched and weeping.

Even to her own eyes, her nakedness was luminous in the streaming sunlight. Replete, nothing mattered now but him and pleasing him. She sought him as lovingly as he had sought her, covering him with the same exquisite silkenness, infusing the same spiraling pleasure.

But he tensed beneath her hands and pulled her face up to his, holding her tightly, his features no longer handsome.

"There's something I have to tell you." He was heaving to breathe.

"Later."

But he held her there, hurting her with his urgency. "God, Kathleen, look at me."

He clasped her face, searching it for things Kathleen didn't understand, asking her for answers that she didn't know the questions to.

"I've been wanting to tell you since the beginning. Over and over I've tried to tell you, but I didn't know how."

His anguish was so prophetic that Kathleen felt the wound of a deep, visceral fear. In the posture of a mother rescuing the lost child, she drew him into her arms.

"I'm here, Nathan," she whispered, holding him to her breasts, rocking him. "What's wrong? You can tell me anything."

He lay for a moment in the solace of her love. Then, taking her into his arms, he sank back to the floor and stared at the dripping crystal of the chandelier.

"Before..." His voice was thin and faraway. "Long before I even knew who you were, Kathleen, I made a pact with someone. It wasn't an agreement, but a sacred vow. I swore on my honor, what little I had, that I would never tell anyone about this. I swore for as long as I lived that no one would know. And now..."

The question of desire was no longer the focus of their love. Whatever it was that he must tell was hurting him, and because she loved him, Kathleen felt the quick of his pain.

Kneeling, leaning over him, searching his face, she kissed him with compassion born from her own suffering.

"You don't have to tell me, Nathan," she whispered. "Let the past stay in the past. Whatever you've done, I don't care. If you're happy, that's all I need to know or ever need to know. And you feel the same for me, I know that. Can life give more than that to two people like us?"

He stiffened, his muscles as hard as steel. He worked his mouth, as if the taste of ashes was there.

"If it were that simple," he declared hoarsely, "I'd leave it there. But people *are* their past, Kathleen. You think you're not, but when you least expect it, it comes at you like a wild dog. The pact was with your mother! I made a vow to Lee that I've got to break. There's no other way."

The faces of men were nothing new to Kathleen—men who knew their lives were a shambles, who were facing the slow death of prison, men who were steeped in guilt and its horrible aftermath.

Nathan's was that of a man torn. His chest rose and fell with the harshness of an anvil accepting the hammer. His hands were like claws upon his knees, and veins stood out on his forehead.

Kathleen suddenly felt that her nakedness was a mockery before such soul-searching. She crossed her arms across her breasts.

"Forgive me, Lee," he whispered, and searched for Kathleen's eyes. "I married your mother, Kathleen," he said dully, "but I was never her husband. She used me to break her word to your father."

What signal marks the changing of a person's heart? What happens when old ways of thinking aren't valid anymore? When there is no longer anything familiar and solid to place the foot upon?

Kathleen was severed from everything she had known before. Things about Nathan that had seemed confusing were made clear. Their love which had been forbidden, was now within reach, yet farther away than ever. They were free, but who knew that except them?

"I don't know what to do," she said, trembling when his hands moved over the veil of her hair, over her shivering shoulders. "What happens now?"

His lungs sounded as if they were corroded and would not allow him to breathe. "We have to decide."

"About what?" Incredulity loomed in her face.

"We have to decide what we want, you and I. What *we* want." He pointed to his own chest and to hers. "Not what someone else wants for us."

"Nathan, how can you oversimplify it like that? Don't you know what people would say? They wouldn't understand. How could they?"

"We'll find a way."

"Rush in like dragon slayers defending truth and honor? Challenge them to a duel if they whisper about us?"

Kathleen wanted to blame something. Him—she wanted to blame him. Why hadn't he known that her love was out there in the world, waiting for him to find it? Why couldn't he have told her mother no?

She began gathering up their clothes. And later, after the two of them lay upon his bed, facing each other, their lengthened bodies aligned, she came to him with the strength of a woman fully grown. Her scent was strong and sweet and good, and he moved his lips over her flesh, tasting the saltiness of her white, white skin.

Her eyes fluttered closed when he kissed her, and then she kissed him—his eyes and his cheeks and his lips. She touched him, and her breath was warm as she learned the answers to all her questions. He was enthralled, and his heart was ready to burst. The pleasure became a test of pain, and when he was ready to despair, she climbed upon him with a blinding grace and lowered herself, her sigh more than words.

Smiling, she bent so that her hair hid her face. She bent over him, and he gripped her shoulders as his own humanity began its sure and certain defeat. With a moan, he felt himself running headlong through sheets of glass that splintered and flew. Things inside his body were ripped free. He was spread-eagled, and he saw himself for what he truly was; in this moment of earth's great time, she was seeing him as no other woman had ever seen him before, and for the first time in his life, Nathan was not ashamed of what he had once been.

"Oh, love," he said tenderly as she lay limp and replete upon his chest. "Oh, sweet girl, my sweet Kathleen girl, I never meant to make things so difficult for you."

"Shh," Kathleen said, for she now knew the secret of love, that it was all-encompassing, capable of the greatest pleasure and deepest pain and the most damning confusion and solemn mystery. She didn't know what to do, only that they would do something.

"I think Kathleen should stay till Christmas," Polly said.

She was standing on a stool, swathed in pajamas, robe and slippers with droll elephant ears on the toes. She was thumbing her way through a collection of video cassettes that everyone had seen until they were sick.

Her remark didn't get so much as a flicker of agreement. Polly moved her eyes over the large room that should have been noisy but was like a tomb. No sounds emanated from behind Nathan's newspaper. Annalee's ears were covered with her headphones, Frannie was bent over her shopping list and Kathleen, on hearing her name, had looked up from the *New York Times* Crossword Puzzle, her expression one of blankness.

"Is everyone around here dead or what?" Polly demanded with a stamp of her foot. She flashed a lethal grin. "If I don't get an answer, I'm going to play *Little Shop of Horrors* again."

All heads lifted, and a chorus of *"No!"* rang out.

Except for Nathan's. All that came from behind his paper was a muffled "Mmm."

Polly giggled, and Frannie shifted her peppermint to the other jaw. "I like Audrey II, honey," the black woman said.

Jumping down from her stool, the child threw her arms about Frannie's neck. "Then we'll go watch on the television in my room, Frannie."

Laughing, Frannie disengaged herself. "I don't like her that much."

Annalee pulled the headphones from her explosion of crimped hair. "Does anybody in this room know how much I hate being on these crutches?" She made as if to suffocate herself with a blue satin pillow and popped up with a wounded look. "Kath, would you please bring me some magazines?"

"She's not your slave," Frannie remonstrated with a sigh, and gathered up several of the most recent slicks and placed them in Annalee's lap. "Anyone who can destroy the country club can get magazines for herself. Is that what you say, Mr. Cypress?"

"Mmm."

"That glass door was already broken, Frannie," Annalee protested. "You can ask anybody there. And besides, they should never have left a golf cart just sitting around like that."

"Okay, okay," Polly gleefully announced, "I've narrowed it down. You have your choice between *Back to the Future* or *Jumpin' Jack Flash*."

"Forget it, Sis." Victoria walked in the front door, her shoes clashing with her socks and her purple pants and green-striped blazer and orange mittens and muffler, and stood in the doorway like a high priestess. "Ken Wohl is on tonight. Nothin', but nothin' comes between me and Ken Wohl. Nathan, tell Polly I get dibs on the *tee-vee*."

"Mmm."

Leaning over the back of Kathleen's chair, Polly pretended to creep up the back of her neck like a caterpillar, making Kathleen wonder what she would do when she had to leave. How she loved them.

"Frannie wants you to stay, too, Kath," Polly cajoled. "She said that maybe now that you're here, I'll get my filthy pigsty of a closet cleaned out over the holidays."

"Did she, now?" Kathleen pecked her sister's cheek. "Then I'll be knocking at your door with a big garbage sack in my hand. First thing tomorrow morning."

Victoria picked up one of the magazines and thumbed through it, her bubble-gum smacking keeping time with the turning pages. "Would you look at this belt?" she suddenly squealed, and danced around, flashing pages of glitz for everyone to see. "It'll be *hard-core* with my jeans. I've got to have it. I'll die if I don't have it. Only three hundred and sixty-five dollars!

"For three hundred and sixty-five dollars, I'll buy you the alligator."

"Animal killer!" screeched Annalee.

As Kathleen sought Nathan's eyes across the room, the ringing of the phone brought another outburst of bedlam with all three girls racing for it. But in the matter of incoming calls, Frannie ruled queen.

Her cool preface belied any and all domestic turmoil. "Cypress residence," she said.

I love you, Nathan's look was signaling.

I know, Kathleen's replied.

"Just a moment, please. Miss Kathleen, it's for you," Frannie said.

Perhaps it was because things were going too well. Perhaps it was the gods, who always got upset when people got uppity with their happiness. With a crack of her heart, Kathleen knew what would await her on the other end of the line.

She looked at Frannie, then at Nathan. Her first impulse was to refuse the call, but that would alarm Nathan, and then she would be forced to explain or to lie.

Perhaps she could pretend it was William, but he would have identified himself to Frannie. Perhaps she could fake a call from Farrell. But either of those would give the caller an edge.

She grimaced at Nathan's quizzical expression and took the receiver, calling upon the performance skills that any good attorney comes by innately. "This is Kathleen Case."

Nothing. *Who is this, you fiend? Damn you to hell for this!*

The moment of hesitation seemed to last an eternity, but in actuality it was only seconds. In the end, she couldn't lie at all. Shrugging, not looking up, she replaced the receiver.

"Wrong number," she said awkwardly, and glanced at her watch instead of at Nathan. "I, uh . . . I think I'd better get dressed for the Packfords' party. Would you excuse me?"

No one said a word when she left the room.

* * *

Lee Bradford Case had been obsessed with her position in society.

During all the years that Kathleen had observed her mother, everything she had seen reflected that obsession—the house with its black enameled doors, its gleaming shutters, its brass knockers and knobs and gracefully curved bowfronts and bay windows, its carved lintels and beveled sills and wrought-iron grillwork.

Every few years, Lee remodeled her suite of rooms, and she always chose the currently in decorator from New York. The rooms had always been off-limits to the girls, and violations were severe. Even now, as Kathleen entered them, she broke out in a sweat.

She stood, unmoving, in the doorway, feeling as if a thousand ghosts were watching her from behind the walls, from under the bed. But she intended to borrow one of Lee's gowns.

"Call it payment for what you did to Daddy," she mumbled.

Entering, shutting the door, she moved unsteadily to the great closet and pushed back the louvered mirrors that fronted it. Over two hundred cocktail and dinner dresses hung there—the most expensive designer labels in the world—plus rows and rows of shoes that would have rivaled the collection of Imelda Marcos. There were handbags and scarves and fur coats and hats, jabots and belts and kerchiefs and boots.

Trembling, Kathleen selected a gown and held it against her body. One look in the mirror told her what she had always known, that she was not beautiful. Before falling in love with Nathan, it hadn't mattered. Now nothing seemed as important.

"Okay, Mother," she said bitterly as she lifted out a slinky sheath of glittering green sequins, "Do for me now what you never did when you were alive. If you can't make me beautiful, at least make me glamorous.''

The Balmain gown was cut to fit like a second skin, the strapless neckline made even more daring by a slashed vee in the enter. Lined with pure silk, the dress had probably cost ten thousand dollars.

She flipped through Lee's collection of albums and selected a Saint-Sëns piano concerto. She put it on the elaborate stereo with its quad sound system and browsed through Lee's private bar that was still stocked with vintage wines.

She filled a tulip glass with wine and took it with her to the tub. For a half hour she soaked, then took her pick of creams and lotions from some fancy spa in Switzerland.

Walking naked over an expanse of carpeting as large as a Broadway stage, she stood before a three-way mirror that was recessed into a wall. After blowing her hair dry, she slipped into silk underwear—loose, champagne-colored panties with wide green lace and a corselette with boning that cinched her waist and was fitted with garters.

She polished her nails and searched through drawers until she found a pair of sheer black stockings. Grimacing with amusement, she sleeked on the stockings, only to discover a tiny run, which she repaired with a dot of fingernail polish.

She was waiting for the polish to dry, when the tap sounded at the door.

''Come,'' she called as she balanced one foot on the vanity stool and craned to see the back of her leg to make sure the repair was good.

So surprised was she by the sight of Nathan in a tuxedo she momentarily forgot she was wearing less than a respectable stripper would wear onto a burlesque stage.

She didn't move as he gave a low whistle. ''I got tired of waiting,'' he said, and grinned. ''I see you're ready to go. Boy, will you be the hit of the party.''

"And you—" she pointed a polished nail "—have no manners." She lowered her foot.

"I make up for it in appreciation, though."

"How did you know I was here?"

She walked to the closet with a sexiness that literally set Nathan's teeth on edge, and he momentarily forgot that he had wearied of roaming about the downstairs and had asked Frannie. Once it had even occurred to him to suggest that she borrow something of Lee's, but he hadn't thought she would.

She was startlingly attractive. Her hair billowing about her shoulders was breathtaking, and the translucent clarity of her skin was as elegant as if she spent half her life in beauty salons. In ironic contrast was the naughtiness of her leg having been propped on the stool with one burnished curl flirting at him from beneath her panties.

As she reached for a dress, the rounded swell of her buttocks winked from beneath the soft panties. "What do you want?" she asked.

Nathan dreaded speaking for fear of breaking the spell. "You."

With a quick glance over her shoulder, she stepped before the mirror and unzipped the dress, preparing to step into it. Nathan's throat tightened, and he had to cough to clear it.

"I, uh . . . I wish you wouldn't do that."

A cool smile contradicted the crimson coloring her throat. She flicked her tongue across her lips. "You know what I look like, Nathan."

Yes, he did. He reached into a pocket. "I have something for you first."

Her gaze followed his hand, and she pulled her mouth to one side, nibbled at the corner of it. He found the sound of her quick breath unbearably exciting.

"Flowers?" She shook her head, sending her hair swirling. "Not in your pock—"

As he withdrew the black velvet box that he'd removed from the safe only moments before, her jaw dropped, and her fingers touched her lips. She started to speak, then stopped.

"I only wish they were mine to give to you," he said, "but they belong to your mother. Somehow I think she would want you to wear them."

Without a word, she took the box and found the nested emeralds, an extravagant display of Lee's indulgent vanity. He only knew their value by the insurance that was paid on them annually, and that was for the sum of three-quarters of a million dollars.

"May I?" he asked.

Positioning herself before the mirror, much more interested in watching him fasten the emeralds about her neck than she was in how desirable he found her long stockinged legs and spike heels, her breasts spilling from the corselette, she sighed as she touched the pendant drooping from two rows of matched diamonds.

"Nathan," she murmured, her eyes as large as saucers.

Nathan laughed, adoring her girlish exuberance. "They make your eyes green."

"They make everything green," she purred, and tipped her chin in a coquettish pose, only to realize the scandalous picture she created with her garters and cleavage. She laid her hand upon her breasts. "I have to finish dressing."

He stopped her from moving away, and studied her until his own neck was stained with scarlet. "I, uh..." He drew in his breath sharply and swiped at his mustache. "I brought some other things."

From his other pocket, he drew out two smaller boxes, and he felt a pang of unexpected sadness watching her thrill and knowing he had little to do with it. He placed the fabulous rings on her fingers and placed emerald earrings in her hand. As she slipped them into her ears, he dropped a kiss lightly to her shoulder.

Smiling, still somewhat shy, she leaned back against him, looking at the reflection of the two of them in the mirror. "We look like the cover of a racy magazine," she teased breathlessly.

Leaning around her, he nestled his jaw into her hair. "Not nearly racy enough."

Her lips parted sensually, and she whispered, "Are you just a little bit kinky, my darling?"

"I'm not a little bit *anything* right now. I'm a whole lot." He took her hand and pressed it to the prominence beneath his trousers, and she wiggled her hips against him in a way that made Nathan nearly gag with yearning.

As she watched, he slipped a hand beneath the lace covering her breast, and a lazy glaze dulled her eyes. Her lips parted, and she watched her nipple leap under his fingers.

"That doesn't mean a thing," she lied.

He grinned, and her shoulders went limp as he tormented the tiny clusters of nerves. "Of course not."

"We shouldn't be doing this. We'll be late for the party."

"Damn the party."

"The girls will wonder."

"Damn the girls."

"Nathan!"

"You know what I mean."

Bewitched, she watched him lift her knee and place her foot on the stool once more. The garters stretched across the white, white inside of her leg, and she licked her lips until they glistened. Her laughter was a feline purr, and Nathan slid his fingers beneath the silk hem, fascinated with the offers she was making with her breath and her sighs and her moist lips. Muscles deep inside her were flexing and tens-

ing, and she moved against his hand, meeting the pagan
burn of his own hungry eyes as she boldly offered herself.

"You know I still don't have an answer," she said weakly.

"It's no one's business what we do."

With a sharp breath, Nathan found her with his fingers,
and the silk of her wetness made speech impossible. He sank
into her tightness and reached for her lips, but she drew back
her head, watching them, watching the desire that stained
them both and shortened their breaths and made them move
in rhythmic pulses, making them imitate the final conclusion of all such acts.

"Does that excite you?" He could hardly speak as he
found flowering warmth.

Her fingernails were sharp upon his sleeves. "You...
excite...me."

With a wantonness that Nathan thought he could not
possibly bear, she reached through the parting of her legs.
Her lip caught between her teeth as she worked his zipper.
He thought he wouldn't be able to last, for she was not
skilled in such maneuvers, and he paid dearly for that lack.
But nothing mattered now except having her.

"Say you love me," he muttered as they watched themselves poised, positioned, aching with the expression of love
in its pure and more primitive form.

"I love you."

As she breathed her confession, she took him in her
hands, and, with the most blinding eroticism, slowly
sheathed him with herself.

It was the seeing of it, he thought—the silly garters that
were so equated with the world's idea of temptation, the
graceful rock of her pelvis, the way she let her head drop
back, arching her throat and letting her hair swing over his
shoulder.

In the end, however, they forgot to watch. They forgot
everything except the search that impelled them forward,

causing her to drape her leg upon his side and to climb him and lift herself closer, ever more joined until they collapsed in each other's arms and she was weak with the return of sanity.

Picking her up, he carried her to the bed. In her embarrassment, she grasped the spread and covered herself, face and all.

"I can't believe I did that," she whimpered.

Nathan adored her shyness and laughed down at her.

"Promise me something," he said, and tweaked the corner of bedspread aside so he could find her squinched-up face.

"Don't speak to me."

"Oh, yes, my darling, I will speak. And speak and speak."

"What d'you want?"

"I want you to say that you love me and that we'll find a way to spend our lives together. I have to go make arrangements with Simon. Wear Lee's sable coat tonight. You think about us some more, but before the night is over, Kathleen, I think you owe me an answer."

Before she could ask why she was the one who had to be the problem solver, he had kissed her and repaired his trousers and was walking through the door.

Chapter 15

SEC Gives Sterling Interbank a Clean Bill of Health—
Headline, page one, *Business Today*.

Something is wrong with this picture," Kathleen said.

She was sitting with Nathan in the back seat of the limousine while Simon drove them to Senator Packford's party.

Decked out in his best uniform and cap, Simon had his brass buttons gleaming, his boots spit-shined and his mustache trimmed to perfection. Thank goodness he was discreet enough to refrain from looking into the back seat through his rearview mirror.

Nathan's arm along the seat was a friendly port to come home to, but Kathleen stroked the fur of Lee's coat, gazed into the bubbles of her champagne and imagined herself dealing with the gossip she and Nathan would create. Many had shared lives under worse circumstances, though. As sensitive as Washington was to scandal, this was 1990, after all.

"Have another glass of champagne, Cinderella," he said. "Maybe the world will look better."

"You know what happened to Cinderella, don't you?"

He touched his glass to hers. "Here's to wicked stepmothers. And if you're Cinderella, I suppose that makes me the prince."

"Sorry." She pulled a gamin face. "I'm afraid you're the frog."

"Then kiss me." Leaning forward, he clasped her neck with one hand and drew her face nearer to his. Touching her nowhere else, he made love to her with his eyes.

Gooseflesh sprang up on her flesh like the harbinger of a fever. "I did kiss you," she reminded him, "and a prince wasn't what you turned into."

"That's because you gave up too easily." His eyes twinkled. "Frog into prince is easy, but everyone knows that prince into frog doesn't happen on the first try. Perseverance, Cinderella, darling. Perseverance."

His teeth were a flash of brightness beneath his mustache as he moved his lips toward hers. As delicately as a hummingbird seeking nectar, he touched his tongue to hers.

Kathleen was too attune to his mind to indulge in this sort of thing before going out in public. Her body was suddenly alive, and his tongue was stroking hers.

"Don't do that anymore," she whispered.

"You know what I want, don't you?"

"Well, you're not exactly Mr. Subtle."

He reared back, miming affront. "I'm not talking about sex. Sex is the easy part. I'm talking about..." He searched for the word. "I'm talking about commitment. A person's life ought to have commitment. You give me that, and I could, if you'd let me, give *you* that."

She closed her eyes and sank against the seat, deeply touched. He pressed his lips to the hollow of her throat, and the caress was not so much of passion but of closeness, at-oneness.

"I know, Nathan," she murmured into his clean-smelling curls. She stroked the back of his neck. "I've thought of nothing else for days. But it wouldn't be easy."

"If I'd waited until things were easy, my love, I would never have left Philadelphia."

"But it could be more pain than we could imagine."

He looked past her eyes and into her heart. With his fingertips he traced the line of her hair, the curve of her brows, the emeralds in her ears.

"Life without you is pain, my love," he said. "Not seeing you is pain."

The limousine was sweeping to a stop beside the curb, and they both knew that neither of them wanted to share this moment with people.

"Your public awaits, Cinderella," he said wryly as he straightened and made adjustments to his clothes.

When they got out, he indicated three levels of steps that approached the Packford house. The mansion resembled a small castle with its soaring turrets and gales, its tiers and tiers of windows that were ablaze with light. The steps were lined with dozens of hurricane lamps that glittered like scattered diamonds in the snow.

Kathleen tucked the sable high beneath her chin. "Just make sure you're the one who finds the glass slipper," she said as she took his arm. "I don't want to wind up with some gouty old man who holds up his britches with suspenders."

"How you wound me!" He drew his tails aside to reveal a pair of white suspenders nestled in the pleats on his shirt.

She gave the elastic a stinging snap. If not for another car braking to a stop, Nathan thought he would have kissed her again on the spot and the world be damned.

"Actually," he said as they moved up the steps in tandem, "this is more like the bride and groom walking down the aisle."

"Except that you haven't proposed."

The top step was beneath their feet, and the butler was pushing the door open. Suddenly Nathan's fingers were a vise on the sleeve of the sable coat. The snowflakes were collecting on his curls. Kathleen knew what he would say.

"That, my darling, is easily remedied. Will you marry me, Kathleen Case?"

The door swept open.

The butler's shoe crunched on sand that had been sprinkled over the step.

For a heartbeat the world was in a different place, and Kathleen's heart was singing. But crystalline laughter, music, the clink of glasses, the thick underpinning of voices, all conversed to drown it out. She descended swiftly to earth.

":Oh, Nathan," she whispered on a silvery sigh. *I want to say yes, but I'm so scared of making another mistake with my life. Don't make me do it just yet.*

The butler reached for her hand and, grasping it, drew her inside. "Do be careful, madam," he warned. "The step is slick. May I take your coat?"

Kathleen hardly realized when the man slid the costly sable from her shoulders. What were jewels and furs and parties when Nathan Cypress proposed marriage?

"Do be careful, madam," the butler was reciting to the next guest who came after her. "The step is slick. May I take your coat?"

"Oh," said the woman entering after Kathleen. "What lovely emeralds. Why, Mr. Cypress, I hardly recognized you. Darling, you know Nathan Cypress. From the *Sentinel*."

"Yes, yes. Nathan, old boy, I've been keeping up with the Sterling thing. Looks like they're off the hook. Just some mix-up with bookkeeping, I suppose. A good thing, because I've got money invested. Introduce us.''

"This," Nathan said testily, "is Kathleen Case."

Words melted meaninglessly until Kathleen wearied of smiling. Was this how it would be every time she went out with Nathan? She imagining everyone waiting until they were out of earshot to say, "He married the mother first, you know. And when she died, he married the daughter. Strange, wouldn't you say? Do you suppose he was sleeping with the daughter when he was married to the mother?"

As if he felt the icy wind that blew upon her dreams, Nathan drew her along an immense marble foyer.

On one of the walls hung an enormous Aubusson tapestry. Against the other stood a lacquered commode bearing a large eighteenth-century porcelain figurine. The ballroom, lit by three matching chandeliers, was filled with people, a number of them dancing, the men in black so that the splendor of twirling gowns were facets of an ever-changing jewel.

Kathleen found no glory in it—a bunch of people with glasses in their hands, everyone tossing verbal glitz back and forth like tennis balls while their eyes searched other faces in hopes of seeing something for themselves. For each floor-to-ceiling mirror that lined the walls, dozens of eyes scanned the images they created, wondering if their fear showed, or their worry about their future, the lies they would tell in order to survive. The artificiality of their laughter echoed throughout the room.

"I don't think I should be here, Nathan," she declared, mocking her nervousness. "My name isn't hyphenated."

"Nonsense."

She was introduced by Nathan to friends of her mother. She smiled. She shook hands. She chatted. She received compliments on the jewels and sloughed the words off with vague remarks about having inherited them, but she didn't say from whom, and no one asked. No one seemed to make the connection between Lee Bradford Case and Kathleen Case.

It dawned on her then that no one thought of her mother as Lee Case but as Lee Bradford.

Nathan swept her onto the dance floor. She wanted to laugh up at him and say, *it doesn't even matter—all my worrying.*

Her laughter was swallowed by a vocalist who had begun to sing "Moon River," a not very accomplished rendition. They leaned back enough to be able to measure the reactions of each other.

"So what's your answer, Cindy?"

Why, he was nervous. As nervous as she was. "Well, Prince, baby—" she cocked her head "—I'm not being trite, but I really have to go to the bathroom."

With a groan, he rolled his eyes to the ceiling. "Good grief, woman! Would you like me to bare my chest so you can run me through?"

Before she could stop him, he anchored his feet to the dance floor, and as everyone whirled past them, he pulled the front of his pleated shirt apart so that she glimpsed a furl of curling brown hair.

"Here," he said. "But keep it below the rib. If there's anything I hate, it's a messy killing."

She squinched up her face. "You're embarrassing me."

"And you're turning me on." His apology was a kiss upon the tip of her nose, and as he caught her close and danced her across the room, he whispered a bit desperately into her hair, "Why do I have the terrible feeling that you're going to break my heart, Kathleen Case?"

Kathleen was as weak in the knees as if he had seduced her all over again. She caught up the skirt of the sheath when he released her, and when she looked over her shoulder and saw his grin slowly disappear, she knew what her answer would be.

Stepping back, she rose on her toes and kissed his jaw. "Yes, Prince Charming, I'll marry you."

Kathleen wasn't surprised to find the bathroom as large as an apartment. It had its own shower and tub and sauna and Jaccuzi. And it was mirrored on all sides.

As she washed her hands and considered the step she'd taken, she decided it was the most frightening, most wonderful thing she'd ever done. Everything was different now, and she couldn't wait to get about living it, relishing it.

She hurriedly freshened her blush and leaned against the sink. How would she tell the girls? What would she tell the girls? She couldn't very well tell them about Nathan and Lee's arrangement.

From somewhere in the bathroom came a stream of earthy vulgarity such as she had never heard issue from a woman's mouth before. A toilet flushed, and heels clicked. The most gorgeous woman she had ever seen walked out, glanced mildly at her and wriggled her fantastic body back into a gold lamé gown that was skintight and whose strapless top hardly covered her breasts.

"Just once before I die," she said as she held her right hand nearer the swag lamp beside the sink, "I'd like to grow a fingernail of my own. I just ripped the thing completely off."

Kathleen stood very still, then she smiled blandly.

"You're smart," the woman added. "You wear yours short. But Curtis adores these mandarin monstrosities, so I trot off once a week to the salon to have them done. And now one comes off in the middle of a party. Wouldn't you know?"

Curtis? Kathleen frowned. "Could I help?" she offered.

"Would you be a dear? I have some glue here in my bag, but I'm right-handed, and I'll make a mess of it if I try."

Bits and pieces of facts fell into place, and Kathleen recognized the face that had been front-page news in Nathan's paper for days—the face that was now as familiar to Wall Street as to magazines about all the savvy beautiful people. Gloria Sterling!

"Of course," Kathleen said, her face as cool as chipped ice.

"You are an angel," cooed Gloria.

It didn't shock Kathleen for Gloria Sterling to look the opposite of what she was. Some of her own clients look innocent and were cold-blooded murderers.

"Actually, I'm not an angel," Kathleen said as she took the glue and positioned Gloria's finger at the proper angle beneath the light. "I'm just a saint working on it."

Gloria tipped back her head in a raunchy laugh. "Who are you, sweetie?"

"Kathleen Castoro." Kathleen didn't have the faintest idea why all her instincts prompted her to keep her identity from the woman. But those instincts were tried and true, and whenever she didn't listen, the price was high.

Deliberately she passed Gloria's bottle of glue beneath her nose and laughed. "D'you think a person could get sauced on this stuff?"

"Castoro?" Gloria shrewdly studied the emeralds about Kathleen's neck, the bracelet that caught the light and shot fire. "You're Italian?"

"Somewhere back in time," Kathleen said. "Hold very still now. I don't want to get anything on that dress."

"What? This old rag— Darling, those have to be the most fabulous emeralds I've ever seen."

Kathleen shrugged, as if emeralds were something she wore to make pancakes every morning. "They are nice, aren't they?"

"Which translates to mean, 'My husband is very rich'?"

"Are you kidding?" As Kathleen applied the proper dot of glue, pressed the nail back into place and squeezed it a moment to ensure that it held, she added in confidence, "Share my money with some man? Never."

"Good thinking, my dear. There're many more husbands than there is money."

"And jewels."

"Lord, yes. You must have someone very elite and prestigious managing it for you."

The lawyer inside Kathleen could sense Gloria's radar homing in. Gloria smelled the money, naturally, but she was much too clever to leap immediately to the bait. She circled it like a shark.

Kathleen calmly released Gloria's finger. "What's the matter, Gloria?" she drawled. "Are you on the prowl for investors tonight?"

They read each other's minds perfectly, and Gloria threw back her head in her famous laughter.

"You know who I am?" Gloria asked.

"Of course. Doesn't everybody?"

"Now I know why you've held on to your money, darling." Gloria held up her hands and inspected them. "You're right, I'm looking for every solid client I can get, and I've been feeding my sales force on raw meat ever since that jerk at the *Sentinel* started waging war. But you do know that the SEC gave us the thumbs-up today."

"So I heard." Kathleen plucked an imaginary piece of lint from her cleavage and readjusted her pendant, which rested there.

Gloria inspected her nail once more and, approving, opened a gold cigarette case and placed a cigarette between her lips. "But the FBI is sniffing around like a dog in heat."

She flicked the lighter, and blue smoke rose toward the ceiling. Then she shrewdly dissected Kathleen. "Sterling is still the hottest investment around, Kathleen. They're such frauds, those other brokers, investing a client's money only to have the IRS gobble it up faster than they can turn a profit. Curtis learned a long time ago how to deal with the IRS. That's why everyone's so upset. They can't stand to see him pull it off.''

Her glamorous face brightened as she stared point-blank into the mirror at Kathleen, then laughed. "Everyone's upset except the clients. They love it! Nah, we're going to come out of this smelling better than ever. All the FBI is going to do is wind up exposing how corrupt the system really is. And I—" she pointed to herself with the nail Kathleen had just repaired "—am going to bury Nathan Cypress in his own garbage!''

The skill of experience warned Kathleen that if she wanted to help Nathan, she must throw out a hook now or forget it. Gloria was too clever, too savvy.

Kathleen gestured to the door to the ballroom as if she couldn't have cared less—about Nathan Cypress or Gloria's passion to act as her broker. As she suspected, her unconcern was irresistible.

Gloria said as the door shut behind them, "Kathleen, darling, I've got to dash down to the Bahamas over the weekend. When I get back, why don't we have lunch? Better yet, why don't you fly down with me?''

Gloria was immediately off on a whirlwind of networking the likes of which a carnivore would envy, dropping a name every ten words as bait. Keeping with her strategy of implacability, Kathleen kept smiling and murmuring nothing in particular.

When the maven was out of breath, Kathleen dragged her feet. "I really couldn't do it anytime soon, Gloria. Actually, I'll be tied up next week with attorneys. So boring, I know, but some things just can't be put off, can they?'' As a final touch, she toyed with the emerald necklace as if it were so much costume jewelry. "One has to spend money to make money, as they say."

She was too tempting to let go, and Gloria nibbled at the bait Kathleen was dropping, then took it with a gulp.

"Then the week after, darling," She fluttered her fingers effusively. "I absolutely insist. Oh, Jack, there you are." Gloria drew Kathleen into a group of people, among whom Kathleen recognized Senator Wiseman and his wife and a television star whose name she couldn't recall. "Do you know Kathleen Castoro? Curtis and I are flying her out week after next to San Francisco for a seafood dinner at the marina. You know that little place we like so much. Nettle's—that's it. We adore their shrimp. Evelyn, darling, did you get the Porsche I had Curtis send over for you son's birthday?... Yes, yes, I know, but it was nothing, really.... Theresa, dearest, have you met Kathleen Castoro?"

Astonishingly—because she was an unknown in Washington—no one made the connection that Kathleen Castoro was Kathleen Case. And as Nathan observed her from across the room, she signaled him with a look so intimate, he took one look at Gloria and understood.

For the next hour and a half, Kathleen allowed herself to be made the darling protégé of the Sterlings. The more distant she became, the more they fawned. Curtis was practically frothing at the mouth, and Kathleen swore that if he put his hand on her waist one more time, she was going to plant the toe of Lee's shoe squarely on his shin.

Eventually Kathleen detached herself and explained that she really must go. Gloria drew her aside to make sure the Sterling hook was truly set.

"My dear, please think over what we've talked about. To let such an opportunity pass would be criminal. Because you're a player, darling, I'll make you a deal. I guarantee that you'll double your money in two months, and if you owe one penny in tax, I'll pay it myself. Fair enough?"

From across the room, Nathan was becoming impatient, and Gloria, piranha that she was, didn't miss the looks Kathleen and Nathan exchanged.

"Do you know him?" Gloria asked with more of an honest ring that anything she had said all evening.

Kathleen felt dismay that she had ruined everything at the last minute. She deliberately modulated her voice and stifled a yawn. "I know he publishes the *Sentinel* and seems to have painted himself into a colossal corner with you, Gloria."

Gloria gurgled. "From what I hear, that's not the only corner he's painted himself into. Juicy, juicy...you can't begin to imagine."

Kathleen rolled her eyes. "Gloria, I don't think I want to hear this."

"No, I'm not kidding. This is for real."

The woman actually lifted a diamond-encrusted hand and whispered behind it.

"You know he's playing around with one of his stepdaughters, don't you? Hanky-panky."

Kathleen's stomach turned over, and she knew that her color must have become ashen.

She quickly smiled and deliberately ran her eyes up and down Nathan's handsome length. "Well," she drawled, "if I were his stepdaughter, I can't say I wouldn't be tempted. He's quite a hunk, even if he is a bad painter."

"Hell, if I could get proof, you think I wouldn't sic the child authorities on him?"

"It's nothing but rumor. I'll bet he doesn't even like women. Look at him. Isn't he stag?"

"He's a lech!" Gloria gave a majestic sniff. "Listen, Kathleen, I know what I'm talking about. He in some legal confrontation with his stepdaughters' real father right now. I just know their real father's trying to prove incest. Why, someone ought to do something. At least I had enough social conscience to try to find out. I hired a photographer to sneak into this big meeting to get the truth, but . . .''

If one of Gloria's friends hadn't rushed up and rudely monopolized the woman, Kathleen was certain she would have given the whole thing away. Her stomach rolled, and her knees threatened to collapse beneath her. Mumbling something about San Francisco, she drifted numbly away. She was so stunned she didn't realize she had wandered out into the foyer until a man stepped next to her and another closed ranks on the other side.

''Miss Case?'' the one on her left said.

In an effort to clear her head, Kathleen blinked.

''Please don't be alarmed, Miss Case,'' the man said. ''I'm Rudy Medina, and this is my associate Ian Raines. FBI.''

They drew her into a portion of corridor and flashed identification badges discreetly. Kathleen's jaw dropped. Nathan was emerging from behind a crowd of people, also accompanied by another man who couldn't be anything other than a third agent.

''Oh, no,'' she said on a defeated sigh as she saw Helen Mason's face superimposed on the entire evening. ''You're not going to arrest me, are you?''

Chapter 16

Grand Jury Dismisses Charges Levied Against Curtis Sterling—Headline, *Washington Sentinel*, morning edition.

Without explanations, without apology, they took Kathleen to a room in another part of the house. Though she should have been inured to such requests, several days in jail left a person with an acute case of paranoia where badges were concerned.

Kathleen gripped Nathan's hands until he winced. "Easy, easy," he murmured, and lifted her knuckles to his lips.

"What's going on?" She released his hand to slip her arm about his waist, unable to get close enough. "What have I done?"

"Nothing."

"Exactly what I said to Helen Mason. It's Leavenworth, for sure."

His chuckle was accompanied by a kiss to her temple. "Then I'll go with you."

"You haven't done anything."

He comically ran his eyes up and down her and wiggled his brows. "That's what you think."

She cut him a sharp-eyed censure. "That's not funny."

"Neither is Leavenworth."

Rudy Mendina opened a door, turned in invitation and motioned for them to enter. Kathleen pressed Nathan's fingers before going in.

One of the sitting rooms, spacious and convenient, had obviously been set aside as a base of sorts for the agents. On a sideboard, a coffee machine had been set up. A silver tray had been laid out by the hostess, piled with sandwiches and doughnuts. A bowl of fruit gleamed from the center of a coffee table. Bone-china coffee cups were scattered throughout.

At a desk sat a fourth man, wearing a set of headphones that led into a tape recorder. Beside him were three incoming telephone lines. The jacket of his dark suit was draped over the back of his chair, and a shoulder holster fitted across his back. He nodded as they entered, stopped chewing his gum for a moment, then returned to his listening.

"Please," Mendina said, "make yourselves comfortable. Can I get you some coffee? A sandwich?"

"I'm not hungry. I just want to know what this is all about," Kathleen said, and adjusted her tight skirt in order to take a chair near the door.

Nathan disdained a chair, choosing the arm of Kathleen's, instead, and he laid his arm across the back so that his waist conformed to her shoulder. Grateful, Kathleen reached for his hand again.

Rudy Mendina was a short man with a short and very precise haircut. His dark blue suit and tie were so neat they were painful to look at. His shoes, black, expensive, were exactly like those of Ian Raines, the man who had accompanied Nathan.

Positioning himself near the coffee table, Mendina braced his foot on the rung of a chair and gripped the back of it. When his jacket flared, Kathleen saw the same type of holster.

"Miss Case, would you mind telling us what you and Gloria Sterling talked about this evening?" he asked.

At first Kathleen couldn't digest the question, and her face showed it. She came forward in her chair. "You dragged me in here for that?"

"We need to know."

She gave him the same frown she would have given Tortorelli. "Look, I'm an attorney, Mr. Medina, and I'm not telling you anything, nor is Mr. Cypress, until you tell us what the hell is going on here. You guys think you can flash a badge and walk on water. Well, you can't, and you have no right to descend on people in public like that. You could've ruined everything."

"Meaning what?"

Snapping her mouth shut, Kathleen sank back into the welcome haven of Nathan's body.

Mendina gripped the chair's back and released it, gripped and released. "Perhaps we trespassed a boundary of etiquette, Miss Case, but we do have the right. We're conducting a federal investigation of Curtis and Gloria Sterling. We're well within our rights to question anyone who does business with them."

"The Securities Exchange Commission said the Sterling operation was on the up-and-up," Nathan said.

Ian Raines emitted a disrespectful sound from between his teeth. "We're not the SEC."

Kathleen crossed her legs and realized that half her thigh was showing. She wriggled around in an attempt to be more modest.

"I'm not doing business with the Sterlings, anyway." She grimaced. "I'm conducting a little investigation of my own." To Nathan, she explained, "I was going to tell you about it, when these men dragged me out. It just fell into my lap, Nathan. Gloria Sterling has no idea who I am. She took one look at these emeralds and started drooling. Why, the woman wants to take me to San Francisco for seafood. If I flashed enough money under her nose, she would probably take me for a tour through the Sterling offices."

Every man in the room, Nathan included, was riveted to what she was saying. She told them, then, what she knew, and when she was finished, the investigators were beginning to do a bit of drooling of their own.

Ian Raines stepped forward, a swarthy man whose dark stubble was the kind that never disappeared no matter how recently he had shaved.

"We would like very much for you to pursue this friendship with Gloria Sterling, Miss Case. You could help us immeasurably."

"Hey, wait a minute," Nathan interjected.

"It isn't exactly a friendship," Kathleen said. "And I was vastly overplaying my hand to her, in any case. I don't have any money. I was shocked that she bought anything I said."

"By the looks of that jewelry, Miss Case, you appear to have a great deal of money."

Kathleen unwittingly lifted the emerald pendant in her hand. "Putting on jewelry is a lot different from talking the language, Mr. Raines. Not that I wouldn't like to, simply because it would help Nathan." She twisted in her chair and laid her hand familiarly upon his leg. "Gloria hired the photographer, Nathan. She's probably been spying on you since you ran the first article in the *Sentinel*."

The thought came to Kathleen that it was possible the blue sedan parked on Nathan's street was watching him instead of her.

Nathan was already shaking his curly head, his brows a network of disagreeable lines.

"That's all the more reason this has a bad feel to me. I don't want you getting mixed up with that woman, Kathleen. When people's money is threatened, they do crazy things. They do things they don't even *mean* to do."

"*You* threatened her," she argued.

"That's different."

"Why? Because I'm a woman?" Color flooded irately into Kathleen cheeks. "Come on, Nathan. You need what I can do. I want to help."

Rudy Mendina said, "Miss Case has a good idea, Mr. Cypress. We could wire her, monitor her every minute she's with the Sterlings. There wouldn't be any danger."

Nathan jumped up. "Damn it, Miss Case is returning to Philadelphia. She can't do it. No, I won't hear of it."

Incredulous, Kathleen lunged to her feet, not realizing that she was exhibiting a large amount of stockinged leg and half her bosom.

She hiked at her strapless gown and scowled fiercely at Nathan. "A few hours ago you were telling me I shouldn't go back. Now you're telling me I should?"

"You're a lawyer. You're not a government operative."

She threw up a hand and rolled her eyes. "You're overdramatizing. Look, I deal with people who would make Gloria Sterling look like a mother superior. And any good investigative reporter does stuff like this all the time."

"And I've got people who're doing it. Let them!" To the FBI officials, he said, "I think I do have a say here, since I started this whole thing. Kathleen isn't going to wear any wire if I have anything to do about it."

"I really think that's up to Miss Case to decide, sir," Ruby said. "There's no danger involved, and—"

"That's what you always say—no danger. What about that woman who was following her son's drug dealer. Did you keep her from getting hurt? Yeah, she's okay as long as no one takes her off the machine. Find someone else, gentlemen.''

The three agents saw that his adamance came from his love for her, and not one of them would have felt differently if their wives or their lovers had been in the same position.

Extending his hand, Rudy Mendina stepped forward, and Nathan, appearing apologetic about his outburst, accepted it.

''I understand, Mr. Cypress,'' he said, and nodded politely to Kathleen. ''If you come up with anything, we'd appreciate your giving us a call. And if you change your mind, Miss Case...''

''Yes,'' she said, and didn't resist when Nathan circled his arm about her shoulder and spread his hand firmly upon her bare arm.

Couldn't he see that she wanted to give something to him? Couldn't he realize that she would have placed herself on any line for him? And that she had not told him the whole of it? That she couldn't marry him now? That Gloria Sterling was already spreading the vile rumor that could damage him beyond repair?

Aside from being the most expensive restaurant on the East Coast, the Napoleon Restaurant in Arlington, Virginia, had the reputation of being the most authentically French.

In their present mood, however, Kathleen would have settled for McDonald's. She had to tell Nathan the truth, and her heart was breaking.

The doorman, in full livery, invited them into an elegant enclosure that held no more than twenty tables, each with starched, powder-blue napery and a blue candle whose dancing flame was reflected in real polished silver.

"Monsieur Cypress," the maître d' exclaimed with a smart bow that exposed the shining top of his bald plate. "Your table is ready."

"You bring all your dates here?" she unenthusiastically teased Nathan.

"Be careful, my love," he warned.

The maître d' led them to a corner table so discreet she didn't think her irony had been necessary; he probably did bring all his dates here.

"*Madam?* Your coat?"

"Oh." She smiled self-consciously and let him take the sable. He took a moment to approve of her jewels, and Kathleen imagined him snapping his fingers for the waiter with a tad more enthusiasm.

"Jean-Claude enjoys his tip as much as the next fellow," Nathan answered as he read her mind.

Nathan ordered a bottle of Montrachet from the hovering wine steward, and as it was being poured, Kathleen met his pensive stare. The moment the waiter was gone, he pushed the bottom of his tulip-shaped glass away.

Neither of them touched the wine. He was waiting, and Kathleen drew arabesques upon the tablecloth with a fingernail. At length, she asked, "Why didn't you love my mother?"

The question sent him slumping back against the velvet-covered chair. "Sweet mercy, woman, what a question."

She leaned forward and reached for his hands, which she loved so dearly. "I know you love me, Nathan. If I had any doubts about that, I wouldn't be here."

"Then why ask a question that has no answer?"

The unhappiness in his eyes prompted her to sip again. He shrugged despite the tension that was weaving more and more thickly between them.

"A waste of good wine, darling."

Over the rim of her glass, she disagreed. "Crisis times aren't known for their economy."

"Am I to take that to mean that the coach did indeed turn into a pumpkin?"

"Worse. *I* turned into a pumpkin."

The waiter arrived and placed in Kathleen's hand a monstrously large menu with no prices. Nathan ordered for both of them: seasoned crabmeat, *choufleur au gratin*, *créme brûlée*.

When they were alone, he hesitantly answered her question. "At first, all I could see in Lee was a way to free myself from my past. Then, as I changed, I realized my past had little to do with the kind of man I'd been. But I've explained all that to you before."

"What would happen if you lost it all tomorrow?"

He made a sound of disbelief. "I don't think that's possible."

"Anything is possible. Could you be happy in another kind of life? Without the daily challenge of the paper? Could you be poor and be satisfied with nothing but me?"

"But I'm not poor, and the question is ridiculous."

The silence was filled with the sounds of other patrons, and Kathleen didn't want to see the truth in Nathan's eyes. His great charm was his ambition. It made him quick and eager and entertaining and appreciative. She wouldn't have loved him half so much if he were apathetic.

"Gloria Sterling knows about us, Nathan," she said quietly, and appraised the way he grew very still.

A muscle flexed in his jaw. "What're you saying?"

"Oh, she doesn't know *who* I am, but she's heard gossip that you're involved with one of your stepdaughters. That's why she hired the photographer."

"What?" He grew pale and taut.

She was right to realize how sensitive his professional and personal life were to scandal. "Right now it's only gossip.

It can die or it can become an avalanche. But if the slightest whisper of authenticity reaches Gloria, she'll bring you down with it, Nathan. She wants your head on a platter. And Curtis will get it for her if he can.''

He was bent forward, and his hands gripped the edge of the table. "Curtis Sterling is a whining little wimp."

She met his intensity with one that was as powerful as his. "Curtis Sterling is a mirage, Nathan. He has a magical tongue that creates an illusion. People go for it like knights after the Holy Grail. I'm not exaggerating this."

Kathleen knew, deep in her aching soul, that what they had between them would never, never work. Far better for him to learn it now, for him to hate her a little now than to watch everything he had worked for slowly disintegrate before his eyes. He would learn to hate her in any case, and over the years would be intolerable.

"Then I'll just have to expose him, won't I?" he said dully.

She prepared herself for something that would make contempt of court seem like a day in the park. "And who told you that the truth could win against a lie, Nathan?" she said. "The truth fairy?"

Somewhere, somehow, it had gone bad.

All during dinner Nathan watched Kathleen suffering a private sorrow, which she tried to hide behind willful, challenging poses that didn't really hide her vulnerability at all, only enhanced it. She seemed unable to touch or be touched.

When they returned home, she changed clothes immediately, retreating beneath her loose pants, baggy pink sweater and socks. The house was dark, for it was quite late, and they huddled on the bar stools in a half-dark kitchen while he fixed hot chocolate.

She tried to drink some, but lowered the cup with a jarring clatter and slid off the stool and slipped her arms about his waist and stood for long moments, holding him until he wondered if he didn't feel her weeping in silent grief.

"It's all right," he whispered, and stroked her hair repeatedly. "It's all right."

But she knew it wasn't. And she raised her arms, her hands on his shoulders as she searched along his neck, placing her lips to his.

"Oh, Nathan," she kept saying over and over. "Please hold me, Nathan."

He did, and he took her upstairs and put on some music. Never had a woman approached him so desperately, as if she were trying to repair the desolation of her past in one act of absolute, supreme love. She was a shadow in the night, melting into the darkness of the room, approaching him before he knew her intentions and moving her hands over him while he stood before the stereo.

She pulled at the buttons of his shirt and couldn't manage them, so badly were her fingers trembling. He helped her and tried to make her see that there was no hurry, that they had the rest of their lives, but she was too desperate. With her mouth she clung to him and moved hungrily over his face, then she pushed her tongue past his teeth and seemed to need the substance of his breath and his bones and blood to keep herself from slipping away.

Sobbing, clinging, she kept saying his name. "Nathan, Nathan, Nathan."

"I'm here, Kathleen," he kept telling her, moving his hand along her fragile jaw.

She was ripping the buttons free and tracing the outline of him beneath his trousers—stroking, stroking, magically freeing him of the restrictions, caressing his muscles with hers, licking his chest and sleeking down the length of him until his heart was hammering so hard he thought his chest would burst. Every fiber he possessed was stretched to its limits, until she ruthlessly taught him that he could stand more and more. She kissed his knees and his legs. She kissed him everywhere, then engulfed him, her hair strewn over his ribs as slowly and wetly she rode him with exquisite silkenness, then writhed upon him, her head thrown back until she lay limp across him, emptied of all feeling.

Later, when she slept, he studied her in repose, her face so peacefully relaxed and so very young. Then her dreams turned troubling, for her eyebrows were pulled and her lips tightened, her teeth ground. Naked, her body was more slender than it appeared when she was dressed. Her pale skin was pulled tightly against her ribs, outlining them clearly, yet her breasts were full and ripe.

When he awakened, the room was bright with a new day and she was gone. Not until he had showered and dressed did he realize she was no longer in the house. Simon told him that a taxi had arrived very early in the morning and that Miss Kathleen had carried her bags to the cab herself.

Deep in his heart of hearts, Nathan was wounded beyond bearing. He felt capable of terrible things, then he felt capable of nothing at all.

So be it, he told himself in a haze of agony. If that's the way she wanted it, that's the way she would get it. He'd be damned if he would go after her.

Chapter 17

Police Instigate Search for John Tortorelli—Headline, page one, *Philadelphia Reporter*, morning edition.

Kathleen had always tried to see the up side of her office, but the fact was, it was ugly. Grim. Hideous.

There was no window, yet she tried to see it as not necessitating the purchase of draperies. The walls were a vomitous shade of green, the floor was municipal rubber-based tiles, but that made any small knickknack outstanding. No one noticed that her desk was a battered prewar reject, because she was so overworked the desk was never visible beneath the stacks of case files and material from Records.

Too, her ivy had finally built up an immunity to the recycled air that had been tainted by cigarettes, cigar smoke and fear. Her telephone, basic black, possessed only a few disfigurements. By wearing a sweater over a blouse and sweats and socks and leg warmers, she could, just barely, keep from turning blue from the lack of heat. In her apartment-size refrigerator presently resided a carton of yogurt for lunch—low fat, without fruit. Plus two pints of ice cream, which she and Farrell had bought to celebrate the winning of the State vs. Grayson. Plus a six-pack of beer, which she kept for clients' emergencies.

A good suit, which she wore to court, hung neatly beside her coat on a rack. Beneath them was the pair of Ferragamo boots she'd bought on impulse and never regretted. They looked ridiculous. As if a phantom were wearing them.

Quite fitting, Kathleen thought, and dropped her head and closed her eyes. She had ceased to exist; Nathan would have read the letter by now.

"Forgive me, Nathan," she whispered, and rose to look at her face, which was splotchy and swollen from weeping.

"But I did the right thing. One day you'll thank me."

She had crept downstairs before she left, while the house was slumbering, and had taken out the family photograph albums and gone through them, retracing her past, remembering her mother and touching the wedding pictures, crumbling at the sight of Nathan so handsome in his white tuxedo, Nathan with Polly on his shoulders, Nathan at Annalee's basketball games, Nathan escorting Victoria to a formal dance, pinning a corsage to her shoulder.

She hadn't stopped crying since. "If it's any consolation, Nathan—" she blew her nose "—I'm the most miserable I've ever been in my life."

When Nathan did his own driving, he took the Thunderbird. It wasn't a new car but a vintage model he treated as tenderly as a newborn baby. He'd rebuilt the engine himself, and he would put it up against anyone's car for sheer speed and maneuverability.

But now it didn't cheer him up or give him a sense of pride. He drove too fast into the city. Images of Kathleen

were superimposed everywhere he looked: upon his wind-
shield, in the front seats of other cars, between the cross-
walks, climbing the steps of the Lincoln Memorial.

All day long no one had appeared to notice he was suffering in a monumental way. Rose was too accustomed to
seeing him buried behind his desk, snarling and growling at
the world. Frannie's brows hardly lifted at dinner when he
pushed back his plate untouched. The girls had scattered in
all directions as usual, giggling and arguing about borrowed clothes and concert tickets for U2.

He tried to replace Kathleen with memories of other
women, of losing his virginity at fifteen to an older woman.
He tried to remember the faceless girls in college. "You're
so good-looking," they'd all said.

Not once had Kathleen told him that, and all the memories ended the same way: Kathleen awakening in his hands;
Kathleen letting him make love to her in the Vega; Kathleen's hair flying in the rotor wash of the helicopter; Kathleen wearing garters and naughty underwear; Kathleen
holding him at the head of the stairs, whispering, comforting, promising that everything would be all right.

Well, it wasn't, damn it! It would never be all right again!

He parked illegally near Constitution Avenue and turned
up the collar of his coat as he walked bleakly past an unac-
cusing Lincoln. "You've got it made, sir," he said.

Glancing at his watch—he was late to meet Paul Escavito
and Jerry Franks—he walked to a bar on a side street, which
catered to college students from Georgetown University and
senators and Capitol employees who were catching the last
train home. Pauly and Jerry were warming bar stools at the
long mahogany bar, munching pretzel sticks and watching
the door for his arrival.

"Sorry," he said when he signaled the waiter and got a
booth. He asked, "What're you having?"

"Martinis," Jerry said morosely. "Did you see the six o'clock news?"

Removing his glasses—his new ones had arrived today—Nathan shook his head, and Paul peered at him from behind the thick lenses of his own glasses.

"They crucified us again," Jerry informed them. "The bastards. My snitch swears the grand jury won't find anything to try Sterling for. Those two are going to come off squeaky clean, and we're going down the garbage disposal."

What would his reporters say if they knew Kathleen had been asked by the FBI to wear a wire and he'd thrown a fit?

Nathan stared morosely at the framed prints hanging on oak-paneled walls. A college student wearing a waiter's jacket appeared, order pad in hand. Someone put an old Kris Kristofferson on the jukebox. "'Lord, help me, Jesus...'"

Nathan knew the feeling.

"How was your day, sir?" Pauly politely inquired.

"Whiskey," Nathan mumbled to the waiter. "Double. Neat."

Jerry sluiced down his own drink and ordered another. "That bad, huh?"

"I know what you mean," Pauly said, and sneezed.

"Jeez, Pauly." Jerry pretended to mop up the table.

Nathan tossed down the drink the moment the waiter placed it on the table, and the young men blinked in surprise. They had never seen him drink like this; he *didn't* drink like this.

"Would you like another, sir?" asked the waiter.

A muscle twitched beside Nathan's mouth as the whiskey hit his empty stomach. What the heck? He would become an alcoholic and Kathleen would be to blame.

"Don't stop till I tell you to," he growled.

"Sir—" prompted Pauly, who had already begun to feel the adverse effects of one martini.

"You got a problem, Pauly?" Nathan snapped, and let his eyes close with remorse.

Pauly gave one of his best trustworthy smiles. "No, sir. No problem at all."

"Good."

As the waiter placed another double whiskey on the table, Nathan sluiced it down, sucking his breath harshly between his teeth. Pauly and Jerry exchanged a look of mutual understanding over the executive editor's head.

"A woman," Jerry mimed.

"A woman," Pauly agreed, and thought that Nathan Cypress had finally fallen off his pedestal and was joining the human race.

"Kiddo, are you in there?"

Farrell Mulhaney's voice jarred Kathleen from the stupor that had waylaid her on the way to the file cabinet.

Coming to herself, Kathleen realized she'd started out for the file cabinet, but had no idea how long she had stood there, her body draped over the open drawer, her hands covering her face and tears falling onto the folders.

Hastily attempting to repair enough damage that a week at Elizabeth Arden's wouldn't have improved, she blew her nose into the wadded tissue and smoothed the skin over her cheekbones and jaw in an effort to work out the haggardness.

"Farrell!" she said overbrightly, and swiped at her eyes and smoothed her hair before turning around. She smiled prettily. "I was hoping to catch you this morning."

"Welcome home, kid—oh, my achin' back, what's happened to you?"

Kathleen's bluff was difficult to maintain. She tipped up the corners of her mouth a little more. "What d'you mean?"

"Don't give me that. This is Farrell, remember? You look like someone fished you out of the Dumpster."

Kathleen braced a hand on the edge of her desk and dropped her head. "Look, Farrell," she warned, "I've caught a cold. Why can't you be like everyone else and simply say, 'Welcome home. I hope your cold gets better.'"

"Cold, schmold. Look at me."

"Farrell, please."

"You've been crying."

"What if I have? What's the crime in that? Everyone cries once in a while. Besides, I've been looking over the work that's piled up." She began gathering up files from her desk, thumping them and putting them back down. "If that wouldn't drive a person to tears, what would?"

Farrell Mulhaney hadn't gotten to be Philadelphia County public defender for nothing. Holding her at arm's length, tipping up her face and wiping her tearstained cheeks, his ugly face screwed up with the gentlest, most wonderful compassion, he was the nearest thing to Nathan that Kathleen had.

"What is it, baby?" he asked.

He folded her into his arms, a totally ludicrous maneuver, because she was taller than he was and bigger. Which only generated a whole new wellspring of tears.

"Oh, Farrell—" she shook her head "—I think I've really gone and done it this time."

"Just a minute."

Releasing her to lock the door, Farell removed the ice cream from her refrigerator and located two spoons. Then he returned to fish her small electric heater from beneath her desk and set it in the center of the hideous rubber-tiled floor, right between the vomitous green walls. He motioned for her to sit.

Kathleen dropped into a cross-legged Indian position, and he followed suit. Huddling near the heater, they ate ice cream without speaking. When Kathleen became so chilled that she was shivering, he fetched her coat from the rack.

When they had polished off a pint each, she leaned back against the peeling, prewar desk.

"So, tell me about him," Farrell said.

Kathleen sat licking her spoon, as if in a trance. "I love him very much. It's just one of those situations where taking it any farther would be destructive."

"He's married?"

"No, but he was. To my mother."

The only sound was the whir of the tiny heater.

"Oh, I see."

"No, you don't, and neither does anyone else. The marriage was nothing but a convenient way for Lee to keep my father from getting the paper."

"Well, it sounds pretty hairy."

"Which is the point."

"You're afraid people will talk?"

"Wouldn't you be?"

When he didn't reply, Kathleen cocked her head at her friend, feeling the sugar hit her blood like a drug. She scraped at the carton and came up empty. "Farrell—" she kept her attention fixed upon the bottom of the carton until the last second "—why did you come here?"

His sudden gravity planted Kathleen back into the real world. She tried to remember who she was, who he was.

"It's not good, Kath."

The muscles of Kathleen's face became pinched. "What?"

"It came over the police radio a few minutes ago. I didn't want to tell you over the telephone. I'm sorry, Kath, real sorry."

"Are you going to tell me?"

"It's Tortorelli. There was an APB out on him, you know, for questioning in connection with some body they found in the Delaware. They tried to apprehend him. An officer was killed."

Nathan's hangover wasn't to be believed. When he finally made it downstairs to breakfast, a feat he felt deserved the Congressional Medal of Honor, the girls had the heartless insensitivity to look at him without pity.

And Frannie had the terribly bad manners to drop her mixing bowl to the counter, wipe her hands and remove his cup from his trembling fingers after he had just managed to pry it from its hook in the cupboard.

"Let me get that for you, sir," she kindly volunteered while three giggles shattered his eardrums.

Moaning, Nathan tried not to allow too much light beneath his eyelashes, but he knew that his shirt was buttoned wrong and the narrow part of his tie hung below the wide. As for his hair, he hadn't been able to bring a brush near it; all the roots were undergoing a metamorphosis like the one Jeff Goldblum suffered in *The Fly*. In another hour he wouldn't even resemble himself, he was sure. He would have melted.

"I think I'm coming down with the flu," he croaked.

"Yes, sir," Frannie said.

"Look's like a hangover to me, Nathan," Victoria cruelly observed.

"Ungrateful child." The movement of his jaws brought unbearable pain to his head. "Ohhh. I have only one request. Don't have me cremated."

More giggles. And more shushes and shakes of Frannie's head.

"Nathan, would you hand me my crutches?" Annalee asked when Victoria pushed back her plate uneaten and announced she would tell Simon they were ready to leave for school.

Nathan was still trying to focus his eyes upon a dangerous-looking liquid in his cup. "Polly, give Annalee her crutches."

The girl was licking her fingers and gathering up her books. "I'm late, Nathan. Frannie, would you get Annie's crutches?"

Frannie was returning to the kitchen from the laundry room, and Annalee's crutches, thank heaven, were in her hand. Frannie thrust them at the thirteen-year-old.

With a number of contortions, Nathan struggled to concentrate on the plates surrounding him. "What's with all this uneaten food?" he questioned. "This is a waste. What're we going to do with this? Do you have any idea of the people that're starving in Cambodia?"

"I cleaned up my plate," Annalee said, chalking one up for herself.

On her way out the door, Victoria called, "I'm on a diet."

"So am I," Polly chimed in, following her. "Is the car ready?"

"You're only eleven years old," Nathan remonstrated, and pressed his temples, then whispered to Frannie, "isn't she eleven?"

"Na-than," the youngest girl whined, "I have to think about the future."

"Anorexia," Nathan yelled after her, and shuddered violently. "That's what's in your future!"

"Oh, Lord," said Victoria. "Come on, Polly."

"And no swearing in this house. That's the rule."

As she thumped past the table, Annalee reminded him, "You swear, Nathan."

With a slam that made the dishes tremble and his own skin seem to shrink until it was too small for his body, Nathan brought his fist down to the table. "When you're the boss, you can swear. In the meantime, don't break any more bones, and don't run into any more plate-glass windows."

"Jeez," whispered Victoria as she poked her head back into the room. "What's the matter with him?"

"Aye-aye, sir," Polly said with a salute.

Nathan felt like belting her for it.

With shaking hands, he patted his pockets and located a pack of cigarettes. The moment the girls left, he lit one, and Frannie turned from the sink.

"What're you doing?" she demanded.

"What does it look like?"

"When did you start that again?" She snatched the cigarette from his lips and ground it out.

Nathan tried to light another and, aiming his finger, mumbled, "Be a friend, Frannie."

One of Frannie's sniffs was enough to bring Charles Manson to his knees. "Yes, sir," she drawled. "Would you like some aspirin, sir?"

He smirked at her. "How do you feel about getting married, Frannie."

Forgiving Frannie for his vile temper when she brought him two aspirin and a fresh cup of coffee, he lit the second cigarette and jumped a foot when the telephone rang.

"I'll get it," Frannie volunteered. There was a moment of silence, then, "Could you repeat that? I can't understand you, ma'am."

"Who is it?"

"For you, I think," Frannie said, and handed him the receiver. "She's very upset."

"'She'?"

On the opposite end of the line were nothing but muffled sounds he couldn't identify.

"Hello?" He heard a small, nervous shuffle, and then something passed through the line that had little to do with AT & T and very much to do with his heart. "Kathleen?"

The sobs stopped for a moment, and Nathan let out a pent-up breath. "Sweetheart, what it is? I'm here. What's happened, my love?"

"Oh, Nathan," she wept. "Oh, Nathan. Oh, Nathan."

A maddening helplessness consumed Nathan, and he wanted to reach through the wire and drag her into the room, to hold her. "Kathleen," he said firmly, "stop crying and tell me what's happened. You know I'm here for you."

"It's Tortorelli. You know, the man—"

"I know Tortorelli. What's going on?"

"He was released. I got him off—"

"I know that. Kathleen, get to it!"

"He killed a policeman, Nathan."

She broke down again, and Nathan stubbed out the cigarette and began buttoning his shirt and tying his tie. "You're at home? ... Stay right where you are, sweetheart," he said gently. "I'll be there as soon as I can. Everything's going to be all right. Kathleen?"

"What?"

"I love you very much."

"I know, Nathan. Please hurry."

When Elsa Case opened the door and peered through the screen, Nathan was consumed with such a garish mixture of emotions, all of them an outrage at life's injustice, that he had to rein himself in to keep from jerking the door from the hinges.

"Nathan Cypress," he said woodenly. "I was here once before. The night Kathleen was released from jail."

Elsa didn't smile, but he had the distinct notion she was glad to see him.

She said solemnly. "I remember you very well, Mr. Cypress."

He felt her artist's penchant for details taking note of the sharp creases of his jeans and his Western boots, his corduroy jacket, the cream-colored turtleneck that folded around his neck.

"Kathleen called me," he explained, acutely self-conscious.

"I know."

"I'd like to see her if that's all right with you."

"And even if it's not?"

Did he actually detect a bit of acidic humor beneath the crusty shell? Was this eccentric woman an ally? "I really think we're on the same side, Elsa," he said. "May I come in?"

Elsa opened the screen, but held out her hand in hesitation. "I should warn you—William wasn't very happy when he returned from Washington the other day."

"Then he has something in common with most everyone I know."

She had been working. Her long peasant skirt and blouse were covered with a smock as paint-spattered as her rags. Her army boots had been replaced with chukkas, and her hair was caught up in a topknot that gave her the look of a Halloween witch.

Smiling, Nathan followed as she picked up a half-smoked cigarette and took a long pull.

"Kathleen isn't here right now." She plucked a shred of tobacco from her tongue. "You look terrible, Mr. Cypress. Sit down. I'll fix you lunch."

"Oh, no." Nathan laughed a nervous apology. "I mean, that isn't necessary, Miss Case. The truth is, I had a bad night, and I don't think I could stand...I'm really not hungry. You don't happen to know where Kathleen went, do you?''

Elsa's canvas was in the very beginning stages, and she paused to swish her brush in turpentine. "I know where she is, but I think my brother wants to talk to her first, Mr. Cypress."

Nathan had been afraid of that. It had to come sometime, he supposed—that moment of truth for every person who loves, that end of anonymity when love has a face and a past due account that must be settled in full.

At the far end of the expanse, a door opened. Nathan tensed as William emerged, as elegantly attired as ever, but even from a distance showing his age in the stoop of his shoulders, the cane that was no longer a dramatic prop but a necessary piece of equipment.

"Mr. Cypress," William said.

With matching formality, Nathan wondered just how much they knew. Kathleen didn't share her whole heart with her father and aunt; the policeman was proof of that. Did they know about Tortorelli?

William aimed his cane at the chairs arranged around the piano and harp. "I suppose this can be done better sitting down."

Nathan clumsily attempted to make idle conversation as they sat. "I can see where Kathleen gets her talent." He indicated the piano.

Too late, he remembered that William wasn't Kathleen's real father, and he nervously scooped up one of William's books that lay upon an end table. On the back flap of the jacket was an old, flattering photograph.

"I want to confide something in you, Mr. Cypress," he said, "but I must have your word that you'll never disclose to Kathleen what I've told you."

Was that all the Cases knew how to do? Nathan wanted to ask. Ask people to enter into secret pacts with them? What the heck? A person could only be damned once.

"You have it," he said with a tight grimace.

"I tell you this because it will dispense with a lot of painful fence-mending between us. First of all, I will never like you, Mr. Cypress—"

"Sir..."

"No, hear me out, please. I knew my wife very well. Too well, perhaps, and she could never forgive me for that. But the one good thing we did together was have children. Our roles were different from other couples'. Oh, it's quite common these days for the husband to stay home and raise the children, but then it was a brow raiser. I was much closer to our children than Lee knew, Mr. Cypress. Being a man of artistic bent..."

He gave a self-mocking shrug, and Nathan wasn't certain if he was meant to offer encouragement or not.

"I'll not weary you with the sordid details," William said. "The bottom line is, I'm not Kathleen's natural father. Kathleen has no idea that I know the truth, nor would I have known it except for Lee's ego. But I'm ahead of myself, aren't I? You see, the woman that you and I married—"

"Sir... look." Nathan bent his head momentarily, then faced the issue. "Mr. Case, I know about Kathleen's paternity."

William dropped his cane on the floor, and it rolled a distance away. Nathan replaced it into William's hands.

"What I'm trying to say sir—" Nathan didn't resume his seat but braced a foot on the rung of one of the chairs "—is that Kathleen has kept her secret all these years because of the deep love she has for you. I would never do anything to damage that. I don't want to take anything from Kathleen, sir. On the contrary, I want to give her something that I treasure."

"You love her, don't you?"

Elsa's voice coming from behind them made both men flinch.

Recovering, Nathan nodded. "Yes, I do. Very much."

"Then you'll be taking her away, I suppose."

Nathan moved to the piano, where he drew his hand along the sleek sensual curve of the lid. He stared, not at them but at the ebony reflection of himself, a man who no longer seemed remotely connected to that ambitious young comer who had arrived in Washington with blood in his eye.

"I hope to, Elsa," he admitted humbly. "But there are problems, as you may have guessed."

Elsa noisily cleared her throat. "There's a little park down the street. Kathleen goes there with Dusty when she needs to think. Are you sure I can't get you some coffee before you go?"

Nathan shook his head, then nodded politely to William and walked slowly to the door. From across the room came a delicate rustle, and Nathan sensed rather than saw the cat pouring himself from table to floor and tiptoeing to strop Elsa's legs.

Removing her cigarette, she lifted him, nuzzled him and said, "Marry her now, Mr. Cypress. Don't wait until all the problems are worked out. The problems are never worked out."

She dropped the cat and anchored the cigarette between her lips. With a jerky move, she picked up her palette and dipped her brush.

Nathan let himself out and walked past the garage, where Kathleen's Vega sat with dreary resignation. In Elsa's eyes he had seen the scars of tragedy. Elsa wasn't strange at all; she had simply had her heart broken beyond repair.

Chapter 18

Tortorelli Rampage Ends in Death of Police Officer—
Headline, page one, *Philadelphia Reporter*, morning
edition.

From a distance he saw her—she sat folded on the steps of
a rickety gazebo, her knees high and her chin resting upon
them.

With a twig she flicked distractedly at a dead leaf on the
ground. Beyond, Dusty had discovered a stick and raced to
drop it at her feet.

Hugging him, Kathleen rose and flung it high and away
so that he was a flash of gold in the dusk. How fine she was,
standing there on the step like a mariner's wife—shading her
eyes, scanning the horizon, her all-weather coat buckled
trimly about her waist, her hair blowing about her shoulders, its crown imprisoned by a small red cap.

As if he had called out, she turned. His steps had quickened until he was running. His legs were churning faster,

faster. His heart had swelled until it felt ready to burst in his chest.

"Nathan!"

Her cry was snatched by the wind. She stumbled down the steps and raced toward him, her hair catching the fire of the sunset, her boots flashing beneath her flyaway coat. She flung herself into his arms and clung as fiercely, as tightly, as a lost child who had been found.

"You came—you came!" she wept.

He lifted her up in his arms, turning with her and crushing her smallness as he pressed his face into her cap and her hair and the life-giving sweetness that was her.

"Of course I came."

They kissed desperately. "Don't ever leave me again."

"No, no, not ever."

"I thought I'd never see you again."

"I'm sorry. I'm so sorry."

When Nathan could finally bear to part with her and they simply clung to each other like children, dizzily, weaving back and forth, he dropped soft kisses upon her ear. "No more bargains, my love," he promised. "No more demands. I don't care how it has to be. Life isn't worth the trouble without you."

She stuffed her face beneath his chin, her arms a wreath about his chest. "Oh, Nathan. Don't say that. My life's such a mess."

"We'll work it out."

"I try to do the right thing, but it just keeps getting worse and worse." She leaned back in his arms and sought an understanding that surpassed the boundary of words. "A man is dead, Nathan. A policeman is *dead*. Because of me."

"Not because of you."

"It feels like it."

Only at Lee's death had Nathan seen a woman so battered by life. Kathleen was wearier and more drawn than he had imagined her—her eyes were haunted and shadowed, a bluish circle outlined her lips: her eyes were red with weeping and her lips dry and chapped.

Yet he could feel her fighting valiantly inside. How could Farrell Mulhaney stand by and let her keep charging at the same foe until she was used up?

"Let's walk," he said tenderly.

Turning her into his side, they set out with no destination in mind. As she explained her grief about Tortorelli and talked about William and Elsa, her loneliness for her sisters, the way she had missed him, the shadows grew long. In the dusk, the great houses looked forbidding, like convents or penal institutions. Lights came on, and the interiors promised warmth, but the cold outside grew even colder.

They huddled together to stay warm. "I learned something about your aunt today," he told her.

Her boots crunched upon the slush, which was freezing. "Elsa's hurting for me. It isn't fair that she should be paying for this."

"If she couldn't grieve for you, she would be forced to grieve for herself. *That* would be more than she could bear."

She smiled unhappily. "You have a way of putting things into perspective, don't you, Nathan?"

"Not with some things."

"Elsa's hard to find beneath the combat boots and cigarette smoke. She doesn't really hate men, you know."

"She's been wounded by one."

In the middle of her stride, she stopped, her breath a plume of mist. "She told you that?"

Nathan placed a soft kiss upon her lips. "No. She's afraid I'll break your heart."

In the gathering darkness, with her palms resting gently upon his coat, she seemed incredibly precious to him.

"Nathan?" she whispered.

"What, darling?"

"What's the worst thing that you can imagine ever happening? Your absolute worst nightmare?"

He wondered if he could expose himself so utterly. He wasn't sure how to say how afraid he was of facing life without her. "That your three sisters should discover that Anne Marie Gabalis has designed a dress that costs over fifteen hundred dollars."

She hit him with a fist and curved her lips in charming, girlish mockery. Her brows arched high. "Why, look at you. You have new glasses, Nathan Cypress."

His fist playfully found her jaw. "The better to see you with, my dear."

She plucked them from his face and anchored them majestically upon her own nose, where they slid to half-mast. Laughter bubbled out of her, then slowly dwindled as she removed them and nervously held them with her long, tapered fingers.

"Do you ever want a baby of your own, Nathan?" she asked quietly.

Until she had come into his life, he would have said an emphatic no. He had seen too many children torn apart by poverty and divorce; even Lee's daughters bore their scars. To picture himself fathering a child and raising it within the social turmoil of the nineties was an illusion that carried its own futility.

But a baby with Kathleen? Retrieving his glasses before she wrecked them again, he thrust them into his pocket and drew her head to his chest. "Listen. What do you hear?"

"Your heart."

"That's my biological clock ticking."

Giggling, she started to turn, but he caught her with a rough urgency. "Are you trying to tell me you're pregnant, Kathleen?"

Her profile was a pensive silhouette against the darkening day and didn't tell him much. "How could I know that? There hasn't been time."

"Could you be, though? Is it possible?" He was shocked at his own need to know, at his wild hope that she truly had conceived.

Flushing, she disguised her self-consciousness by busily poking her hair beneath the cap. "Elsa has a saying—If you're exposed, it's possible. If you're asking me how fertile I am, I don't know. I haven't had a lot of experience in that particular area."

The darkness was upon them now, allowing them to open new and more secret doors.

"I don't think either of us needs that problem just now," she mumbled. "Not that I don't want this to work between us—you can't know how much I want it to work."

"Sometimes babies settle priorities, my sweet."

"I wouldn't do that to you."

"Hey." Didn't she know how much he wanted her in his life?

They had begun to walk to keep from freezing, migrating toward his car. "I've been thinking about Lee the past few days," she admitted.

"She wanted very much to make peace with you, Kathleen. Though she never said it in so many words, I think she took all the blame upon herself."

"I'm so tired of hating her, Nathan. I wish...I wish I could do some things differently. I wish I hadn't been so righteous, so quick to judge."

"I think that's called growing up, darling. I've a few wishes of my own."

The sidewalk had cracked and buckled, causing their feet to stumble. Catching themselves, they found each other in the darkness.

"Marry me," he said on a thick, guttural breath. "Right now, Kath, and the world be damned. Make a life with me. Have a baby with me. I don't care if I lose the paper or lose everything else. What's it worth without you? Let William have the miserable *Sentinel*."

The silence was tempered by the low moan of the wind, and she rose up on her toes and stroked his face and the new stubble sprouting on his jaw. "Oh, if it were only that easy, my love. Don't you have any idea what my presence would do to your life? I've got a dangerous man thinking I betrayed him. I can't just sweep you and my sisters into that guilt by association. I couldn't live with that. I need a little more time. I need to put my life in order."

"Life is never in order, damn it!" Elsa's words came crashing down upon Nathan like an avalanche. "We'll never have the problems worked out. That's what life is—problems. Love is two people facing them together. Love is people being better together than they ever were apart." His despair matched hers as he caught her in a fierce grip. "What do you want?" he groaned into her cap. "Just tell me what it is. I'll get it. I swear I will."

A sob escaped her. "You," she confessed as she tightened her arms hungrily about him. "I want you."

Dusty was nowhere in sight.

"Oh, he deserts me all the time, the rascal," Kathleen complained sometime later. "It doesn't really matter. He'll have found his own way home by now."

Their drive back was one of uncertainty. Neither of them knew exactly what to say. Kathleen wasn't even sure why she directed Nathan to park on the street in front of the big house. To give them the added moments alone, she supposed. To exchange a final intimacy before going in.

For long moments, they kissed, allowing chemistry to speak its own familiar language. Their caresses grew more urgent, however, and soon they were straining for that eternal solace of release in each other.

"We'd better go in," she whispered as he studied her face in the shadows.

"Lady, I ain't sure I can walk just yet." His lips found hers in a final slaking kiss.

Their feet crunched softly in the new crust of ice, and Kathleen glanced aimlessly for Dusty, and in doing so spotted the big, black car before Nathan did. With hairsplitting reflexes, she stopped.

Immediately finding the object of her concern, he pulled her into the safety of the cold shadows. "Who is it?" he asked.

Kathleen shrugged. "I don't know."

She started to walk over and find out, and he held her back. "Just a minute, just a minute."

His precaution unnerved her, and she caught its fever. "What's wrong?"

"Nothing probably," he said. "Where's Dusty?"

Ordinarily Dusty would have been curled up in a ball of golden fur at the back door, waiting for it to open.

Alarmed, Kathleen gripped his arm. "Nathan—"

"Shh."

"Do you see Dusty?"

"No." Nathan pressed her against the frozen branches of the hedge and placed his mouth against the ribbing of her cap. "There's a man standing beyond the porch. He's dressed in dark clothes. You can just make out the brim of his cap behind the shrub. In the shadows beneath the frame of the window. Do you see?"

She nodded, but what she didn't have any trouble making out was the shape at the man's feet. "Oh, no," she murmured as heartsick dread rose in her mouth like bile. "Oh, Nathan, it's Dusty."

Nathan planted his hand over her mouth, shutting off the sound, and Kathleen forced back the grief that was bursting in her throat. Dusty, Dusty! She brought his head down to her ear. "I never told you this, but someone was watching me when I was in Washington."

He gave her a sharp, cross-examining look of disbelief.

"I wasn't sure it was Tortorelli at the time," she confessed. "There were some phone calls, too, but then there was that thing with Gloria and the photographer, and I thought maybe the sedan on the street was someone she had hired. And it may have been, Nathan. But, then, maybe it wasn't..."

He made a swift reconnoiter of the big house and the garage and the stable and the shrubs and the car. "Well, I don't think *this* is Gloria."

"He killed Dusty." Kathleen was shaking violently now, and she bent until her head touched her knees. "He killed Dusty."

He gave her a harsh shake. "Get ahold of yourself. Dusty may only be drugged to keep him quiet. Someone's probably in the house, too."

Kathleen forced herself to concentrate. Against the light, an occasional shadow passed, but she couldn't identify it. A voice was audible as it rose and fell, but again, she couldn't identify it as male or female. It could've been her father.

"Is there a way we can come up from the back?" Nathan was saying.

"Do you think Elsa and Daddy are in trouble?"

"I think it pays to take precautions. We can get behind the garage, then we can make sure. Is there a way to come up from behind?"

They could circle the block and climb through the hedge at the back where the lot behind adjoined them.

At once, he was guiding her out the driveway, holding her hand so that he was practically dragging her as they raced down the block and up the next, around the corner and past houses until they were aligned with the stable. Then they tromped across the property of a man Kathleen knew only in a vague, impersonal way.

The dividing line was honeysuckle and privet. By abusing some of the branches, they were able to crawl through, though it seemed to Kathleen that the sounds they made were loud enough to wake the dead.

"They'll probably be gone by the time we get there," she whispered, gasping for breath.

"Then we won't have a problem."

But the car had not gone, and they still had a problem. Kathleen prayed that she would see that familiar bundle of gold streaking through the cold night. But they were met by silence. Taking her hand, crouching, Nathan ran with her to the back of the garage, and their steps seemed to thunder like a legion of horses.

He flattened her against the stones, and they waited until their breaths had steadied. He nodded then whispered, "Okay, okay. We're okay."

Kathleen had no idea how he could say such a thing. Seconds turned into an interminable stretch of time. When Nathan at length inched around the corner, she clutched his hands and drew him back. "Nathan, it has to be Tortorelli."

"A good guess."

"Then why don't I talk to him? I could explain that I didn't tell Helen Mason anything."

He rolled his eyes. "One man is dead already, Kathleen. Do you see Tortorelli sitting down for a pleasant chat?"

"Then we've got to call the police."

Before the words were out of her mouth, somewhere a pane of glass shattered. Kathleen lunged, and Nathan slammed her against the stone so hard, the breath was knocked from her body.

"I'm sorry," he whispered, and clasped her tightly. "Are you all right?"

"The police," she gasped.

"It will take them a while to get here."

"We have to do something!"

"Throw rocks at the guard?"

"We need a weapon."

"Sure. And I can hold them at bay with a tire tool." Pushing her away, he stripped open her coat and stared at her, and Kathleen, aghast, thought he had gone mad. "That shirt," he whispered. "Take it off."

"What?"

"Get it off. As we were taught in the military—" he showed his teeth in a flash of self-mockery "—I'm going to create a diversion."

Prompted to haste by another dreadful sound from the house, Kathleen snatched off her coat and, shivering, peeled off the shirt. As she shrugged back into her coat, her teeth chattering, she gaped as he twisted the cotton fabric about his hand and, crouching, moved swiftly around the corner and disappeared into the garage.

Afraid to follow for fear of being detected by the man, she couldn't remain outside alone, either. As quick as a flash she followed, and found Nathan muffling the sound of the gas cap being unscrewed.

Her eyes widened. What on earth . . . ?

He sniffed, then blew into the cavern of the gas tank and stuffed her shirt as deeply inside as was possible. He patted over the pockets of his trousers and pulled out a book of matches. Why, he intended to make a bomb out of her car!

She grasped his arm, shaking her head. "You can't do this! It's against the law."

"So is holding innocent people at gunpoint."

"You'll wind up in jail!"

"It won't be the first time." He grinned. "You can be my lawyer. You got Tortorelli off. Surely you can get me out of Alcatraz. Now when I light this," he warned, "the moment it catches, you run like hell toward the hedge we just climbed through. Go to one of the neighbors and call the fire department and the police.

She pounded at his shoulder. "But my car."

"The world will thank me. Now do as I say."

"But—"

"Do you want to get them out of that house?"

"Yes, but—"

With a savagery that was as frightening as the terrible risk he was about to run, he kissed her hard upon the lips. "I'll be all right." He grinned recklessly. "I was a 'bad boy.' I know what I'm doing."

There was nothing to do but obey, and the sure terror of loving someone so deeply overwhelmed her. What if she never saw him again? What if she had lived this long to find a man she could love with all her heart, only to lose him before they had their chance? Suddenly all the things she had imagined keeping them apart seemed a child's game.

A groove appeared briefly between his brows as he struck the match. Slowly, the tiny flicker of flame caught her shirt and began to burn. Horrible scenarios flashed through Kathleen's mind as she slipped out into the darkness and began to run, not daring to turn back to see if some faceless monster was lumbering after her. She ran until her side was hurting, and still the hedge seemed miles and miles away.

Just as she reached it and was scrambling through tangles of honeysuckle, battling for every inch, it seemed as if an atomic bomb had detonated behind her. There was a sound like the sucking of air, once, twice, and another sound that struck her eardrums with a painful pressure.

Without meaning to, she screamed Nathan's name and tumbled headlong through the brush, losing her cap in the branches. She scrambled to her feet just in time to see a huge burst that sent flames shooting to the treetops.

Adrenaline surged through her. She clamored up the back steps, where a light shone dimly from one of the back windows. She imagined Nathan suffering horrible, unspeakable things. She imagined him thrown by the explosion and lying lifeless upon the ground. She experienced the agony of bullets as he was gunned down by the stranger in the shrubbery.

To her relief as she clattered up the steps, she saw that the man who lived there—a small, redheaded Irishman who smoked a corncob pipe and was so covered with freckles that his face appeared to have rusted—had come to the back door and opened it.

"Please," she cried, stumbling toward him.

When she couldn't find the strength to explain, she grasped the poor man by the front of the shirt and shook, waving distraughtly at the holocaust now visible to the entire neighborhood.

"Fire department!" she gasped. "Police!"

Without a word he disappeared into the house, and not knowing if she should follow him or not—perhaps he was deaf and had not heard her; perhaps he was unfriendly and didn't want to get involved—her instincts told her to trust him. With tears wetting her face, she raced back to the hedge and began to crawl painfully through.

From a distance came the sound of a fire engine. The smell of burning was a stench in the heavy night air as thick smoke billowed out of the garage, which had lost part of its walls and roof and was now an inferno. Flames shot over the bare trees as she pulled herself through the hedge and came to her feet.

As she ran nearer, the heat became unbearable and the air filled with pieces of ash and sparks.

"Nathan, Nathan!" she screamed until there was no more breath to scream.

The car was no longer there. In a haze of despair she stumbled around the garage, getting as near to the hellish furnace as she dared, scanning the surrounding ground with streaming eyes.

"Nathan!"

Did she hear him with her ears or with her heart? Not with her ears, she thought, for the sound of the fire was deafening. When she felt herself falling and sank to her knees, only to be lifted up in powerful arms, she didn't question if she was dreaming. He was alive. He was holding her. Everything would be all right now.

Chapter 19

John Tortorelli Continues to Elude Authorities—
Headline, page four, *Philadelphia Reporter*, morning
edition.

William and Elsa refused to leave the house for a safer
place. Throughout the endless questions by the police and
the prowling of the grounds by detectives, the probe into
Kathleen's relationship with John Tortorelli, the statements taken and signed, Elsa clomped about in her combat
boots and shook her head.

"No gangster is running *me* out of *my* own house," she
grumbled. "Whatever the stars say is the way it'll be. No
running will change that. No, sir. I'm staying put."

The police said they would keep the house under surveil-
lance. "Actually," a detective explained to William, "it's
unlikely that John Tortorelli will ever come back. Why
would he? The risk isn't worth it."

As Nathan suspected, Dusty had been drugged, and as he came awake in Kathleen's arms, weakly wagging his golden tail, he thought he had gone to doggie heaven, and wouldn't have had it any other way.

"Dusty, you probably got the best end of it," Kathleen cooed as she cradled his head in her lap and rewarded his gallantry with tiny scraps of Elsa's cooking.

Nathan's entanglement with the police was not so cut-and-dried.

After a series of grilling questions and an agreement to pay a hefty service fee to the fire department, Nathan agreed to plead nolo contendere to the charge of disturbing the peace and burning inside the city limits, and was let off after promising to appear before a county judge.

"He'll dismiss the charges, Nathan," Kathleen promised, still petting Dusty. "Take my word for it."

But the police warned that the next time Nathan should let them "do their job" and not be "such a hot dog."

"What would you have done," Nathan countered in annoyed self-defense, "without that gun on your hip?"

"I'm not saying it wasn't an effective ploy, Mr. Cypress," the officer retorted. "But you ran a great risk, besides, violating a half-dozen city ordinances. The fines will hit you pretty hard."

"Fines I can live with. Having the homicide department out here now, carrying two people away in body bags, is something I couldn't have."

The man saw his point, but wasn't about to admit he might have reacted the same way.

The next morning Kathleen was grateful that Elsa was alive to brew her bitter coffee and cook her terrible food. As she sat sipping the brew, she exchanged long, wordless looks with Nathan. Elsa was already preparing her easels, but

William was in his chair, staring into space, not having eaten a bite.

"I don't know what to do," Kathleen admitted to Nathan with a shrug, stealing glances at her father.

"The first thing is to tell him about us," Nathan said. "Putting it off won't help, sweetheart."

Watching William's face when she told her father about her true feelings for Nathan was not an experience Kathleen wanted to go through ever again. Even more ghastly was William's reaction to Nathan's admission about his marriage to Lee.

"Oh, I knew she hated me," William grieved after he had taken in the implications of Lee's last months, "but to go so far? How afraid she must have been, how tormented."

"Oh, Daddy." Kathleen wrapped her arms around him. "You're the only man in the whole world who would look at her side of things now. Try to see the truth. You're a kind, loyal man, and she was selfish and thoughtless. Forgive her, but don't take the guilt upon yourself."

"She's in the past, William," Elsa observed with brutal honesty as she set out her paints and brushes. "Bury the past with Lee, and wish these two young people Godspeed."

Kathleen was reassured that William and Elsa would be all right. These two aging siblings would see each other through whatever was to be borne. Since the Vega was mercifully dead and buried, Nathan left them his Thunderbird. So with tears and the inevitable regret of hindsight, she left them and returned to Washington with Nathan.

As the plane made its descent, however, she sat stroking Nathan's hand, smoothing the large strong knuckles and the fine peppering of brown hair across its top, and his beautiful, strong wrists. When she looked up, he was staring at her.

"Nathan," she whispered, "what're you thinking?"

"All my life I've been decent with words, and now I don't have any to tell you. 'I love you' seems so...inadequate."

With a shift of his knee over hers, Nathan shut out the passengers with his back, content simply to lose himself in watching her—the flaming radiance about her head, the top of her breasts beneath her blouse.

She moistened her lips with an earnestness that drew him closer.

"All my life I've gone contrary to nature." She stared wistfully at their laced hands. "I don't know why—maybe to prove to myself that I could do it. I used to like being a rebel, out of step with the world, but now I want to do a few of the normal things." She looked up. "Nathan, I want the trust Lee set up for me."

There was a moment of quiet as they both allowed themselves to be shocked by this last statement.

Nathan laughed. "You're kidding." He puckered his lips beneath the mustache. "Sure. Okay. I'll set it up."

Kathleen set her jaw with determination. "I want the money, and I want my own place. I want..." Her eyes grew misty, and her voice was a husky whisper. "I want you to come courting, Nathan. No, now don't laugh. I want to cook you lovely dinners. I want to dress up for you. I want to go shopping and buy you cuff links."

How could he laugh? Nathan wondered. He felt more like crying.

Sighing, she leaned against the seat and moved her gaze dreamily over his face. "I want us to enjoy a little of that sweet rush while it's still there to be had," she said softly as she traced his nose and brows with a fingertip. "I want to enjoy falling in love with you. Can you understand that?"

Great tears trembled upon the ends of her lashes, and he pressed his lips to the pulse in her neck and felt her blood surge against his mouth.

"I didn't think it was possible to love you more than I do," he murmured. "Now I see I've only just begun."

For quiet moments they held each other, not speaking, content to drift and let dreams work their magic.

As the pilot touched down, Kathleen pressed Nathan's fingers with a new and quickened demand. "But there's something else I want. I want you to let me work with Rudy Mendina and Ian Raines. I want to wear the wire, Nathan. I'm perfect for it, and you know it. I want to do something for *you*. Please don't say no."

Oh, but he wanted to. He wanted to be the macho tyrant and lay down the law and declare, *This is how it's gonna be. No wires, no Rudy Mendina. Forget Gloria.* But she was much too set on her purpose. If he loved her, he had no choice but to give her the freedom to move, to be her own person.

By a stroke of luck, one of Jerry Franks's friends had a friend who had a friend who was connected to the embassy and had a house for rent in the heart of Alexandria's Old Town across the Potomac.

The owners were wintering on the Riveria. The house was magnificently furnished. He and Kathleen agreed that for three months she could present herself to Washington society as Kathleen Castoro, heiress. If, in that time, she could not cause Gloria to incriminate herself and give the FBI a reason to open a full-fledged investigation, she would let it go.

They were trailing behind the realtor's high heels that clicked up the sidewalk. The grounds were kept private by a sixteen-foot fence of wrought iron on the outside and a dense growth of bamboo on the inside.

"Can I afford this?" Kathleen was wondering, astonished at the luxury. "They said it was nice, but mercy..."

Nathan was reminded of old Southern mansions that had movie producers drooling to use them in films. The interior decorator had had honest-to-goodness good taste. If the truth were known, he rather liked the idea of Kathleen having her own house. Sweethearts could never have too much privacy.

"Darling," he chided, "can't I get it through your head? You're a very wealthy woman. It's no longer necessary to squeeze the copper out of the quarter."

"I won't ever get used to it." Kathleen listened to the realtor extol the virtues of the kitchen, with its expanses of wood and copper. "I've been a miser too long."

"If you insist on traveling in fast company," he observed, "you'd better learn to look the part."

When they climbed the stairs to see the bedrooms, Kathleen stole a quick inspection of herself in the mirrors. She *did* look the part, dressed in smart winter white, a cashmere sweep cape enfolding her. Her gloves matched the delicate buff of her boots and wide-brimmed felt hat, beneath which she had crammed her hair.

"It's true," she said to Nathan as she took a critical view of her backside. "Clothes make the woman."

"If you think that—" Nathan planted a firm slap upon her buttock "—you're not as smart as I gave you credit for."

Pretending a growl, she reached up and removed his glasses. "I always knew you couldn't see an inch before your nose."

Holding them out, she squinted through them with a laugh, then blinked at him with comical amusement. "They're different."

He shrugged. "Old age. Now I really do have an astigmatism."

"Serves you right," she said, giggling, and poked them back onto his face.

The realtor was waiting for them in the corridor. "Well, have you come to a decision?"

Both stories had been examined, plus the pool that was covered for the winter, as well as the double garage. The woman lit a cigarette and blew smoke at the white walls surrounding them.

"It's an absolute steal," she said. "I could have already rented it if the owner—"

"We'll take it," Nathan said, interrupting.

Swinging around, Kathleen said, "Y-yes, we'll take it."

The agent was surprised to have the deal finalized so quickly, and she extinguished her cigarette.

"We'll want immediate possession, of course." Nathan told her as Kathleen removed her checkbook.

"Of course." The woman lifted her brows. "I have the contract in my case."

While Kathleen signed the contract and wrote the check, Nathan amused himself by removing dust cloths and stacking them in the corridor. Once the realtor had gone, they stood alone in the huge house, gazing at the high ceilings and finely crafted fireplaces and leaded windows and marble floors.

Laughing, Kathleen hugged herself and rotated in a circle. "My first act will be to have you and the girls over for dinner," she announced, and proceeded to the kitchen, where she swung open the cabinet doors and peered into their secrets. "Frannie, too, naturally. And Simon."

"Are you sure you wouldn't like to invite the entire staff of the *Sentinel*, Cinderella? And the FBI, as well?"

"Don't be rude."

"I wouldn't dream of it." He plucked off her hat so that her hair tumbled about her shoulders.

She watched the hat go sailing across the room, then found herself lifted from the floor and left to slide slowly down the front of his body. Beneath his trousers was the evidence of arousal, and his eyes plumbed hers with growing warmth.

"It's getting late," he said, and drew her fragrance deep into his lungs. "Tomorrow the maid will come and help you get settled. Frannie, too, if you need her."

"Maybe we should be leaving now, Nathan."

"I thought we might stay a moment longer."

"There's no food in the house. Aren't you getting hungry?"

"I'm starving."

They read each other's minds and laughed. They had all the time in the world to love each other. Kathleen gathered up the papers and stuffed them in her bag, while Nathan moved through the house, turning off lights and making sure things were locked.

As the lights went off one by one, the sense of isolation returned. Kathleen was waiting beside the front door, her hand resting upon the switch.

He looked rather like an errant prince as he came toward her, Kathleen thought, with his curls and his leather jacket and wool sweater, his dark slacks and leather-soled loafers. When he took her into his arms, she laughed nervously and doused the light.

"What's the matter, counselor," he murmured, and located the facing of the door in order to get his bearings. "Scared of a little dark?"

"How can you ask me that after I crawled through fences and let you blow up my garage?"

His laughter was warm and sweet on her cheeks. "I owe you a car, don't I?"

"You owe me a lot."

"Good grief, I hope you're not going to be one of those mercenary wives and divide everything into mine and yours."

Tension was building along the inside of Kathleen's thighs. How could something so simple as the texture of his voice do it?

"Absolutely." She leaned against him. "This is mine, and that—" she wriggled erotically against him "—is yours."

"What's mine?"

A sudden urgency was in the bend of his head over hers, and Kathleen trembled as she made herself available and he searched for her beneath the soft cape, following the contours of her breasts and her sides, drawing her nearer and straining with the abandon only a strange, empty house could trigger.

"You know that I want it all, don't you?" he muttered. "I only went through the motions before, but I want the real thing this time—the rings, the ceremony, the best man, the bridesmaids. I want a honeymoon that lasts six months."

"Why, I do believe you're anxious, Nathan Cypress."

"It is for your deep perceptions that I love you," he said, and lifted her cape from her shoulders to let it slide to the carpet in a pool of white.

Their eyes were used to the darkness now, and she watched him step back, saw his nostrils flare. The room was chilled, hardly conducive to romance—no music, no candles, no good food, no exotic wines, only the two of them and their deep need for the other.

They were like two healthy animals under the spell of nature, taking cues from body language and the heightened senses of taste and smell. He touched the buckle of his belt. She reached for the button at her own waist. His gaze remained riveted to hers as he removed his jacket. Kathleen flicked a button free on her blouse. He watched her fingers moving down, down, down, and Kathleen swore she could feel all the roots of her hair, all the pores of her skin.

When her blouse was loose, she twisted the tiny clasp of her bra and waited, going no further. The ritual was growing strained, and he took a step to one side, then around, making her turn with him. In a last surge of uncertainty, Kathleen sucked in her breath, and she thought she murmured his name.

Suddenly he had her in his arms and was kissing her and pulling her down to the carpet upon the cashmere cape.

"Nathan," she whispered as he was freeing himself, as he was finding her, touching her in the ways that were now familiar and in the ways she would be exploring for the rest of her life, "do you really love me?"

"There aren't enough ways to tell you."

"Then make me a baby," she gasped as she clung to him very, very tightly. "I want a baby, Nathan. I want your baby."

Every good lawyer was, by necessity, a good actor. Timing was an art form by which whole cases could be won or lost. The lucky ones to whom the talent came naturally could enhance their skills of subterfuge and were, when the final gavel came down, champions that no one could gainsay.

Kathleen was a great actress. Not only had Lee given her the genes, she had developed the potential. For the next weeks, in a subtle, unhurried manner, she worked on Gloria and Curtis Sterling. With Nathan's connections, she got herself invited to all the best parties, but her escort was more often than not an FBI official.

Like bait, she dangled herself, always turning up where Gloria was, refusing to talk money, yet not falling into the trap of flaunting it; nothing gave away new money so

quickly as flashing it. Since Gloria was such an avid pursuer of philanthropy, Kathleen supported the same charities, and she made sure that no one knew of her gifts except
Gloria.

"Have you always been a patron of the arts, Kathleen,
darling?" Gloria would coo.

Kathleen's smile would be a cunning tell-no-evil smile.
"It's my opinion that once you tell about your gift, Gloria,
it's no longer a gift."

"We should get together sometime," Gloria insisted.
"Come with me to the Bahamas next Tuesday."

"Tuesday? I'd love to, but some friends and I are running up to 21 after dinner. Maybe next time."

Once that seed was planted, there was the hair-raising
frenzy of having Rudy Mendina arrange for a proper entourage at the celebrated club. Kathleen had never been to
21 in her life, and by the time the limousine pulled to the
curb, it was nearly midnight. If Gloria didn't take this bait,
she probably never would.

When Kathleen stepped to the sidewalk in front of the
club she was on the arm of an FBI man who was the spitting image of Sam Elliot. She was wearing Lee's Russian
lynx coat that had, back in the eighties, cost three hundred
thousand dollars. Beneath it were Lee's ten-thousand-dollar
alligator jeans. Adding that to the lynx coat, there was
enough to incite the SPCA to crucify her.

Even though people didn't know who she was, they recognized style, and once Rudy's planted photographers began flashing strobe lights, the fever caught and whispers
raced through the crowd. Who is she? A foreign princess,
someone said . . . the mistress of a Greek shipping magnate.

The doorman hurried them into the restaurant, where
socialites and jet-setters from all over the world stared at

them from the banquettes. As Kathleen suspected, Gloria and Curtis were holding court at their table.

She drew in her breath. "Easy, easy," warned her escort, who had introduced himself as Winchester.

"I'm okay, Winchester." Kathleen pasted an artificial smile on her face. "Gloria is drooling."

Knowing it wasn't in her to assume the facade of haughty wealth, Kathleen pretended an elegant disdain as she moved through the club—polite but thoroughly disillusioned and nonsensical. When Winchester took her cat, she let the lynx drop from her shoulders as if it were a rag she cared nothing about.

A gasp rose from nearby tables as her sapphire pendant and earrings shot fire. Embarrassingly large, the jewels had been purchased from the collection of a deposed European princess and reset for Lee by a Swiss jeweler. Aside from the necklace and earrings, Kathleen wore no other jewelry.

Hardly had she been seated than Gloria raised her brows from across the room.

"Perhaps you should go by her table," Winchester suggested.

"No." Kathleen accepted the fawning attention of the maître d'. "She has to come to me."

There were times when Kathleen thought that Gloria would refuse to do it. In such a public place, it boiled down to a ceremony of rank.

Finally Kathleen couldn't bear it any longer. "To hell with this," she muttered to Winchester. "She's not going to bite, and I'm tired. Let's leave."

Rising, not caring at this point if Gloria choked on her food, Kathleen waited as Winchester fetched her coat. She wanted Nathan. She wanted to forget the whole idea and get on with her life.

As they were proceeding to the door, to Kathleen's surprise, Gloria came out of her seat and glided across the floor. "Darling," she murmured, and ran an intimately approving eye up and down Kathleen. "I've been trying to get away all evening to speak to you."

Liar, Kathleen thought. "Hello, Gloria."

"Everything's so noisy here," Gloria said. "Why don't I send a car for you tomorrow? You really must come and see our new offices, my dear. I absolutely insist. We've redecorated, and I think you'll love the new paintings Curtis bought. Oh, did I tell you? We've opened a new branch in London. We're very excited."

It was better than nothing, Kathleen thought, and said, "What a good idea, Gloria. Do you know, I've been thinking all week that I should call you?"

"Really? You look tired, sweetie. Do I detect the shadow of a cloud in those eyes? A raindrop? I won't stand for it."

Kathleen forced herself to laugh. "I've only lost two accountants to suicide this past week. Honestly, I think it's time I did something."

"Of course it is." Purring, Gloria exchanged a look of triumph with Curtis and walked Kathleen to the door. "I'll be expecting you."

The next day, as Kathleen was being given the grand tour through the Sterling complex in one of the chic International Plazas, she wasn't sure what she'd expected.

True, Sterling's offices were intimidatingly ornate, with private elevators and special computer rooms and expensive antiques and art pieces on the walls. Catered food was brought in on a daily basis, and the security system would have made the Pentagon sick with envy. Gloria let her know up front that what Kathleen saw was only the tip of the iceberg, that Curtis was doing so phenomenally well that they owned a number of foreign sports cars and two jets and several homes, one a penthouse in Manhattan. Everyone was involved with the new British-licensed bank.

But Kathleen found a disappointing lack of activity going on at the Sterling complex. Secretaries were on the phones, yes, and salesmen were working with clients, yet a vague sense of futility ran through the building, a desperation that came close to panic.

Kathleen smiled as Gloria finessed her and introduced her to everyone, bombarding her with proof of how their off-shore bank in the Bahamas could protect her millions from U.S. taxes. Knowing that FBI agents and Nathan were sitting in a van parked down the street, Kathleen made as many audible remarks as possible into the microphone taped to her ribs and kept smiling.

"Sit here, Kathleen, dear," Gloria said. "I'm going to find Michael now and let him explain our contracts. Then we'll dash up to New York for some of Alfredo's grilled octopus."

"Isn't Curtis here?" Kathleen inquired mildly.

"Oh, no, darling. He had to go home for a private meeting. Some of our clients are so discreet they don't even come in. That's the beauty, don't you see? We can come to you."

"This is his office?"

Without waiting for a reply, Kathleen peeped inside the elaborate suite. Sophisticated equipment lined one entire wall, the screens a blur of cathode rays and phosphor dots, but not a soul was in the office. The chairs were empty; the telephones were silent.

Kathleen thought of all the brokerage houses she had known—not many, admittedly, but all of them with brokers glued to the screens lest a second slip past that might make the difference between loss and gain.

"Y-yes, this is Curtis's den of lions," Gloria said, and hurried Kathleen on to another suite that was even more elaborate.

She was placed in a plush chair, given a cup of coffee in Spode china and a brochure lauding Sterling Interbank.

"This is *my* private office," Gloria explained. "No one but *no one* comes in here. Except you, of course."

Kathleen had worn Lee's largest diamond about her neck—one with enough carats to dazzle a king. Gloria had to tear her eyes away from it.

Gloria had obviously been in the middle of paying bills, for several checkbooks were spread across the desk, along with electric bills, telephone bills, insurance bills, water bills. As cool as a margarita, she raked everything into a drawer and smiled as she was leaving to fetch Michael.

Cup in hand, Kathleen smiled with equal coolness and rose to wander negligently about the office.

"Nathan, if you're listening," she intoned under her breath, "this is a bust. This woman's like a locked safe. She doesn't let anything get past. And that theory you had about Sterling not paying its bills? Forget it. They're writing checks this very minute."

Inching around the desk, leaning against it in a demure pose, she flicked her eyes over papers stacked haphazardly upon the surface.

"Sterling letterheads with the Bahama address," she mused into the microphone. "Letterheads with a London address, memos to clients, hype for the sales force, tons of paperwork. Nothing, nothing."

The stationery was quite stately, tastefully engraved, and Kathleen gazed from it to dozens of plaques of commendation to Gloria and Curtis covering the walls. She furtively turned the page of a personal telephone directory with a fingernail, sending a page flipping over: the Bahama bank, the new London bank, Japan, flick, flick, flick.

But still nothing.

Gloria passed outside the door in search of Michael and laughed. "That man is never around when I need him."

"No hurry," Kathleen said with a gelatinous smile.

When Michael finally appeared, Kathleen was condemned to another hour of smiling through one high-voltage sales pitch after another on why she should invest at least a half-million dollars in Sterling.

"Well, Michael," she said at last, glancing with marked impatience at her diamond wristwatch, "I find this all very tempting, truly, but before I sink a half-million dollars into this, I do have one request."

"I'm your man." He flashed a salesmanlike grin.

"I'd like to know why no one is supervising the computers in Curtis's office."

The aggressive facade paled. "Ahh—" he licked his lips "—well, I'll tell you, Kathleen, that's an excellent question, but I think you should talk to the man himself. Nothing like going to the horse's mouth, don't you agree? Why don't I just have the switchboard ring old Curtis and you can talk to him?"

The last person in the world Kathleen wanted to talk to was Curtis Sterling. She crossed and recrossed her legs as Michael buzzed the receptionist.

"Get Curtis on the phone, will you?" Michael snapped. "Miss Case would like to speak to him. Yes, sweetie pie, didn't I just say that? At home, damn it—555-4521. Yes, thank you, Marie. Thank you very much, indeed." With a grimace, Michael added to Kathleen, "Secretaries! They go to school to learn how to screw me up."

"Why don't you let me look at one of your contracts, Michael?" Kathleen said.

While the man pinched the phone beneath his shoulder and jaw, he rummaged in the desk drawer for a contract and, in a moment of exasperation, hauled out all the checkbooks and bills and dumped them inelegantly to one side, causing several to fall on Kathleen's feet.

"Oops." He made as if to rise and pick them up.

Waving him back into his chair, Kathleen stooped and gathered up the bills, furtively attempting to get a look at one of the bank balances in the process. The balance would necessarily have to be large; the telephone bills were in the four figures.

And as quick as the click of a snapping camera lens, the answer flashed from the bill, taking Kathleen's breath away for its beautiful simplicity. The bill was for the installation of phone service in the new London branch Gloria had been bragging about. Right in the center of the charges was the bold-faced heading Remote Call Forwarding. Also given was the number in London and the number in Washington where all incoming calls would be forwarded: 555-4521. Curtis Sterling's home phone, which the switchboard was ringing this very moment.

Feeling as if she had caught hold of a naked wire, Kathleen flinched and swiftly arranged her expression and let shutters drop over her eyes. With slow, careful moves, she replaced the fallen bills and checkbook to the desk.

Then she sat straight—tall, unmoving. Her smile broadened until it hurt. No wonder the SEC had missed it! It was too obvious! Right in plain sight, like masking tape across the lock of a door in the Watergate Hotel. The proof of Sterling's fraud wasn't in figures on some ledger where funds had been misappropriated, though she was sure they had been. The proof wasn't in the failure to register investments and bank deposits, though she was sure that such existed.

The proof was in the telephone billing. There was no bank in London!

And she would wager Lee's emeralds that all Curtis's other banks were nothing more than bronze plaques on some office door and a telephone that could forward the calls back to the United States. There was only Curtis Sterling, swindler: 555-4521.

She hardly knew what she said to escape Michael, something about having parked her car illegally and having stayed much longer than she'd intended to, that she would come again later and would call Gloria.

Poor Michael looked as if she had struck him across the face with one of his checkbooks. In alarm, he rushed to another office and alerted Gloria that the prize catch was escaping the net.

She heard a feminine shriek. "Kathleen, *dar-ling*," Gloria cried, hurrying after her, her beautiful chin sagging. "Where in heaven's name are you going?"

"I have an appointment to keep, Gloria," she said sweetly.

"But what about lunch?"

"I don't really care for grilled octopus, Gloria."

Kathleen was certain she heard a long colorful spiel of cursing as she strolled out onto the cold, windy street and recounted into the microphone everything she'd learned.

Nathan knew, even before Rudy Mendina smiled and pulled off his headphones, that Kathleen had stumbled upon the key they needed to unlock the door to the Sterling vaults. Coming to his feet, he cracked his head against the top of the van and winced.

He rubbed his head gingerly. "Well, gentlemen," he said with a crooked grin, "I don't know about you, but I think I've got some real ammunition this time. I'll see you later."

With his usual deadpan face, Rudy Mendina stalled. "Wait a minute, Mr. Cypress. We can carry the ball from here. We do appreciate your offer to help, though."

Laughing, Nathan opened the door and stepped into the cold. "You do your thing, guys, I'll do mine."

As she walked down the sidewalk at a brisk trot, Kathleen rounded the shrubbery and fancy planters of the plaza. The euphoria was like a magical enchantment as they waved at each other from opposite ends of the plaza.

They knew that they had done exactly what they had set out to do. They had faced circumstances that were hopeless, and they faced rough weather ahead. But they were no longer afraid, because they had each other, and whatever the future held—be it scandal or misunderstanding or money or career compromises—they would work them out together. Whatever price tags were attached, they would pay.

But together.

Laughing, Kathleen grew dizzy with the wonderful sight of Nathan's curly head as he strode toward her—so handsome and so fine, his grace so princely that people were turning to take a second look. She was suddenly impatient to be with him and hear his congratulations. She wanted to bask in his approval and feel that good warmth of having played her part so well.

She broke into a run and was spun around by the figure that moved quickly from out of a building's doorway. She stumbled over her own feet and lost her balance.

"This way, Miss Case," a gruff, familiar voice said.

Strong hands took her by the shoulders and walked her quickly around the corner in the direction from which she had come.

"Oh!" she cried, stunned and trying to jerk free, to look back for Nathan.

"Please don't do that, Miss Case," John Tortorelli said as he pushed her along the side of the brick building, whose back opened onto an alley that was in stark contrast to the elite chic of the plaza.

Garbage cans and debris surrounded them now. And worse things. Kathleen looked up at the man she had defended and knew that her small flush of happiness for the future had been an illusion.

Slumping against the wall, she tried to perceive the ending of her life, but couldn't do it. This wasn't right. It wasn't supposed to end like this. She couldn't even fathom summoning the adrenaline to fight; she could only think of Nathan, who was walking toward her and who would, in another second, turn the corner and face John Tortorelli. Dear God!

With superhuman strength she lunged free of Tortorelli, and felt his hands grabbing at her coat. Yet she gained a second's head start just as Nathan burst into the alley on a dead run, his face that of a man in terror.

"Kathleen!" he roared, bringing John Tortorelli to a sharp standstill. And Kathleen, too, for one of John's arms was now a vise about her waist.

Kathleen screamed. She twisted to face Tortorelli, fully expecting to feel the impact of a killing shot.

"Keep back!" Tortorelli shouted to Nathan, and kept Kathleen pinned to him. "Don't come any closer! I'm warning you!"

Still pressed against the man, Kathleen pleaded with Nathan. "Do as he says, Nathan. Please, don't come any closer."

"She's right."

Tortorelli's words grated against her ear.

"Stay where you are, and no one will get hurt."

She didn't believe Tortorelli. He was a killer, and he thought she had betrayed him. And why would he not? All the circumstantial evidence a person could want was there.

But her forte was circumstantial evidence. Slowly she worked herself around and peered up at the man she had saved from the hard fist of the law.

"John," she said with a raspy whisper and shake of her head. "Oh, John, you don't want to do this. I know you think I ratted on you, but I didn't, John. That man standing over there paid fifteen hundred dollars to get me out of jail. He did it because he loves me, John. It had nothing to do with you. Please believe me."

John Tortorelli's past was written on his face, but as Kathleen spoke a strange, tortured gentleness passed over his craggy features. He shook his head.

"I just wanted to tell you something, Miss Case," he said with puzzling courtesy. "That's all. I don't want to hurt you." Releasing her, he stepped back and held out his hands as proof. Then he showed them to Nathan, who was poised in the opening of the alley as menacingly, as dangerously as the cocked hammer of a pistol.

Kathleen's jaw dropped in astonishment, and she lifted her hand to her mouth.

"I was trying to tell you before, but he—" John inclined his head, indicating Nathan "—he blew up a car before I could talk to you."

A feather could have toppled Kathleen. "Tell me what, John?"

"I know you've been afraid of me, and you had good right at the beginning. But things are different now. You were kind to me, Miss Case. You helped me when no one else would have. Whatever I've done, I'm grateful for that. I just want you to know you have nothing to fear from me.

I've got my own troubles now, and you don't have to keep looking over your shoulder for me. I have to go now.''

With a skip backward and a quick-footed spin on his heel, Tortorelli shouted before he sprinted down the alley toward the corner, ''By the way, I didn't kill that policeman, Miss Case. That's the truth.''

Before Kathleen could speak or move, he was disappearing around the building, and Rudy Mendina and Ian Raines were appearing at the head of the alley alongside Nathan.

''Where did he go?'' they demanded as they rushed up.

In all honesty, Kathleen could say with a shrug, ''I have no idea, Mr. Mendina.''

They were instantly in pursuit, and Kathleen fell into Nathan's arms as if she had come home after a long, long absence. She let herself be held until she could gain her bearings, and then she reached beneath her coat and through her blouse to where the microphone was taped to her midriff.

The tape rasped when she pulled it free and disconnected it, folding it into her fist.

''Nathan Cypress,'' she said as she leaned weakly upon his arm, ''I'm not cut out for this. If this is any indication of what it means to be married to you, I'm not sure I won't die before my time.''

The smile had not yet reached the steely blue of Nathan's eyes, and his body was as taut as stretched wire. He was as dazed as she was.

''I'll be damned,'' he said in bafflement as he looked at the place where John Tortorelli had been only seconds before. ''I'll be damned.''

''We might both be if we don't get out of this alley.''

Then he was gathering her as if she were the missing half of himself. He was taking her into his side where it was warm and safe and the cold wind could not touch her. He was rocking her against him.

"I want to go home," he said, and lifted a hand to her face and slipped it into her hair.

With a sigh, Kathleen closed her eyes. She guessed they would have stood like this even if John Tortorelli had run back into the alley and shouted that he had changed his mind. Beyond them the dome of the Capitol was glistening in the cold. The monuments were making their statements and the wheels of the System were turning once again. It was business as usual.

"There's only one thing I've got to know," Nathan was saying as he walked her to the curb of the plaza, inserted his fingers between his teeth and whistled an ear-shattering shrill. "Taxi!"

Kathleen had not yet emerged from her daze. "I have a feeling you're going to tell me what it is."

A yellow cab whipped to the curb and screeched to a stop, revving its engine impatiently. Ignoring the cab, Nathan took her by the shoulders and tipped her face to his. He probed her with a series of doubtful looks and opened his mouth to speak, then stopped.

Presently he said as he held up his finger and thumb, a small space between them, his expression was winsomely cajoling as a boy's, his eyes worried behind the glasses, "Kathleen, don't you find me even a *little* handsome?"

Turning her head, Kathleen let her laughter ripple merrily into the cold afternoon. Passersby turned to see, and she smiled happily at them, and they at the pretty woman being held at such urgent length by the handsome man.

Signaling the taxi driver, who was about to leave and go where normal, sane people could make up their minds, she opened the door for Nathan.

"Ask me in forty years, Nathan Cypress." She flung out her arm in a facetious invitation for him to enter. "Now get in the cab."

* * * * *

Silhouette Intimate Moments®

COMING
NEXT MONTH

#325 ACCUSED—Beverly Sommers

Anne Larkin was assigned to defend her former law professor, Jack
Quintana, on a murder charge. Jack was innocent, but Anne was
guilty—guilty of falling in love with her client. When the verdict was
handed down, would it be life without parole—in each other's arms?

#326 SUTTER'S WIFE—Lee Magner

When Alex Sutter and Sarah Dunning met, the air crackled with
electricity. If only they could find a way to merge their lives.... Could a
cynical, semiretired intelligence agent who was accustomed to a no-
strings-attached lifestyle and an independent, settled young woman find
permanent happiness together?

#327 BLACK HORSE ISLAND—
Dee Holmes

Keely Lockwood was stuck between a rock and a hard place. She was
determined to fulfill her father's lifelong dream to work with troubled
boys, but she got more than she bargained for when she hired Jed Corey.
Could she mix business with pleasure and succeed at both?

#328 A PERILOUS EDEN—
Heather Graham Pozzessere

What do you do when the man you've fallen in love with may be a traitor
to your country? That question haunts Amber Larkspur when she finds
herself held hostage in a terrorist plot. Suddenly she has to trust Michael
Adams, not only with her heart but with her life.

Silhouette Special Edition

proudly presents

Taming Natasha
by
NORA ROBERTS

In March, award-winning author Nora Roberts weaves her special brand of magic in TAMING NATASHA (SSE #583). Natasha Stanislaski was a pussycat with Spence Kimball's little girl, but to Spence himself she was as ornery as a caged tiger. Would some cautious loving sheath her claws and free her heart from captivity?

TAMING NATASHA, by Nora Roberts, has been selected to receive a special laurel—the Award of Excellence. Look for the distinctive emblem on the cover. It lets you know there's something truly special inside.

You'll flip . . . your pages won't!
Read paperbacks *hands-free* with

Book Mate • I

The perfect "mate" for all your romance paperbacks

Traveling • Vacationing • At Work • In Bed • Studying • Cooking • Eating

Perfect size for all standard paperbacks, this wonderful invention makes reading a pure pleasure! Ingenious design holds paperback books OPEN and FLAT so even wind can't ruffle pages— leaves your hands free to do other things. Reinforced, wipe-clean vinyl-covered holder flexes to let you turn pages without undoing the strap...supports paperbacks so well, they have the strength of hardcovers!

Pages turn WITHOUT opening the strap

SEE-THROUGH STRAP

Reinforced back stays flat

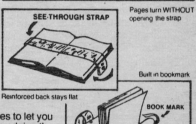

Built in bookmark

BOOK MARK

BACK COVER HOLDING STRIP

10 x 7¼ opened
Snaps closed for easy carrying, too

Available now. Send your name, address, and zip code, along with a check or money order for just $5.95 + .75¢ for postage & handling (for a total of $6.70) payable to Reader Service to:

Reader Service
Bookmate Offer
901 Fuhrmann Blvd.
P.O. Box 1396
Buffalo, N.Y. 14269-1396

Offer not available in Canada
*New York and Iowa residents add appropriate sales tax.

BM-G

At long last, the books you've been waiting for
by one of America's top romance authors!

DIANA PALMER
DUETS

Ten years ago Diana Palmer published her very first
romances. Powerful and dramatic, these gripping tales
of love are everything you have come to expect from
Diana Palmer.

In March, some of these titles will be available again in
DIANA PALMER DUETS—a special three-book collection. Each book will have two wonderful stories plus an
introduction by the author. You won't want to miss them!

Book 1
SWEET ENEMY
LOVE ON TRIAL

Book 2
STORM OVER THE LAKE
TO LOVE AND CHERISH

Book 3
IF WINTER COMES
NOW AND FOREVER

 *Silhouette Books*®